A DEADLY FLAME

DOUG SINCLAIR

Copyright © Doug Sinclair, 2024

The moral right of the author has been asserted.

Ebook ISBN: 978-1-80508-512-6
Paperback ISBN: 978-1-80508-513-3

Cover design: Blacksheep
Cover images: Shutterstock, Depositphotos

Published by Storm Publishing.
For further information, visit:
www.stormpublishing.co

ALSO BY DOUG SINCLAIR

DS Malkie McCulloch Series

Blood Runs Deep

Last to Die

For my mum, who never stopped believing in me, and did as good a job at bringing/dragging me up as anyone could have.

ONE

'Why are you calling this number? I gave you that other number for a reason, you idiot.'

'It's done.'

'And?'

'No problems. I didn't even have to reset the alarm. It wasn't enabled.'

'You're sure there was no one there? No one got hurt, right?'

'You should have worried about all this before asking me to do it, but aye, I checked as much as I could. No one was there.'

'What do you mean "as much as you could"?'

'Calm down. The office door was locked but I checked through the glass walls. There was no one in there.'

'You're certain?'

'I checked, OK? Why did you want this done, anyway? Are you that desperate?'

'Not that it's any of your business, but I'm just tired, OK? I'm tired of being tired. And I'm tired of seeing my—'

'Your what?'

'Like I said, none of your business. We're done now. You'll drop that phone in a loch somewhere, right?'

'Maybe.'

'Why "maybe"? I want nothing left to connect us. What's not clear about that?'

'I'll dump it when I'm happy there's no comeback from this, that you haven't missed something that could fuck us both up.'

'I haven't.'

'Please understand if I take that with a healthy pinch of "aye, right". Besides, I might decide some other kind of remuneration is in order.'

'You've been paid.'

'Ah, but I didn't do it for the money. Well, not just for the money. You know I've fancied you since school, right?'

'Don't.'

'Maybe we can catch up socially sometime. I'd like that.'

Click.

TWO

Malkie stared at Steph's empty chair. He could swear it stared back at him.

He'd often heard that dogs came to resemble their owners or the other way around; same way people said you can tell a lot about a person from their music collection.

Could someone's workplace desk absorb their personality? He glanced around his own desk and decided, hell yeah. His had been remarked on previously by his DI, Susan Thompson, and his DI before her, Gavin McLeish, and – of course – by his DC, Steph. Technically his subordinate officer, but she never seemed to get that memo. His colleagues had stopped laughing with him when he claimed that the calamity his desk represented was actually a finely tuned and efficient system only he could navigate. As so often these days, he found himself wondering if he needed new material.

Post-its covered Post-its, three deep in places. Coffee-mug rings decorated what actual desk space could be seen between piles of papers, sheaves of vital and critical administration papers and forms that had been awaiting his attention for anything from that same day to weeks ago. He made sure –

because otherwise Steph would – he adhered to the current incarnation of the Police Scotland Clear Desk Policy, because he handed Senior Damagement enough ammunition to boot his arse without needing to violate the critical strictures of Policy. Policy mattered. Policy kept hands clean. Loose Policy could sink careers.

Steph's desk couldn't be more opposite – and mutely critical – of his if she took night classes in Showing Up Scruffy Bosses In The Workplace. The bloody woman even kept her own supply of screen wipes and a miniature USB keyboard vacuum-locked in her drawer. Malkie had learned that if he left his own desk dusty and messy enough for long enough, he'd arrive one morning to find it cleaner and tidier than he ever left it, and Steph sitting at hers with a look that promised violence if he dared thank her.

At the moment he felt her absence more than he thought he could handle for much longer. He even missed her brutal – if well-intentioned and completely deserved – gob tearing him a new arsehole most days.

'She'll be back on Monday.' Susan Thompson spoke from her office doorway. Malkie jumped, and even that made him miss Steph, her and her unpleasant habit of appearing behind him without a sound and making him jump at every opportunity.

'Aye, I know, boss.'

Thompson pulled Steph's chair out, turned it towards Malkie's desk, and sat.

'Is it true that you tell Uniforms not to call you "sir" during shouts?'

Where's she going with this?

'Aye. Why?'

'You and I go back further than most of our department, don't we?'

'Aye.'

'This is like pulling teeth. It's late, both of us should have gone home an hour ago, and both of us have had a bellyful of the usual, all week. How about you pretend I'm a human being as well as your superior? You know, when it's just you and me here?'

Malkie sighed, held his hands up. 'Sorry. I'm just rattled, you know? Worried.' He glanced behind her at Steph's desk.

Thompson smiled, and he knew her well enough to read the affection in her. They'd been close during their cadet days at Tulliallan, but when he'd got himself booted back down to DS the previous year she'd become his superior, and he'd learned that the further up the greasy pole someone climbed, the more they got pressured to put career before nostalgia, which could turn even the strongest friendships bad.

'It's not like her. I know she's going through some family stuff at the moment, but I hoped she'd let me in, you know?'

'I know, but remember she asked me to tell you – specifically – if she needed someone to get pissed with. She wouldn't say that about many people.'

Malkie saw the gleam in Thompson's eye and smiled. 'Cheeky mare. She knows I don't drink.'

Thompson raised an eyebrow. 'Don't?'

'Fair point. Can't. But I'll find something, one day, I can stomach, then I can start listening to jazz and buy a classic car that costs more than I make in a year and then I'll be a proper copper, right?'

'Cheeky bastard. You're just jealous.'

'I am. What's it feel like, getting hammered and forgetting for a few hours?'

Thompson opened her mouth to answer but they both stopped when a tone chimed from Malkie's computer, a sound they both knew and dreaded because it always carried the possibility of a shitty shout. Some poor woman nicked because she'd stabbed her pig of a husband with a bread knife after years of abuse. Or a child found dead in its crib while its parents slept off cheap booze and even cheaper coke. Sometimes even worse: some poor kid found hanging from a curtain rail. DC Rab Lundy had once confided to Malkie that his nephew had suffered the funerals of two school friends before they turned eighteen. The lad had written and played songs for both funerals that broke every person there, but he still blamed himself because nobody saw it coming, until all he could do for them was write songs they'd never hear.

'Malkie? Need you back in the room, mate.'

Something in Thompson's tone ripped him from his chronic habit of dwelling in places he shouldn't.

'Sorry, Susan. We got a new shout come in?'

Thompson stared at him for a few seconds, and Malkie braced himself for bad news. A lump of dread formed in his guts. 'Whatever it is, don't piss me about, Susan. What is it?'

Thompson studied him for a second more, then pointed over his shoulder at his PC screen.

As expected, he saw notification of a new shout, a new call-out that needed CID attendance.

A warehouse fire. One fatality.

Malkie's mind strobed on memories he'd been fighting to drag into some kind of clarity for eight months: his mum and dad's bungalow, a fire, him not being there for them, him recalling his stupid, fateful part in the chain of events that led to his mum dying and his dad in hospital for six months.

'Malkie? That tells me enough. I'm calling Pam Ballantyne out.' She pulled her phone from her pocket.

'Like hell you are. Shit, sorry.'

She put her phone back. 'Seriously, Malkie? You still worried about giving her leverage on you? You still think she's out to get you, that McLeish is pushing her to nail you? Really?'

Malkie held a hand up, his head bowed. He needed her to

stop before he said anything else unprofessional or, worse, hurtful.

'It's not that. Not just that.'

He took a breath through his nose, held it, let it seep out through his mouth, slow and controlled. Thompson waited.

'This had to happen sometime.' He skim-read the details on his screen. 'It's a warehouse fire. A house fire I might have passed on, but an industrial property is nothing like a private home. I'll handle it.' He read on but stopped at the last paragraph. 'Fuck.'

'What?'

'The fire was called in on 999 by someone, but it was noisy and they couldn't make anything out but loud crashing noises and coughing, then a thud like a handset being dropped, then nothing more.'

Thompson did him the favour of not asking if he was up for the job, but she studied him for long seconds more.

'Who's on with you this shift?'

'Gucci. Lou Gooch.'

'I know who Gucci is, Malkie.' She smiled at his constant need to ensure his comments were interpreted correctly. 'She's good, and she knows how to handle you.' She yelled over her shoulder to the back of the CID room. 'Louisa. New shout. Can you assist Malkie, please?'

Louisa 'Gucci' Gooch's head popped up from behind her screen, like a prairie dog. 'Do I have to, boss? What kind of mood is he in?'

Thompson grinned. 'She wants to know what kind of mood you're in.'

Malkie smiled back, his face a mask of sarcasm. 'She's hilarious, isn't she?'

Gucci appeared at his desk and glanced at the screen. She took a moment, looked at both Thompson and Malkie, then recovered. She punched him on the arm, just like Steph always did. 'Let's go get 'em, boss.'

As he stood and grabbed his coat, Thompson placed a hand on his arm. 'Steph is OK. She's a survivor, more than anyone else we know. I have no doubt she'll tell you as much as she feels ready to, on Monday.'

Gucci held the door to the stairwell open for him. He barked at her as he walked through. 'You drive, Detective Constable Gooch.'

THREE

Even having had recent experience of what to expect did nothing to lessen the battering Malkie's self-confidence took at the first flash of blue strobe, lighting up the sky from three blocks away.

He couldn't seem to pass the flashing lights of an ambulance or a fire engine or even a roadside recovery truck without triggering the worst kind of thoughts – memories that still threatened to unman him a full eight months after the night he failed so spectacularly to save his mum from the event that killed her.

Gucci would suspect exactly what assaulted his mind right now, and he wished her a silent thank-you for not trying to pry.

'About five minutes away, Detective Sergeant McCulloch.'

Malkie groaned; he deserved that. 'Ach, I'm sorry, OK?'

She feigned ignorance. 'For what, sir?'

'Oh, cut it out, Gucci. I said I'm sorry.'

'You hate being called "sir", and I hate being called "Detective Constable" like I'm a walk-on bit-player in some crap pot-boiler. I learned that from you, you know?' She grinned.

Malkie felt his strop ease off, but none of his tension, none of his fear.

He harboured zero doubt that he would be calling Gucci 'ma'am' one day and he hoped to a god he never believed in that promotion wouldn't change her. He also harboured zero doubt that Steph wouldn't change when she finally moved from DC past him on her way to DI, or rather, she would change but almost certainly in ways that would make Malkie laugh himself stupid. The senior ranks had no clue what they were in for if Steph decided to 'go career'.

Gucci turned a final corner inside the Houston Industrial Estate and a massive, brutal shit show assaulted Malkie's eyes. Three appliances, hoses blasting water fifty feet into window openings in the now fire-gutted shell of what he knew to be the remains of the William Galbraith Independent Bonded Whisky warehouse. He could imagine the Scottish Fire and Rescue crews would have their hands full with several hundred barrels of Central Scotland's best home-produced whisky feeding those monstrous flames.

Gucci parked outside a Fire Service cordon and turned to him. He loved her to bits for it, but it still rankled that he felt such a need for assurance from a junior officer, even Gucci. Although this wasn't just any officer. This was Gucci, Malkie's unofficial young protégé, keen as hell but grounded with it, and altogether Malkie's idea of a perfect officer.

'I have zero doubt you can handle this just fine, Malkie. I'll be right behind you, every second though, OK?' She waited.

He turned a weak smile on her. 'Thanks, Lou. Let's go start on this one, shall we?'

She grinned. 'We got this, boss.'

They threw their doors open and stepped out of the pool car. Malkie felt the heat hit him, and nearly crumbled, already. Even from the cordon, fifty metres back from the building, the blast of scathing air from the flames felt like a tangible thing, almost like a thickening of the air he pulled in through his mouth, now gaping, his chest heaving.

The single-storey building stood ablaze, flames gouting from the windows like a living, grasping thing, clutching at fresh air to feed itself in its battle against the efforts of the firefighters who risked everything to get close enough to fight it. Judging by the report of the 999 call and the possibility that someone may have been trapped inside, they'd be venturing into it too, and Malkie shivered to imagine the danger these people put themselves in. As he and Gucci watched, part of the roof fell in with a massive crash and sent sparks exploding out of the now-glassless window openings. Malkie's stomach turned over at the thought of any firefighter getting caught under such a collapse. He remembered flames creeping along the ceiling of the hallway as he fought to push through searing heat and choking black smoke to enter his mum's bedroom.

He never made it. The flames won. Took her from him. From him and his dad. All the poor sod had left now was Malkie, who had to believe he could yet be the son his dad needed to weather the rest of his life without her.

He'd been beaten back by flames then, and yet here he stood, only metres from a blaze ten times the size of the one that—

Fuck's sake. What the hell was I thinking?

Gucci, as promised, appeared beside him and stood shoulder-to-shoulder. She made just enough contact to remind him she had his back.

They stood and reeled under an onslaught of sights and sounds: the roar of the fire as it consumed the building, the noise of the appliance pumps and the deluge of water being thrown at it, steam rising from the tarmac around the immediate edge of the building. Malkie nudged her with his elbow. She seemed to realise he was there all over again and smiled at him, and together they approached the cordon.

A woman Malkie assumed to be Health and Safety checked their warrant cards and signed them in, and they approached what looked to be the Command Vehicle. A whiteboard hung outside with a table of information scrawled in black marker. Malkie knew from previous shouts to assist the Scottish Fire and Rescue Service, the SFRS, that it detailed the zones that the building had been subdivided into so they could coordinate and record the entry and exit of the firefighters, along with various other bits of jargon and acronyms he never bothered to learn. They approached the man who had to be the Incident Commander, judging from his hi-vis jacket and IC tabard pulled on over his fire tunic.

'Evening, mate. DS McCulloch and DC Gooch.' They flashed their warrant cards, but the man barely glanced at them, his attention switching between the burning building and a board of details and plastic tokens hanging from the Command Vehicle door and occasional commands spoken into his headset mouthpiece in calm but urgent tones.

Malkie pocketed his warrant card and waited for the man to find a second to look at him. 'Can I assume you're the Incident Command on this one?'

The man appraised him, seemed to recognise him. 'Ah, hello DS McCulloch. Sorry, didn't recognise you. I mean I know your face, like. Aye I'm IC on this one. Jeremy Lees, watch commander of Livi SFRS Blue Watch. Red Watch is in attendance too, round the other side of the building, led by Pete Fairbairn. We found only one viable entry point on this side, so they've gone to look for another around the back.'

'Seriously? How quickly did it go up if they're still looking for entry points?'

Lees stared at him. 'It's a bonded warehouse. Whisky. Hundreds of barrels of it, mate.'

Gucci shuffled her feet. Malkie had the decency to feel as much of an idiot as the man must think him.

'Fair enough. I'm a flatfoot, not a firefighter. Point taken.'

Lees laughed. 'Only pulling your plonker, mate. I'm

guessing the fire started in the barrel storage to have lit up so fast. We've called your command structure for resources to evacuate every house in a two-block radius in case it all goes up.'

Malkie asked the last question he felt like asking. 'So, the report of the 999 call indicated the possibility of someone trapped inside?'

Lees's face darkened. 'Aye, our initial entry team spotted a casualty from twenty metres away – very obviously already well gone – but couldn't reach the person before having to fall back because an interior wall collapsed in, nearly caught them. Reaching the victim wouldn't have been feasible without jeopardising their own lives. They had to withdraw.'

Lees took a breath that turned into a long, tired sigh. 'But we've had another casualty. One of our own. I don't know the details yet because his partner is pulling him out now, but it sounds like one of them declared a BA Set emergency.'

'A BA Set emergency?'

'Breathing apparatus. Loads of safeguards are built in to make sure no firefighter runs out of air or even gets close to it, but one of our men declared an emergency, which means a serious issue and immediate withdrawal. That's all I know for now. Sorry. I need to stay focused. Talk to me later.'

Malkie had feared this and his stomach sank. Any fatality required Police Scotland attendance, so he and Gucci would have to be 'it' until they brought the fire under control, safe access established, and backup arrived. Which looked unlikely to happen this side of daylight. A long, long night stretched ahead for both of them.

His gaze returned to the burning building. The furious flames erupting from every window, the occasional soft, muffled boom of another barrel igniting deep inside the warehouse. The torrents of water directed through window frames and up under the roof seemed to do little to assuage the hunger of the flames.

He felt himself pulled towards it, into the conflagration, like a child creeping too close to the glowing embers in the bottom of a bonfire. He and fire had history.

A harsh screech from IC Lees's walkie-talkie shocked him back to the present. Lees listened, and Malkie saw his shoulders slump. He leaned back against the side of the Command Vehicle and lowered his head. He looked about to buckle, to fold at the knees and slide to the ground. Malkie's blood turned cold.

Lees looked up at them, seemed to remember his professional obligations. 'Casualty is being brought out, now. Suspected cardiac arrest.'

Malkie closed his eyes. *Oh, for fuck's sake, how much worse is this going to get?*

FOUR

Malkie watched Lees collect himself. He rallied visibly when he noticed Malkie watching him, as if appearances mattered, as if his professional performance mattered.

He disappeared into the Command Vehicle, left Malkie and Gucci with nothing to do but call in what they knew so far. Thompson sighed down the line, promised them some backup, then she hesitated.

Malkie put her out of her misery. 'I'm fine, boss. I can see the big scary fire from here and it's nothing like my mum's house and yes, it triggered me, but I've got a hold on it, and I'll be fine. I promise.'

'OK. Stay on it for now. But first sign of any stress-related symptoms, you talk to me. Deal? Agree or I pull you from this one, Malkie.'

'Deal, Susan. Gucci's here to look after me, too, so I'm in good hands, OK?'

She listened for a few seconds, probably trying to gauge the truth of his words face-unseen, then she hung up.

Malkie turned to Gucci. 'You feel like rustling us up some

coffee, Lou? I think the Salvation Army usually set up something to feed emergency workers at these incidents. I'd go myself, but I want to stand here and stare into the fire as if mesmerised then suffer a complete mental breakdown.'

Lou studied him for a second, and Malkie had to wonder if he'd gone too far.

She rolled her eyes at him. 'This is gonna be *such* a long night.' She wandered off.

Malkie watched the smoke and flames pour out of the blackened shell of the warehouse. Was he imagining it, or did they look just a tad less violent than before half the roof had caved in? He wondered what might wait for him once they were permitted to enter, and found himself hoping it would take hours yet. He knew from previous fire scenes that it might take another full day of damping down until the SFRS would declare the fire fully extinguished, but he hoped Health and Safety might decide the air was clear enough for the Scottish Forensics Service to examine the casualty.

A commotion interrupted his thoughts, from off to his left. Four firefighters barged through various other operatives as they carried a fifth towards two waiting ambulances. Malkie walked over, and braced himself for stepping right into something he feared would test him beyond either of the two major cases he'd handled since the night he lost his mum. Every copper had to learn to deal with violence towards their colleagues, and no amount of experience ever dulled the grief and fury at a good officer being hurt or worse by some waste-of-oxygen mouthbreather. It couldn't be any less traumatic for these people to witness injury to one of their own while trying to do their best to save people and property.

Paramedics took over, removed the man's breathing mask and helmet. One of the firefighters who'd carried him snatched the mask and cylinder from the paramedic. The medics worked on the man on the ground, repeatedly pushing down onto his chest then squeezing a bag to force oxygen into him. They battled for twenty minutes, and Malkie could do nothing but watch the efforts to save the man and the worry on the faces of the four firefighters who'd delivered him.

He noted one stood apart, the one who had grabbed the face mask from the medic. While the others leaned on each other, whispered words of encouragement, muttered to themselves, their eyes locked on their colleague, the fifth man stood silent, his eyes down, his fingers working their way around the rubber seal around the breathing visor. Grey-haired and pale even through the smoke and soot staining his face, Malkie watched the man breathe hard but make no effort to join his watch mates. At one point he closed his eyes and tilted his head back, held it for long seconds, then lowered it. As he did, he caught Malkie staring at him. He reacted with anger, as if Malkie had no right to – to what? To even be there? To share in such an intimate, if tragic experience? Malkie got the oddest feeling that the man looked ashamed, as if he considered Malkie to be standing in judgement on him. He had no reason to form any such feeling, but the man's attitude smacked of something Malkie had become far too familiar with. Guilt.

The man stomped away towards the Command Vehicle, but he went the long way around, behind the ambulances, rather than directly past Malkie.

Malkie's imagination kicked into overdrive, and he had to warn himself for what felt like the millionth time to keep his feet on the ground and his mind on the job. The casualty inside the warehouse would only become his problem if arson – fire-raising, he reminded himself – was suspected, and any such finding might take days while the SFRS and Fire Investigation Unit conducted their investigation. Whatever had befallen the firefighter would only become his problem if the manufacturer of the confiscated breathing gear found evidence of equipment-tampering or other indications of willful harm, which could also take days. With a bit of luck, the whole thing might go the way of a Fatal Accident Inquiry with minimal input required from Police Scotland. If his luck held, he might get through this one without triggering too much past trauma again.

A sob sounded from the scene at the back of the ambulance. One of the firefighters, a woman, burying her face in a colleague's chest and sobbing.

The paramedics loaded the injured firefighter onto a gurney and into the ambulance, and Malkie felt his heart ache for the whole squad. If an SFRS squad grew to be anything as tightly knit as the detectives he knew he could rely on in his own department, he understood their distress. He'd heard firefighters describe their bonds as being stronger than brothers, less than lovers. He'd love to think his own colleagues felt something like that for him, but he harboured no delusions on that front. Steph, Thompson and Gucci excepted, he reminded himself.

One of the firefighters who looked to be the youngest stepped away from the group and looked around. When he saw where the man with the BA Set had gone, his face grimaced and he clenched his fist at his side. The lad took one step in the same direction, but an older colleague grabbed him by the arm, pulled him back to his squad and spoke to him, looked stern but gentle. The lad took long seconds to calm down but deferred to his older colleague. He glanced up, happened to meet Malkie's stare, and held it. This made his colleague glance in the same direction. He seemed to appraise Malkie for a second, then stretched a comforting arm across the young man's shoulders and guided him back to his watch mates.

What the hell? One man looking like he wants to tear lumps out of another? Why?

Malkie could see no chance of being any direct use to the crowd trying to save the firefighter's life, so he wandered off in the direction of the Command vehicle. He told himself he just wanted to be where any important communications would be centralised, but he also felt himself slipping, again, into Columbo mode.

He stood with his back against the outside of the Command Vehicle, one foot crossed over the other, stuffed his hands into his pockets and tried to look no more suspicious than a man taking five minutes off from an intense situation. When he saw no one paying him any attention, he glanced around the corner to the back of the vehicle.

The firefighter he'd followed sat on an equipment crate, his head lowered, looking for all the world like the most broken man Malkie could ever remember seeing. There was no sign of the breathing gear removed from the injured firefighter. As Malkie watched, the man rubbed his eyes with the fingers of one hand and looked about to weep.

'What the hell are you doing?'

Malkie jumped. Steph had appeared behind him. Again. Like some rotten game she liked to play on her favourite DS. Malkie thought about pulling rank on her, trying to put her in her place, but his mind saw in seconds how that would play out and talked himself out of it.

'Fuck's sake. Again, woman?'

She's fine. She looks fine. Good grief, I've missed you, Steph.

She grinned, then peered past him. Malkie turned to study the firefighter. He'd heard them and looked appalled to see them standing there. He stood and stomped off in the opposite direction.

Oh, there's something bugging you, isn't there, mate?

Steph punched him on the arm. 'Malkie. Pay attention. What are you doing skulking around back here? I saw Gucci, she said there's one confirmed fatality and a possible second? We need to be where the action is, mate.'

'Aye, I know. It's just...'

She eyed him, ready for one of their 'talks'.

'Nothing. Just some poor bastard handling his grief in his own way, I suppose.'

Aye, and he didn't want anyone to see his attention on that equipment, did he?

He turned away and they headed back towards the knot of firefighters.

As he approached them, one left the group and walked towards him, a big bloke, thick hair and what some people would call handsome and rugged features. Malkie hated him immediately, on principle.

The man held his hand out and Malkie shook it, surprised to find his grip firm but devoid of any bullshit macho finger-crushing. Always a half-decent early sign.

'Hi. Graham Cormack. Blue Watch. Our Watch Commander Jeremy Lees is IC on this one and will be up to his eyes in it, so if you need anything, ask me or one of the others, OK?'

He turned to Steph and greeted her. He looked tired and gutted, a man determined to observe professional etiquette despite what must have been a shock for him and his colleagues.

'Detective Sergeant Malcolm McCulloch. I know we can't interview your colleagues now and we'll need to wait for the cross-agency briefing, but we'll need to hang around in case H&S gives the OK for entry so our SOCOs can examine the scene of the casualty, aye?'

'Aye, sounds fine. But bear in mind, even if we don't need to go back in when Red Watch comes out – we only ever do two hours at a time – as soon as we're stood down, we'll be taken back to the station for a hot debrief.' He nodded at Steph, who smiled back. Smiles never looked natural on Steph but she managed one for a man going through what this one must be. Malkie smiled too at Cormack's veiled reminder that Police Scotland had no jurisdiction. Yet.

As all three spent an awkward few seconds nodding and smiling and working out who would walk away first, they heard a furious roar from the crowd around the casualty.

'Where is he? Where is that fucker?'

Back at the ambulance they found two firefighters struggling to hold on to the female he'd seen earlier, the only woman he'd seen in uniform so far tonight. Tears poured from her eyes as expletives poured from her mouth. Six inches shorter and at least thirty pounds lighter than both of her colleagues, she still threatened to break free. She thrashed and screamed and eventually collapsed, folding at the knees to fall to the grass, soaked into a muddy mess by the spray coming off the hoses. One of the men who had tried to hold on to her looked at the other, scowling. The second man shrugged. Both looked down at her, and both looked worried.

Cormack turned and leaned into Malkie and Steph, his face grim. 'That's Sian Wilson. The man on his way to hospital is...' He stopped, swallowed, had to take a second. 'Duncan Duffy. She and Duffy were close friends, knew each other before joining the service.' Malkie heard the man's voice thicken then choke off as he spoke. His eyes remained dry but looked racked with pain. He lifted Sian back to her feet and hugged her. She buried herself in his chest and sobbed. The others looked helpless.

Aye, these people form tighter bonds than anything we see between coppers. Fuck's sake they must be hurting.

'Just friends? Poor woman's in pieces.'

'SFRS prohibits relationships between firefighters, in the same watch or in the same station, and some rules we never bend let alone break, or people can get hurt.'

Malkie noted Cormack's careful statement of regulations without actually answering the question.

Sian Wilson stood. She looked down at Duffy. Her chest

heaved. With a massive effort, she raised her head and turned to her squad.

'Where's his BA Set?'

A look of confusion and something else Malkie couldn't identify darkened every face in the huddle, on both squads.

Wilson walked away.

FIVE

Malkie took Cormack by the arm and headed away from the crowd. Cormack started to turn, but then faced back towards the burning building. No doubt about it now; the smoke had turned blacker but flames no longer erupted through the window openings.

Cormack stepped back to his colleagues and had words with them, hushed and exhausted. The firefighters who had pulled Duffy from the building donned their helmets and headed back towards it. Cormack glanced at Malkie. 'Sorry, Detective. Blue Watch has to go back in to relieve Red Watch. Regulations. They need to continue damping down to stop the flames from flashing again.'

He turned to walk away, to join his colleagues already on their way back into the building, but he offered Malkie one more comment first.

'We'll grieve later. For now, we keep going, finish the job.'

Cormack frowned as if disappointed in himself, then walked away.

Malkie looked around for Steph and Gucci, spotted them

talking to the IC, Jeremy Lees, just inside the Command Vehicle. He joined them.

Steph asked the questions while Gucci scribbled in her police-issue notebook. She, like Malkie and Steph, preferred pen and paper to carrying around yet another electronic brick in their pockets.

'When did Mr Duffy first indicate a problem?'

Lees scanned a laptop screen on a desk inside the Command Vehicle, next to a similar laptop into which a woman wearing a headset typed as she listened.

'23:07. Paul Turner and Duncan Duffy went in first because of the possible risk to life.' He scanned the notes. Malkie looked over his shoulder and saw a screen full of transcribed messages received over the firefighter comms channels. He noticed that the comments were attributed to multiple identifiers, not just separate two-way conversations.

'Is it an open comms line, Mr Lees?'

Lees turned to look at him. He seemed not to have noticed his arrival. 'Aye. Every comment from every firefighter can be heard by every other firefighter. We zone the comms sometimes but not for a small fire like this.'

Malkie gaped at him calling what he'd seen earlier a 'small fire' but didn't want to further reveal his ignorance, so he continued.

'We'll get a copy of all the transcripts, aye?'

'The Operational Incident Log. Aye. Tomorrow.' Lees turned back to scanning the transcript. 'Here we are. There are numerous regular timed updates – we record every action, every new space entered, everything. At 23:22, Duffy reported seeing what looked like the suspected casualty.

'Duffy and Paul Turner tried to get closer, but they were forced back, the flames too intense and the interior walls had started collapsing in. Plus, they must have been nearing their turnaround pressure. They could see the casualty was too catastrophically burned to have survived, and when there's no imminent risk to life, we never take chances. They withdrew.'

Lees frowned. 'I didn't hear this come in, or I didn't pick up on it.' He leaned closer, as if to confirm his first reading.

Malkie prompted him. 'Mr Lees?'

Lees took a few seconds, seemed to need to arrange his thoughts, or perhaps decide how much to say. Malkie's Columbo-meter buzzed at him.

'I don't know how I could have missed this. Either I had to remove my earphones, or I got distracted but...'

Malkie saw a man struggling to voice something awful, something he almost couldn't get out.

'23:27, while they were deciding to turn around and withdraw. Duffy said "My BA. My fucking BA." Then I heard some garbled shouting, then...'

Malkie waited. Whatever he needed to say next had to mean trouble for someone. Possibly Lees himself, from the look on his face.

'Duffy seemed to have a coughing fit, and Paul alerted us that he was bringing him back out immediately.'

Malkie chewed over the words, felt a scenario forming which could only complicate matters massively.

'BA. Breathing apparatus, you said earlier?'

Lees shook himself out of some dark thoughts. 'Aye. If a fire-fighter believes there's a problem with their breathing apparatus, they declare a BA Emergency, but when you're in the middle of a burning compartment and under air – that means an oxygen cylinder and a full BA Set – limiting what you can see and hear in all the noise and the lethal environment, well, any kind of catastrophic event can make someone temporarily forget to use exact terminology.'

Lees stood so quickly both Malkie and Steph had to step back. Lees pushed between them and out of the Command Vehicle.

Malkie called after him, 'Mr Lees, has Duncan Duffy's BA Set been given to you and sealed as evidence?'

Lees scowled at him. 'Of course it has. It's stored securely beside the BA Board.'

'The BA Board?'

'Used to record entry and exit of BA wearers, but neither of those is of any concern to Police Scotland for now, is it? Unless you already have reason to believe Mr Duffy's accident was suspicious? And if you do, you know more than I do.'

He held a hand up to fend off any further questions. 'I need to look after my watch right now, Detective. We'll answer all your questions tomorrow, after the briefing at the station. You know you're only allowed to formally interview me as the Incident Commander and the BA Entry Control Officer, aye? You can talk to the others but go easy on them, please. No formal questioning.' He strode away.

Steph started to follow him, but Malkie stopped her with a light touch on her arm. 'He's right but let's at least try to have a chat with them. But later. It's that bloke we saw behind the Command Vehicle I want to talk to right now.'

'Why?'

'Because I'd bet my pension he was checking Duncan Duffy's BA Set before he took it away. And he did not look happy.'

Gucci reappeared with coffees. Malkie tasted it then tipped it out on the grass. Gucci shrugged. 'All they had, boss.'

Malkie waved a hand at her. 'Not your fault, Lou.'

'Steph, with me, please.'

SIX

They watched Lees speak to his watch members from a discreet distance. They watched as they responded to him. Hands were planted on shoulders, heads were nodded, words spoken. He hugged Sian Wilson and held her as she buried herself in the front of his fire tunic for long seconds. After speaking to each in turn, he returned to the Command Vehicle.

'I'm too soft for this job, you know that?' Lees sounded exhausted and broken.

Malkie unfolded his arms. 'Sorry, mate?'

'That's Duncan Duffy they just took away to St John's. He and I go sailing on Hillend Loch most weekends during the summer. I've known him thirty years.' Lees swallowed, but then seemed to remember he had a job to do. He straightened his slumped shoulders, glanced at the laptop screen he'd shown them earlier, then turned back to them, every inch the competent professional.

'The fire's nearly out, burned itself very intensely in the first hour or so, all that whisky. Initial reports are that much of the roof has collapsed, which smothered the fire to some extent and which is hopefully venting most of the inevitable toxic gases.

When we can enter safely, we'll do our checks and see about accompanying you in, but that'll still be a couple of hours away.'

'Hours?' Malkie scowled at him.

'Hours, Detective, maybe through to morning. It's not just some health and safety bollocks. The casualty is in a room right at the back of the building, furthest away from our entry point, so we need to make sure none of the few remaining ceiling beams are going to come down on anyone's head before we can let you anywhere near it.'

'Fair enough, mate.' He hoped the 'mate' would take the sting out of his obvious annoyance.

'Nae problem. I've dealt with worse than you, mate.' He smiled, but it didn't reach his eyes. 'You realise, of course, that you'll probably get bugger-all decent forensics from the casualty, right?'

Malkie had suspected as much, but allowed the man to advise him anyway.

'The amount of water we've been pumping in there and the debris that must have fallen in from the roof and internal floors, I dread to think what quality of evidence you'll get from the scene. Our own fire investigator is on his way, and they usually manage to read the source and spread of the fire despite the mess we make of it, but a human body? Not sure what will be left of it because we had to leave it in there while we fought the fire.'

'Aye, thanks, Mr Lees. I figured all that but thanks for clarifying.'

Malkie gave Lees a second to make sure he had nothing more to say, then asked his question.

'Did you see one of your firefighters come this way, shortly after they pulled your man out? He was carrying Mr Duffy's BA Set.'

'That was Peter Fairbairn.'

'And he is?'

'Same as me for Red Watch. Why do you ask?'

Malkie picked up on Lees's fraying patience. He knew he had to tread carefully, until – and only if – reason was found to suspect malicious actions had caused the incident.

Malkie studied Lees for a second; his ignorance seemed genuine. 'He walked behind your IC van, had a seat for a while, saw me watching him and scarpered. He can't leave the scene while your lot are still trying to shut that fire down, can he?'

Lees looked troubled. Malkie saw competing emotions in his eyes.

Malkie pushed him. 'Thing is, he grabbed your man Duffy's helmet and BA Set and took it with him. Given that Duffy's condition looked to be breathing-related, just wanted to make sure his BA Set was OK. Am I saying that right? BA Set?'

'Aye, every firefighter is issued one at the start of each shout, but only two use them at first, for the initial entry and assessment and only if risk to life is suspected. Duncan Duffy and Paul Turner were first in. Fairbairn wouldn't be on initial entry, just like I wouldn't be. We should both be on operational matters, decision-making, that sort of thing. We pitch in when needed but we often don't get a chance to.'

'He took your man's helmet and BA Set when one of the paramedics removed them. I assume to let them work on him. When the paramedic pulled it off over his head, Fairbairn grabbed it, so he got it to you OK?'

Lees scowled at him. 'I already told you he did.'

Malkie realised too late that he'd pushed Lees into a defensive position.

Lees stepped past Malkie. 'I need to do my job now, Detective. I trust you'll understand.'

Malkie knew he couldn't force Lees to stay and keep talking without risking alienating him completely. 'Of course. Please.'

Lees re-entered the Command Vehicle.

'Oops.'

Malkie jumped. Again. He'd forgotten Steph stood behind him. Again.

'Fuck's sake. You're going to be the end of me one day, woman.'

He expected a punch on the arm and some sarcastic come-back, but she said nothing.

What's wrong, Steph? If I ask, will you tell me?

'Are you OK? Thompson said you weren't due back until tomorrow morning. Did she ask you to be here in case... You know?'

Steph sighed. Not one of her usual long-suffering expres-sions of exasperation but a genuine, unhappy and bleak expres-sion of something painful.

She cast her eyes around, nodded at Gucci standing a respectful distance back from the two Livi crews, looking like nothing more than someone bored and feeling like a spare part, but probably taking in every word.

'Not here.'

Malkie followed her behind the Command Vehicle. She stood, as he had earlier, with her back against the outside panel of the van and one foot braced behind her. Malkie took up an identical pose beside her, and waited, gave her the long seconds she needed, didn't try to pull it out of her.

'You know I told you about my "uncle", Barry Boswell?' She laced the word with more feeling – venom and disgust and quiet fury – than Malkie would ever expect from her. The man wasn't her real uncle, more of a decades-long friend of the family who'd committed the worst of atrocities against Steph's mother.

'Aye. The animal who—'

Shut up, you idiot.

Steph smiled. 'Good save, mate. This time.' Her smile faded. 'I told you he's my biological father. And I told you why. What he did to my mum.'

Malkie waited. She didn't need to be reminded he'd be hanging on her every word.

'I kicked the shit out of him, Malkie.'

Malkie's stomach sank. Steph had a reputation throughout J Division for being one of the most dangerous officers most could remember. Probably because of her brutal childhood surviving one of the worst sink-estates in Edinburgh, she didn't stop at the basic self-defence needed to qualify for her uniform in the first place. She'd gone on to qualify at mid-level in three other martial arts and self-defence disciplines, and most now believed she could disable the biggest and worst mouth-breathers and knuckle-draggers without even breathing heavily. Malkie dreaded to hear what might come next, what she'd done to the fucker.

'I didn't hospitalise him. I'm not stupid.' She rubbed her fingers and Malkie noticed for the first time near-healed bruises on the knuckles of both of her hands.

Fuck's sake, Steph. How many times did you hit him?

'I went to visit my stepdad. I know, I know, I should have known better, but I wanted him to know I know, you know?'

She paused. Malkie knew she wouldn't have any problem describing to him whatever she'd done. After all, she'd seen more of the worst of him than any other human being, his father included. She seemed more to be overcome with a weariness, an exhausted recognition that she'd lost control. If Malkie knew her at all.

'I wanted to throw the bastard off my dad's balcony, Malkie.' She turned to him, her eyes now more afraid and vulnerable than he'd ever expected to see. 'That's not me. I don't do that. I don't lose control. Never.'

She went quiet again, hung her head as if ashamed. Malkie waited.

'It's like finding out how I even came to be on this rotten planet has damaged me. Inside. I've never felt fury like this. Not even when someone shivved my mum in her cell in Cornton Vale. That upset me, yes, but I dealt with it. Why is finding out that animal raped my mum making me so...?'

She shrugged. Whether she couldn't find a word for her feelings, or if she just ran out of the will to say any more, Malkie couldn't know.

When he decided she looked ready, he risked sticking his infamously error-prone oar in.

'Is it because, you know, he's... in you? His rotten, manky genes? Is that it?'

She looked at him, a look that surprised him, laced with affection and even pride, and accompanied by a small, sad smile. 'For a complete idiot, you can be really bloody perceptive sometimes.' She leaned her head sideways to rest on his upper arm, too short to reach his shoulder. 'Am I half-rotten, Malkie? Have I always been half-rotten?'

Malkie sighed. He knew nothing he could say would take her pain away quickly. He recalled advice she'd given him the last time she'd lectured him about bloody men always bloody charging in and trying to find bloody solutions to every problem a woman could have. She'd told him to just listen, then listen some more, then finish on a laugh.

'Maybe a quarter. Rotten, I mean. Not a full half, though.'

SEVEN

Steph rallied with an obvious effort, and they nodded to each other, ready to get going again. She'd given him something, the bare facts to satisfy his concern. As so often happened between them, there would be more to say, but later.

When they returned to the one remaining ambulance, the firefighters had disappeared. Malkie turned back to Jeremy Lees and held his hands out as if to say *What the hell?*

Lees pointed past them to the burning warehouse. Malkie spotted them just inside an open pair of massive sliding doors. He could make out flames still burning deep inside, but the fire crews seemed to be winning. He turned to find Gucci had joined them. She shook her head: nothing to report.

'Lou. No point in all three of us hanging round here all night. Steph, you OK if I send Lou home? You OK to stay?'

He couldn't miss a knowing glance between them; Lou happy to leave Steph to support Malkie through what might prove to be the most difficult scene investigation he would have faced in years. He'd already proclaimed himself safe to attend, even safe to enter the burned-out shell of the building when the time came. He'd assured Thompson because he had to; Steph and Lou because he knew they cared.

Lou checked her watch. 'OK. I'll grab a few hours' sleep at home then head into the station for morning briefing. If you're not there, I'll give an initial update.'

She glanced at Malkie. 'Good luck, boss. Might be rough in there.'

Malkie laid a hand on her upper arm and smiled. 'I have Steph to pick me up if it gets too much for me, Lou. Now sod off, please?'

She grinned and walked away towards the pool car she and Malkie had arrived in. Steph would drive him home in her own car later.

Steph and Malkie turned back to watch the firefighters move deeper into the building, watched the last visible flames gutter and die under the deluge of water their appliance hoses blasted at it. Malkie decided that regardless of his own recent experiences of fatal house fires, he could never do what these people did. Coppers like him and Steph faced the occasional knife waved in their faces by some drunk or coke-addled idiot who didn't feel like accompanying them to the station, but not often. These guys regularly faced the hell of burning buildings. Not every day, he knew; the SFRS wasted far too much time dousing fires in refuse bins and farmers' fields, chip-fryer fires and cheap imported curling tongs left plugged in, but he doubted he could do what these men and women did all too often. All of which pissed him off even more to think of the reception they got from local youths during a shout. Same with ambulance paramedics. The very people doing the hardest and most traumatising of work to protect the great unwashed public, and too many of the worst of that same unwashed public thanked them by throwing stones and nicking their gear or drugs or anything else they could get their hands on.

He roused himself; that way lay the slippery edge of a deep, dark hole he'd worked hard to stay away from his whole life. Tonight, he had personal demons to keep leashed while he faced his worst nightmare listening to his mum die.

Stop that shite. Dad doesn't blame himself for that night so why should you, you idiot?

He caught Steph staring at him.

'I'm fine. At least it's not a house fire. That might have been tricky.'

She punched him on the arm, her go-to gesture of comfort. 'You're tougher than you think you are, mate. I wish you'd believe that.'

He didn't deserve her. 'I'll believe it if you believe the same about yourself. Deal?'

A shadow fell across her face, the moment ruined. Too much, too soon? She stared at her feet, sighed, breathed. 'Can't promise anything. Not yet, mate. But I'm OK for now.'

I'll take that, Steph, but I'll be watching.

Lou appeared again, two paper beakers in her hand. 'Decent coffee, boss. Some enterprising owner of the snack bar at the entrance to this industrial estate has opened up to support our brave heroes in uniform. Very altruistic of her, I thought.'

Malkie scowled at her, but they all knew his heart wasn't in it. 'Thanks, Lou. Now piss off home before I put you on report.'

She flapped a hand at him as she walked away. 'Yes, boss. Sorry, boss. Pissing off now, boss.'

Malkie turned back to find Steph watching him, her eyes alive with an amused twinkle.

'Shut it, Lang.'

As they sipped their coffee, so much better than the rubbish they'd had earlier, a van drove through the cordon after signing in, and pulled up beside the remaining ambulance. A man in full firefighter gear got out and stretched, and Malkie felt his stomach sink.

Steph noticed. 'You know him?'

Malkie sighed. 'Fire Scene Investigator.'

Steph's face turned serious. 'Is he...?'

'Aye. Callum Gourlay. He attended the fire that killed my mum.'

She seemed to debate whether to speak again, but – as always – did. 'Are you going to be OK? I mean... you know? This is the first fire scene you've attended since that night, and now this bloke turning up?'

Malkie smiled at her. 'Same shit, different day, Steph.'

The man entered the Command Vehicle then reappeared outside. He hung a plastic tag amongst others on a board hanging on the vehicle's door. When he approached Malkie and Steph, he flashed them his ID. 'Evening. Callum Gourlay. FIU. I'm guessing you'll be Police Scotland, aye? Waiting to get in for a look?'

Malkie stared at him. Steph nodded. 'Aye, and to chat to the firefighters – aye, I know we can only formally interview the guys in charge. I'm Detective Constable Stephanie Lang. We have some Uniforms on the way to assist.'

Gourlay nodded at her, then glanced at Malkie, a question on his face.

Malkie roused himself again, for the second time in as many minutes. 'Sorry, mate. Hang on.' He fished inside his coat for his warrant card but stopped when he saw recognition dawn. Gourlay held out a hand. 'DS McCulloch. I wish I could say nice to meet you again, but...'

The air hung thick with awkward silence.

Malkie shook his hand. Gourlay held it for a second, seemed to study Malkie. 'Will you be assessing the scene? Like, inside?'

Malkie smiled at him, appreciated the man's concern. 'I will. I'm SIO. Need to tick that box, right?'

Gourlay laughed, his relief apparent, and Malkie felt all three relax. He turned back to watch the firefighters again, but found they'd progressed deeper into the building and out of sight.

'If they're that far in, it shouldn't be long before they can start checking the structural integrity to decide if you can enter. Are your SOCOs on the way too?'

Malkie glanced at Steph. She nodded, a small smile on her lips.

Gourlay didn't miss it. 'Who's actually in charge here?' Malkie tried to look offended, but Steph raised an enquiring eyebrow at him, and he crumbled.

'Me, nominally. Apparently. Allegedly.'

All three took another second then grinned, the tension well and truly broken. Malkie would want a word with Gourlay about his own past case, and Gourlay would expect that, but for now all three needed to remain focused.

And Malkie needed to build himself up, steel himself, for walking into just about the biggest and most brutal trigger location he could remember. This warehouse fire would feel nothing like the cramped, fire-gutted remains of his parents' bungalow, but he harboured no doubt he'd be assaulted by sights and smells that would test his resolve to the limit.

He'd promised Thompson he was up for this. Now, he needed to convince himself.

EIGHT

The SOCO van arrived. Malkie updated them and advised them of the expected length of wait to be allowed entry. After two more hours of standing around, observing and taking notes, both crews emerged, looking broken. Malkie thought they looked beaten, too. Defeated. He had to wonder if just putting fires out was never enough. Did they rate themselves on how much of the building they managed to save? In this case, the answer to that might explain their apparent mood.

Then he realised his short-sightedness. While they'd been in there, on the job, thoughts of Duncan Duffy would have been displaced by adrenaline and sheer survival instinct. People like them couldn't do their jobs without being able to compartmentalise, much as police officers had to on too many occasions. With the fire apparently beaten, they would now crash. They'd want an update on Duffy. This made Malkie realise he hadn't seen Jeremy Lees for some time. He glanced back at the Incident Control van and saw him sat on the fold-up steps into the van. His posture told Malkie he did have an update and would be dreading his crew asking the inevitable question.

'Fuck.'

Steph looked up from her phone. 'What?' She looked around her for the source of Malkie's considered comment.

'Lees.' Malkie nodded towards him as he stood. 'Poor bastard has a difficult conversation ahead of him.'

Steph watched Lees, grim. 'Be gentle with him, mate. Sorry, you didn't need that.'

'It's fine. I'll dig up a scrap of tact from somewhere deep inside.' He started towards Lees.

Lees looked up at Malkie before he reached the van, and his face told Malkie all he needed to know. His eyes were wet, and Malkie thought he might never before have seen a more broken and desolate shell of a man.

Lees pre-empted Malkie's question. 'Died in the ambulance five minutes from St John's. Resus worked on him as long as they thought it worthwhile, but...'

Malkie half-smiled, an admission of the miserable task ahead for Lees. He stood back a respectful distance.

Lees stood to face his crew.

Malkie backed off further. As much as we wanted to hear every word said and see every reaction from every firefighter up close, he couldn't bear to think he might risk intruding.

The crew walked up to Lees, gathered in a semi-circle around him. Their uniforms and their faces were stained black with the fire's assault on them all. Each held their helmets by the straps, hanging at their sides. Someone had handed them bottles of water which they drank from and poured over their faces to try to wipe off the worst of their fatigue and the inevitable heavy landing from the end of their two-hour adrenaline rush.

Lees took seconds to tell them, ripped the sticking plaster right off, as he'd expect from people of their obvious resilience. Sian Wilson buckled at the knees, but Cormack had positioned himself ready to catch her. She sobbed on his chest for a few seconds then went quiet, collected herself with an obvious effort and stood apart again.

Malkie had to wonder if a firefighting crew losing a colleague they'd been into battle with and had to trust with their lives hurt more than telling some poor parents their son had killed himself doing a ton up the motorway in his dad's BMW. Had to be a different kind of hurt. After more than twenty years facing the shit he'd had to, he wasn't sure that kind of pain could be graded. He'd never managed to feel anything but sick to the stomach after the – thankfully few – deaths of his own colleagues.

Malkie gave them a minute, then stepped forward. Only when he reached them and they turned weary and desolate looks on him did he realise he hadn't the slightest bloody clue what to say to them.

They watched him for a second, which only compounded the pressure to come up with something that wouldn't piss them off and embarrass himself.

'We're here to investigate the death of the first casualty, the person inside the building, but I want to express my sympathies. The last thing I want to do is intrude on your grief and I won't insult you guys with some trite words. I'm sorry. That's all.'

After a few of the most uncomfortable seconds of blank stares, a couple of them smiled and muttered a few words, enough to let him believe he at least hadn't made their pain any worse.

NINE

Malkie left them as they headed for a nearby minibus which he guessed would take them back to the station for what Cormack had called a 'hot debrief'. He returned to the entrance to the warehouse, but nearly turned back as the interior came into clear view through a door that looked to have been forced open to reveal a mass of furniture and storage boxes that must have been stacked against it from the inside. That explained why Paul Turner and Duncan Duffy had to traverse the full depth of the building from the front doors to confirm the casualty, and why they both still had some distance to withdraw after Duffy announced his BA Set issues.

A wave of fear like nothing he'd felt before sluiced through him. His guts turned over and he tasted yet more bile.

Callum Gourlay spotted him and approached. 'The building has been declared safe to enter from a fire door we've forced open at the back, next to where the body was found. When you're ready...'

Malkie's stomach sank.

'Great. Thanks, mate. We'll get suited up, join you in a few minutes.'

'Not much point suiting up, but I know rules are rules. Forensically, the whole of the inside of the building has been pretty much wrecked. We can do our investigation, but I'll be amazed if your lot gets much. You'll need one of our face masks though, might still be a wee trace of smoke and other fumes in there.'

After dressing for entry, they followed Gourlay to the doorway. He held some kind of measuring device in one hand, and he checked the readings before entering. He saw Malkie's enquiring eyes and showed him the backlit LCD display. 'Measures carbon monoxide, which will kill you slowly, and hydrogen cyanide, which can kill you in just a few deep breaths, plus a load of other toxins. We're clear.'

He led them inside.

Malkie had to swallow bile and stuff his hands in his pockets to avoid anyone seeing how much they shook. Steph stood before him and placed her hands on his arms.

'We got this, aye?'

He couldn't answer her. *I can't fucking do this. I have to do it.*

This back corner of the building seemed to have survived complete destruction. He could still see that the SOCOs were going to struggle to isolate any evidence from the surrounding structure or the contents of the rooms. Black soot stained everything. The floor lay covered in soaked, extinguished embers and chunks of ceiling that had fallen in before being completely consumed by the flames. Metal strapping on shelving units had twisted into knots as if agonised by the intense heat where they'd spilled their contents to the floor. Insulation material hung in tatters from ceiling space exposed by the fallen timbers, like shredded skin hanging off a burn victim.

Dad's legs looked like that.

His world lurched and he stumbled. He clutched a doorway

to regain his balance and hung his head, his eyes screwed shut, his throat constricted, his mouth dry.

'Malkie?' Steph's voice, her concern clear.

He straightened. 'I'm fine. I stood on a lump of masonry or something.'

She studied him, gauged him, then nodded. Yet again, more to say. Later.

He continued. Embers crunched under his firefighter wellington boots. Black water dripped from ceilings and tick-ticked against his hard hat. Every inch of the floor looked covered with traps to trip him. Flaps of half-burned carpet tried to snag his feet. Wires severed from their sources, their plastic melted and twisted, lurked under piles of ash and embers, like tripwires ready to pitch him face-first to the floor and a mouthful of black charcoal nuggets.

He tasted ash even through his face mask, nearly choked despite it reaching nowhere near his throat.

Fuck's sake, I remember all of this.

Gourlay stopped at an office doorway, the door lying propped against an adjacent wall. He held his device up again, satisfied himself with the readings, then turned in the entryway as if to block it, as if to hide what lay within.

'Mr McCulloch. Detective.'

'Malkie...'

'OK. Malkie. I wouldn't insult your intelligence by warning you what's inside is... distressing. But...'

Gourlay's words trailed off. How could anyone put it into words?

'It's fine, Mr Gourlay.'

'Callum.'

Malkie smiled but knew he'd fool no one. 'This isn't a bungalow, and...' The words stuck in his throat. He couldn't push them out past a lump of nausea. 'Chances are, that's no one I know in there. I'll manage, but thanks.'

'Far left corner, OK? When you're ready.' Gourlay stepped aside and Malkie entered, Steph close behind him.

'I'll be back soon, need to check the barrel racks. That's where most bonded warehouse fires start. Be back soon.' He turned to go but hesitated. 'Unless you want me to hang on here?'

Malkie smiled at him. 'I'm fine, Callum. Honestly.' He watched Gourlay study him again then nod to himself and disappear down a short corridor.

Malkie entered the office space, the first fire-damaged room he'd been in since his life fell apart eight months ago.

An office space. Half a desk, pitched to the left where the wooden surface had burned away, and what looked like paper ash. Filing cabinets, all drawers closed. Underneath and between them, scraps of paper, brown and scorched but only partly burned. They looked like they might have slid off the table into places where the flames hadn't reached them. He wondered if the contents remained intact, then reminded himself to stop looking for distractions. A plant pot, barely the remains of a single blackened stem of something stuck out of scorched earth. He spotted something he couldn't have expected: what looked like the charred and twisted frame of a camp bed. Beyond that, a pile of what had to be the remains of a sleeping bag. Which led his mind to the very thing he'd been trying to ignore.

In the far-left corner, just where Gourlay had warned him it would be. A corpse. Blackened and charred almost beyond recognition, but horribly recognisable too, its skull exposed where skin had burned away, a smell rising from it he could taste but couldn't describe, an odour that seemed to leave a coating on the roof of his mouth. The body lay on its side, its back to the room, foetal and pathetic, as if the victim had huddled into the last remaining space he or she could find as the flames reached for them and choking, acrid smoke snaked its way into nose and lungs.

Back off. Compartmentalise. Objectify if I need to. Just get a grip.

Malkie's mum hadn't been burned as badly as this poor bastard. When he'd had to identify her, he'd seen no burns or other scarring from her neck up – all that the mortuary sheet had left visible. She'd died of smoke inhalation. Horrible, but he'd been reassured she'd fallen unconscious quickly, before the fire had eaten away at her legs and her torso.

He felt his coffee surge up the back of his throat and choked it back down, rather than embarrass himself by running outside to throw up like some newbie Uniform. Steph stood motionless, watching the body. She'd always had a stronger stomach than Malkie, but even she had turned pale.

'You OK, Steph?'

She dragged her mind back from wherever she'd gone, to process what she saw. 'Aye. It's just so... I can almost imagine that poor sod's last moments. But I can't imagine...' She stopped, gaped at him, her eyes horrified. 'Oh, Malkie, I'm sorry. You don't need to hear that.' She reached for his arm but he held a hand up. She stopped, understood. Time and place, not now. He needed to keep a grip for now. She'd be there for him later.

Malkie forced himself to stand over the body and look at the hidden side, the front of the body, curled into the corner. It couldn't look more like a baby in a womb; arms and hands tucked in as if to protect them, chin tucked in, knees drawn up almost to the chest. He couldn't stop an image of the poor bastard. Did they scream? Or cry? Could he hope to find out that they – like his mum – had succumbed to the smoke before the flames licked at their back? Steph stepped beside him. He heard her sigh.

'I'll get the SOCOs in, boss. I seriously doubt there's anything more for us for now.'

Malkie smiled at her; as usual, she had his back.

They retreated, followed their own incoming footsteps as much as they could, to where Gourlay had reappeared in the doorway.

Malkie moved beside him. 'Anything?'

'Aye. Sometimes the seat of a fire is obvious. A charred wall socket overloaded with high-wattage devices plugged into too many extensions. Or an overturned cigarette and ashtray on an old sofa. Sometimes, the ignition method and the fuelling of the fire are set up by someone who knows what they're doing, and it takes a trained eye like mine to see it. This one may fall into the latter category.'

'So, arson?'

'I didn't say that. Look, anything I say now is subject to change and you can't quote me on anything until I sign off my official report...'

'Aye, we get the same from the SOCOs all the time.' They shared a mutual long-suffering raising of eyebrows.

Gourlay crossed back to the door, studied the hallway outside, then returned. 'Aye, I think we're going to find the fire started down there in the storage room. Most whisky warehouse fires start in storage. Any decent whisky has to mature in oak barrels for years before being bottled. You'll know that, being a good dram-loving Scotsman, I imagine.' He grinned and raised his eyebrows as if expecting an answer.

Steph failed to suppress an amused 'Hmm.' And Malkie scowled at her. She pretended to suddenly find something of interest to investigate on the other side of the room.

Gourlay seemed to catch that he'd missed some internal joke, but continued. 'Over those years, ethanol fumes leak out into the environment. Never catastrophic leaks, but enough that any storage facility storing products that contain ethanol has to be ventilated and equipped with decent sprinkler systems. If the barrels get too hot the metal hoops can expand. The weight of the liquid separates the staves, and the ethanol leaks out. That's dangerous, because although a large volume of it will likely just douse a naked flame, a spray or pressurised leak can ignite on contact or when it spreads across the floor. Happened in Glasgow in 1960. Twenty-eighth March. Cheapside Street. Fire started in the storage room, no decent sprinklers, barrels ruptured, caused a BLEVE. A boiling liquid expanding vapour explosion. Eighteen firefighters died trying to save that building and other commercial properties around it, and half of them were crushed under masonry when the blast blew the walls out.' He seemed to drift for a few seconds. 'Some of us still attend the memorials in the Glasgow Necropolis every March, it caused that big a black mark on Scottish firefighting.'

He roused himself from painful thoughts. 'Anyway, that's the basics. The barrels get hot, the hoops expand, the staves separate, the ethanol leaks out in small-enough quantities to vaporise in the super-heated air, and...'

Malkie could find no words. He almost felt himself obligated to attend the Necropolis in March, only a few weeks away.

He cleared his throat. Found his mouth had dried out. 'So, is that what happened here?'

Gourlay turned to him and fixed his stare. 'Can't tell you yet... I know, I know, but I mean I *can't*. Not yet.'

Malkie sighed. Gourlay held his hands up.

'I can see no sign of accelerant on the floor of the barrel storage, but that's not surprising given how intense the fire would have been in there. Everything flammable will have been consumed.'

'Any signs indicative of arson?'

Gourlay shrugged. 'We call it wilful fire-raising, but no, nothing conclusive.'

'Nothing *conclusive*?'

Gourlay stared at him. His eyes spoke volumes but his lips remained closed.

Malkie knew better than to push for more. 'I know, I know. Briefing only after investigations have been conducted. Like you say, rules are rules, right?'

Steph spoke from the far corner of the room. Malkie turned to find her staring into the top corner. He joined her, looked where she did.

What looked like the melted remains of a CCTV camera hung on blackened and melted wires from a bracket and socket.

They glanced at each other.

Steph said what they were both thinking.

'Mr Gourlay, do you happen to know if this place has active CCTV, and if it's recorded within the building or remotely?'

Gourlay wandered over and looked up. He raised his eyebrows. 'If there's nothing in here, I can't imagine where it'll be, but I'll keep an eye out for recording equipment when I do my full search.'

'Thanks, Callum. I want to know why someone was sleeping in a camp bed in here and wasn't wakened by the alarm or the sprinklers or a bloody great fire raging at the end of a short corridor. Until it became too late, that is.'

Gourlay held his hands out as if to mime a *no comment*, and Malkie decided to stop making the poor sod's life difficult.

'Can I see the barrel storage?'

Gourlay thought for a second. 'I suppose you need to ascertain if there's been any foul play, right?'

'Aye, but only that Hercules Parrot bloke says *foul play*, mate.'

Malkie couldn't see Gourlay's lips behind the face mask, but his eyes smiled for him. He led Malkie down the corridor.

Gourlay checked the air again, then allowed Malkie to enter the storage area.

Wooden racks, some remnants on the ends still three shelves high but most now no more than ashes and charred timbers soaked and strewn across filthy grey puddles that covered most of the floor. Gourlay glanced at one wall, then looked away when he saw Malkie watching him. Malkie studied the wall and the floor beneath it. He saw what he guessed Gourlay had noticed too. Three double electrical sockets at floor level. Three huge metal boxes with louvre-style sides hung on the wall above them. The power cables hanging from all three led to a single extension block plugged into just one of the sockets, now blackened and melted messes of plastic and copper wires. The remaining five sockets were empty, but years-old grime showed that one of each pair of sockets normally had plugs inserted into them at some time.

Malkie glanced at Gourlay. 'Air conditioning?'

'Climate control to keep the barrels at the optimum temperature for maturing the whisky.'

Malkie scanned the wall around and above the units. He saw a skylight above the middle unit, wide open.

'A wide-open window right above a climate control unit?'

Gourlay said nothing.

Malkie looked around the rest of the area. He saw sprinkler pipes and nozzles at regular intervals across the ceiling. He followed them to where they all seemed to flow into a junction box, then he traced a single, wider pipe down to a valve wheel. He glanced at Gourlay again. 'You checked this.'

Gourlay hesitated before answering. 'I did.' His tone told Malkie that asking more questions would elicit no further answers. But he was damned sure that if Gourlay had confirmed the valve was open and functioning OK, he would have had no trouble in saying so.

Malkie nodded to him.

'Thanks, Mr Gourlay. I'll look forward to reading the first draft of your report.'

Again, Gourlay said nothing, but allowed Malkie to walk past him, then followed him out to the cold, fresh night air.

TEN

Back outside, Malkie tore off his paper face mask and gulped down huge breaths of air. He hoped it would clean his lungs out, sluice out the stink of smoke and burned upholstery and interior joinery. And the stink of charred flesh, of course.

The air outside smelled clearer, but still tainted – like the air for a hundred yards in every direction would be – with the odour of smoke. Not the almost pleasant smell of wood smoke at a bonfire, but the rank and cloying stench of fire-damage, of a building gutted and life taken.

Compartmentalise. Or remove yourself.

Steph appeared beside him. 'That was...'

'I know.'

She gave him a few seconds. 'And?'

He gave her unspoken question the consideration it – and she – deserved. 'I'm going to be OK. If it had been a domestic, someone's home, I might not have coped as well, but that's a problem for another day. Tonight is one fucking horrible bridge crossed, and I'm on the other side of it now. Aye, I'm sure.'

Her eyes glowed, and he chose to believe he saw affection.

Gourlay had returned inside the building; he had a long

night ahead of him and his investigation would probably take days, not hours. Three Scottish Forensics SOCOs and a Uniform he didn't recognise approached them from where their kit van sat beside the Command Vehicle and the remaining ambulance.

'Have the SFRS OK'd us to enter yet, DS McCulloch?' A huge bear of a man, his plastic onesie stretched tight over his shoulders. Bruce. Malkie could never remember his surname for some reason, and he'd also learned that the man had hated Malkie calling him 'Big Daddy' in the early days of their working relationship, after he'd looked up the wrestling reference from the seventies.

'Hi, Bruce. Aye, they gave us the all-clear to take an initial look, so you should be OK. SFRS had to enter at the front of the building, straight through the storage area where the worst of the fire seemed to be burning. The first two in – they'd already established a possible risk to life – confirmed the whisky barrels in the storage room were burning out of control, but they had to push further in to confirm a fatality in what we believe is an office at the back of the building. They had to return before reaching the office, though. Some kind of issue with their breathing gear, but then they forced a fire exit at the back that had been padlocked and blocked on the inside with a pile of old furniture. That gave us external access to the corridor right outside the office. That door there.' He pointed to the obvious gaping space in the wall.

Bruce looked up from scribbling in a notebook. 'And one fatality? Male or female?'

Malkie swallowed, pushed back images still too vivid in his mind. 'Difficult to tell.'

Bruce's shoulders slumped. 'I hate these ones. Always get to me. Burning is a bloody awful way to go.' He seemed to realise what he'd said and gaped at Malkie. Malkie patted him on the arm. 'It's fine, mate. I managed OK.'

Bruce appraised him. 'Good. That's good to hear, Malkie.' The huge man turned towards the doorway.

Malkie took his chance. 'Mind your head, mate, aye?'

Bruce turned back to him, leaned in close. 'I'll give you that one, Malkie. Now piss off, eh?' He grinned, and Malkie released a sigh of relief.

Malkie asked the Uniform his name and shook his hand, then asked him to set up crime-scene access control the best he could. He and Steph left him looking a tad overwhelmed but eager to please. They walked back to the makeshift parking area. The firefighters had been bussed back to the station for their debrief. Jeremy Lees remained, busying himself at the Command Vehicle, looked to be doing a handover to a firefighter from another station, someone Malkie hadn't had cause to talk to yet.

When he finished, Lees's face fell and his shoulders slumped when he found Malkie and Steph behind him.

'I have to go back to the station, officers. The debrief won't start without me, and I want to let both watches get away home as quickly as possible.'

Malkie held his hands out to placate the man. 'I know, Mr Lees. I just wanted to check in with you before you leave. Our SOCOs are inside now. Callum Gourlay gave me a tour of the barrel storage, though.'

Lees seemed to realise Malkie hadn't said all he could. 'And? Anything noteworthy?'

'Not to my untrained eye, Mr Lees, but I'll be keen to read the first draft of the report at tomorrow's initial briefing. If some bastard set this fire on purpose, I mean to make sure he or she is brought to book for it. We have no idea who the casualty in the office is, but I'm sure your man didn't deserve what's happened to him. None of you deserve what's happened to you tonight.'

Lees considered him, then held his hand out. 'I appreciate your kind words, Mr McCulloch. But now I have to go.' He removed his Incident Commander tabard, tucked it under his arm, then walked away towards a waiting car.

'Sorry, Steph. I didn't let you lead much on this one, did I?'

'Oh, good grief, Malkie. When have I ever been that thin-skinned?'

Never, but you're not yourself right now, are you, Steph?

He stared at her. She buckled.

'Stop that. I'm fine. I will be.'

Malkie knew not to keep digging but added her to his to-do list.

ELEVEN

Two hours later they returned to the near-deserted Police Scotland CID room in the Livingston Civic Centre. They found no one at any of the desks, which surprised neither of them at 5:30 in the morning.

Each took a half hour to freshen up, grab a cup of what the vending machine called coffee and a sandwich, then sat back-to-back at their own desks to gather their thoughts.

Steph turned to Malkie long before he felt ready for the conversation.

'Shall we make a start, mate?' She checked her watch. 'If we rattle through them to note down any obvious actions for follow-up tomorrow, we can maybe both get a couple of hours' sleep and a shower at home before morning briefing?'

Malkie sighed but swivelled his chair to face her.

'You start. Get me in the mood.'

Steph grinned and opened her notebook. 'Right. Blue Watch Commander Jeremy Lees. Seems competent enough and opinions of his squad seemed very positive. I got the impression he's a bit soft, but he seems to have the respect of his people. Loyalty, even. Good sense of humour, apparently.'

She turned a page. 'Graham Cormack. The big, dishy one.'

'Can't say I noticed but carry on.'

'Really? I wouldn't say no. Anyway, I got nothing from him. Respects Lees and his colleagues. Nothing else I picked up on, no conscious evasion or anything like that. He just didn't have anything to add.'

Another page. 'I found out that a guy called Steve Grayson is their resident techie, their Watch Engineer I think they called him, checks and signs off on all the gear, safety checks, that sort of thing.'

Another page. 'Paul Turner, the guy who went in with Duncan Duffy. He's what they call "Whole Time", apparently. Means he was full time not just on call, but he claimed he had nothing to tell me. Not sure I believed him, something bothered him, more than just having lost a colleague. Duffy was Retained, which I now know means part-time, on-call only, and apparently desperate to go Whole Time. The elephant in the room is that he and Sian Wilson are obviously close, to say the least, even though SFRS regulations prohibit relationships between colleagues. We need to find out just how close.

'Peter Fairbairn is Whole Time too, but I didn't speak to him because he kept disappearing.'

She closed her notebook. 'Duffy and Turner went in first. Always two go in first, with breathing gear apparently, but only if there's thought to be a possible risk to life. Turner says they went in the front door because they found the back door blocked by a pile of old furniture and joinery waste from a recent refitting of the place. By the time they negotiated their way past the storage area deeper into the building and spotted the fatality in the office, Duffy said he'd reached his turnaround pressure, meaning he'd used a third of his air tank, and when that happens they have to turn back so they have a safety margin if they encounter problems exiting. Halfway back, he yelled something about his BA Set, collapsed, and that's all

Turner can tell us. He dragged him out, and the rest of the crew carried him to the ambulances.'

'And the others that pulled him out, they corroborated that?'

'Aye. As soon as the two men staggered out of the door, Turner tore his own mask off, then moved Duffy's to the side to check his breathing. He found a pulse, so they carried him straight to the ambulances rather than attempt CPR immediately. The rest you know.'

Malkie chewed this over. 'So, Lees, Turner and Cormack seemed to have nothing to add, and you got no sense of anything they were specifically not saying? But you think Grayson had something he didn't want to say, right? About Duffy's breathing gear?'

'I wouldn't put money on it at the moment, because they were all a bit knackered and stressed, but...' – she took a second – 'Aye. There was something there he didn't want to talk about.'

Malkie opened his own notebook. Steph's eyebrows lifted. 'You took notes? In your notebook?'

'Piss off. I can when you're not around to do it for me.' He gave her a look, which only made her grin even more.

He opened his notebook. 'I left Fairbairn to last because I wanted to hear from the others, get as much info *on* him before I talked *to* him, if that makes sense?

'Donald McCallum. Seems generally very well liked. Like everyone's favourite uncle.'

Steph smiled. 'Have you been doing that thing you do again? To make sure you don't forget people's names? That's so sweet that you don't want to offend people.'

'Shut it, Lang. Kenny Donaldson. Oldest member and longest serving of either crew. Due to retire seven months from now, and seems solid and dependable. I suppose doing what these guys do for forty years either breaks you or turns you into the kind of person who can handle anything that gets thrown at them.

'Stuart Simpson. Poor sod barely said a word to me. He kept glancing over at McCallum. I didn't get the impression we'll get much of use out of the lad, probably stretched to his limits just doing his job and not letting his crew down.

'Sian Wilson. Like you said, what's the story between her and Duffy? Graham Cormack told us they were just old and close friends, but I saw more than just that in her when she broke down. And remember what she said?'

Steph nodded. '"Where's his BA Set?" or words to that effect. Specific focus on Duffy's BA Set.'

Malkie nodded. 'Aye. So, Fairbairn grabs Duffy's BA Set, seems to feel a need to check it himself before handing it over to Lees, then Wilson seems fixated on the self-same BA Set.'

'Did you ask Lees about that?'

'Aye. He said the same as Cormack thought he might: Fairbairn grabbed it to keep it safe for inspection.'

Steph waited while Malkie recalled Fairbairn's manner earlier.

'But I saw him check the rubber seal. No doubt about it, he wanted to check that BA Set for something specific. I'd bet your pension on that. This will need at least a Fatal Accident Inquiry, and our Police Scotland authority will only kick in if they find someone tampered with Duffy's equipment or if they find any irregularities in Fairbairn's behaviour before he handed it in to Lees.

'Apart from that, Fairbairn's story matches the others. Turner dragged Duffy out, they checked his breathing and carried him to the ambulances. I didn't get any variation in that version of events from any of them.'

Steph sighed. 'No, me neither. So, we need to talk to wait for Callum Gourlay's report. I can't think of anything more we can do until the briefing tomorrow?'

Malkie leaned back in his chair, stretched and groaned. 'As for the deceased in the office, we'll only have a homicide to investigate if Gourlay's investigation turns up evidence of "foul play". I saw some really dodgy-looking electrics in the storage area, looked like someone had plugged three climate control units into one extension and left a skylight open right above them. I'm no expert, but it occurs to me that a skylight shouldn't be wide open in the middle of February, and certainly not above three high-powered climate control units that would go into overdrive if cold air was pouring in on them?'

'Good grief. Sounds dodgy, right enough. What did Gourlay say?'

'I couldn't really press him. Jurisdiction and process, etc. But he gave me a very obvious "no comment" look. I couldn't tell if he genuinely had no opinion yet or he did but was refusing to indulge me.'

Steph stretched now and yawned. 'So, we don't even know if either of those deaths will actually land on our desks, unless our forensics turn something up on the first body, or Callum Gourlay's investigation indicates something other than just fatal accidents?'

'Aye, that about sums it up. Take yourself home for a few hours. I'll write up what we have already and log actions for the briefing tomorrow. I'll get Gucci on background checks on all of them just in case, first thing. And find out how we proceed from here. We don't want to be stepping on SFRS or Health and Safety toes. I'll check in with Callum Gourlay in the morning, too. It'll be too soon for him to give me anything concrete but no harm in asking.'

Steph had started to clear her desk, but she turned back to Malkie. 'If he was the Fire Scene Investigator who did your parents' home, will you be OK working with him?'

Malkie considered this, needed to be sure for himself. 'Aye, I think so. He did his job then and the inquiry found no reason to take it any further. That's all done and dusted, really.'

He realised what he'd just said. 'Formally, anyway.' He tried to smile at her, to reassure her, but her expression told him he'd failed.

Malkie switched on his computer. He got barely fifteen minutes into typing up his notes when his phone rang. He put it on speaker.

'McCulloch here.' He forced himself not to sigh despite seeing his hope of even a few hours of sleep evaporate.

'Sorry to do this to you, Malkie. Call just came in from Uniforms. Assault in a domestic property, and you were called for by name.'

With a feeling of dread he asked, 'What are the details?'

'Someone has attacked a Mr Peter Fairbairn at the gentleman's home. He said "she" smashed a bottle over his head. Fairbairn's still at home, refuses to be taken to St John's for some reason despite needing ten stitches.'

Malkie thanked the caller, then ended the call and placed his phone on his desk.

'Fuck's sake. I'll attend at Fairbairn's address, see if he recognised who attacked him.'

Steph still hadn't left for home. She stared at him, now. 'Which woman did we observe seeming to have a big problem with Fairbairn right after Duffy was taken away?'

'Exactly. You want to check she's OK?'

'I'd better, right? Just for a chat. For her own welfare.'

TWELVE

Steph knocked on the door of Sian Wilson's flat. A call to the SFRS station revealed that she had left in a state after the debrief. A look through the letter box showed nothing noteworthy. Tidy hallway, prints hanging on both walls. But no Wilson. She did notice, though, a light in the living room at the end of the hallway, too bright to be just a single lamp left on for security.

Steph let the letter box flap swing shut with a sharp metallic clack and held a finger to her lips, and Davie Semple, the Uniform accompanying her, nodded his understanding.

She eased the letter box open again enough to see the light from the living room.

It took only three minutes. She saw variation in the light; someone moving about. She gave it another few minutes, then Wilson peeked around the door.

Steph spoke through the letter box. 'Ms Wilson, please open the door. I can't leave without talking to you.'

Wilson stepped into the doorway, her shoulders slumped. She looked back into her living room and sideways into some other room to her left, as if her subconscious refused to believe she had no other way out of the flat. It took her only seconds to give up. She walked the length of the hallway and opened the front door.

Her face was still smeared with soot and ash. She glared at Steph.

'Why are you here?'

Steph held her hands out palms down. 'We had a report that Peter Fairbairn was attacked in his own home. By a woman. I'm sure you can understand we need to talk to you, given your reaction to him at the scene of the fire?'

Steph stepped forward and placed a hand on the door, and Wilson stepped back and to one side. Steph and Constable Semple entered the living room. She noticed two bedrooms and a bathroom as she passed, all as well-decorated and clean and tidy as the hallway. The living room, too, suggested Wilson took pride in her property. The room contained a two-seater sofa, a separate recliner chair, and an antique-effect timber coffee table. A TV cabinet in one corner held a flat-screen TV, but not an enormous one, and tall, flourishing yuccas sat in pots on either side. The room looked immaculate except for Wilson's firefighter jacket thrown across the back of the sofa and an open bottle of gin and a glass on the coffee table. Steph thought of her own flat. The exact opposite. A riot of pot plants, the bigger and more expansive the better. Knickknacks everywhere, mostly gathered during a single year she spent bumming around the continent with nothing but a backpack and four thousand quid her mum had managed to hide from her so-called stepfather. She'd hidden it in the pocket of Steph's one and only proper dress, where she'd found it on the day her mum started what turned out to be her last spell in Cornton Vale.

Wilson entered after Steph and Semple. She slid her gin bottle and glass to the opposite corner of the table and sat on the recliner. She indicated for them to sit on the sofa.

'May I call you Sian?'

'No.'

'Fine. Have you seen Peter Fairbairn since leaving your debrief at the station, Ms Wilson?' Steph laced her voice with a touch of steel.

Wilson looked from one officer to the other and back again, then shrugged her shoulders. Her mouth opened, then closed again. She took a gulp of her gin and sat back in her chair. Steph didn't swallow her affected air of nonchalance for a second.

'No. What I said back at the scene of the fire. Whatever I said about Peter Fairbairn, he had it coming.'

Steph stared at her for only a few seconds and saw what she wanted: Wilson swallowed, then rubbed her nose with her fingers, thinking on her feet, or rather on her backside. She wanted to ferret out whatever Wilson really meant by her comment but reminded herself that the woman had just lost someone who she – for whatever reason – no doubt cared about very much.

'I do want to say how sorry I am about Mr Duffy. You were obviously close. I got the impression everyone on both crews is hurting, and I expect they'll be worried about you. Please accept my sympathies.'

The sudden change in tone had Wilson searching Steph's eyes, as if suspecting some kind of cynical tactic to put her off her guard. In the end she appeared to accept Steph's comments as intended.

'Thanks. I appreciate that.' She stared down into the gin glass clutched in her hands. Steph waited. Tears fell from Wilson's cheeks onto her arms. Steph pulled some tissues from a box on the table and handed them to her. This small act of kindness set Wilson off, and she sobbed, quiet and miserable, for long seconds until the episode passed.

'I'm sorry. I—'

'Don't be. Were you and Mr Duffy very close? Or had you

been previously? Are firefighters in the same squad allowed to, you know...?'

Wilson studied Steph's face and smiled, barely. 'He was the best friend I ever had. We've known each other since our school days.' She nodded at a framed photograph on the TV cabinet. She and Duncan Duffy in shorts and T-shirts, squinting in the sun, wine glasses in their hands, laughter in their eyes. Behind them a static caravan on some seaside field, a table and chairs on which sat lunch and glasses and a wine bottle all under a canopy, a huge expanse of grey sea in the background with white-tipped waves rolling into shore. 'That was just a few months ago. Was bloody freezing.' She tried to smile but her voice caught on her last word, and she lowered her head again.

Steph studied the photograph for a minute, gave Wilson time to gather herself. Unwelcome thoughts intruded on the moment. She wondered if she could ever feel so happy just to be in someone's company to act the fool as they did in that picture. She envied Wilson for a second before remembering that the woman's sense of loss right now must eclipse Steph's current struggles. Wilson losing such an old and close friend had to hurt so much more than Steph's fury at her so-called uncle and the betrayal he'd inflicted on her and her mother.

'DC Lang?'

Steph roused herself. 'Sorry, Constable Semple.' She turned back to Wilson, who had been watching her.

'Ms Wilson. Sian. What do you remember about tonight's events?'

Wilson sat back in her chair, her face set hard.

'You must know that I can't discuss anything with you without my Watch Commander and an FBU rep present.'

'FBU?'

'Fire Brigade Union. Maybe even a lawyer, too.'

'I know, and I do sympathise, Sian. But I was talking about

after your debrief. After you were all dismissed. Not at the scene of the fire or what happened to Mr Duffy.'

Wilson gaped at her. 'Seriously? I came home. What else do you think I would want to do after—'

'I'm sorry, but I need to ask. So, you haven't seen Peter Fairbairn since you left the debrief?'

Wilson's head snapped up, her expression defensive. 'No. Why would I? Did he say I did? Don't believe a word that fucker...' She stopped, sat back, folded her arms.

'So, you know nothing about some woman attacking him on his doorstep an hour ago?'

Steph hoped for surprise. Even a hint of curiosity which would allow her to believe Wilson knew nothing about it.

Wilson stood. 'Please leave. I've had a rotten night and I want you to leave.'

Steph stood. 'OK, Sian. Do you have someone we can call to stay with you?'

Sian nodded without lifting her head. 'Graham Cormack is coming over to stay the night with me. On the sofa. He and I go way back, too. He got me into the SFRS in the first place.'

Steph and Constable Davie Semple left her to her grief.

Steph sent Davie to clock off for the day and she headed home for – she checked her watch – a shower and coffee and an hour on the sofa, she hoped.

THIRTEEN

Fairbairn's home sat in the town of East Calder, to the southeast of Livingston. Detached villas, large gardens, most well-tended with only a few that hadn't seen any attention in a long time. Livingston properties cost a wodge more than similar homes in the smaller towns further out from the Edinburgh city boundary. An SFRS Watch Commander must earn a healthy salary to be able to pay a mortgage on something like this given they tended to retire from front-line duty in their fifties. Either that or they enjoyed a better pension than Police Scotland paid.

Malkie's line of thinking led him back to his own precarious financial position. When his dad's house had burned down eight months ago, his insurer had refused to pay out, only too happy reject his claim because of an undeclared and unfinished conservatory started before the fire by some builder who'd left a bad job half-done then disappeared with most of his dad's retirement savings. With nothing but the value of the land, albeit not a small sum given its location in Old Livingston Village, and Malkie already paying a hefty mortgage on his own flat, both he and his dad had agreed to renovate and move into the old holiday-let cabin they'd owned for decades on the shore of Harperrig Reservoir. A work in progress, it seemed a fitting abode for two people trying to rebuild their own relationship after that brutal night his mum died and the long months of convalescence for his dad, Malkie unable to face the poor old sod because of the irrational feelings of guilt that assaulted him twenty-four seven, and the inevitable self-loathing that such negligence of his own parent – both parents – had brought upon him.

'Sir?'

Malkie realised the constable had been speaking to him. With his eyes closed, his head against the patrol-car window and his mind eight months in the past and flogging him, he'd not heard a word he'd said.

'Sorry, mate. Are we there, yet?' As he asked the question, blue strobes from patrol cars and an ambulance hammered into him and threatened to trigger a relapse of the anxiety attacks that had plagued him since that night. 'Ah, OK. Aye. Right.'

He rubbed his face, as if that could perform some kind of reset on his exhausted mind.

'Thanks, mate. He climbed out of the patrol car and stretched his back.

'Alex Crichton. We've met once, I graduated middle of last year, sir. Boss.'

Nine-plus months in the department and I didn't know your name. Where the hell has my head been?

Malkie shook the man's hand, then they entered Peter Fairbairn's home.

The inside of the house was a mess. Cluttered and untidy. Not to the point of suggesting Fairbairn might be a hoarder, the sort that a lot of TV programmes loved to beam into the homes of people who would never 'get as bad as people like that', under the flimsy pretence of wanting to help them fix their rotten wee lives. But untidy enough to suggest the man lived alone. Malkie always avoided assuming a tidy home meant a woman in residence; Police Scotland's mandatory reading hammered the dangers of subconscious bias into them every six months, most of which he forgot again, the necessary box ticked. But Malkie's experience of never seeming to learn to communicate with 'normal' people over the four decades of his life so far had made him a more receptive reader of the material than most of his colleagues.

But a messy house like Fairbairn's reeked – to Malkie's not-at-all-subconsciously biased mind – of a single man.

As he turned into the living room, he glanced into the kitchen. Again, nothing like the worst of early-evening voyeuristic TV programmes; more like he always imagined a student flat might look. Dishes washed every few days as they ran out, cereal boxes, coffee jars, bag of sugar, biscuit packets left efficiently lying on the worktop to avoid wasted effort in opening cupboards.

Fairbairn sat on his sofa. An IKEA single-bloke special, which Malkie found himself troubled to admit he liked. The paramedics had started packing their kit away, and two Uniforms stood just outside the doorway, looking weary and bored. Malkie recognised the look from too many domestic violence call-outs where some poor woman would sit, clutching a screaming child, repeating 'No, I don't want to press charges' as her partner stood over her to make sure she stuck to her script.

'Mr Fairbairn. Firstly, are you going to be OK?' Due care and diligence observed, Malkie waited for whatever answer Fairbairn might come out with before a statement could be taken.

'I'm fine. It's no big deal.'

Malkie's bullshit-detector rang loud in his mind. 'Ten stitches is no big deal? Really?'

Malkie looked to the paramedics, who wore a similar expression to the constables: *We can't force him to go to hospital.*

'I'm guessing Mr Fairbairn didn't lose consciousness, then? Would you then be obliged to take him to A&E?'

One paramedic stepped past Malkie, looking like he'd had enough of this kind of call-out. 'Nope. Short of sectioning a patient we can't force any treatment on them that they refuse.' The man turned back to Fairbairn. 'Can you please confirm one more time, Mr Fairbairn, whether or not you agree to follow our advice and attend St John's A&E for your own safety?'

Fairbairn removed his hand from a dressing on his forehead and examined his fingertips. 'No. For the third time, I do not wish to be taken to A&E.'

The paramedic shrugged at Malkie then stepped past him and left the property. Malkie returned to the hallway and indicated Crichton and the first responder Uniform, Julie Faulds, to join him. Julie had attended his return-to-work call-out two months previously, a hit-and-run that turned into a shitshow of lies and bigotry and ugly family secrets that put an innocent man, Walter Callahan, in the ground and the repellent guilty fucker estranged from his equally loathsome son but free of charge and still walking around.

'Hi, Julie. Are you well?' He shook her hand, held it for a second to communicate his respect for her.

'I'm good, boss. Malkie.' She grinned. 'How are you, after...'

Are you talking about losing my mum or that disaster of an investigation you watched me fuck up, Julie?

'On the road to recovery, Julie. Managing.'

'Such a shame, that poor man.'

Ah. Callahan.

Guilt flooded Malkie; guilt that he hadn't saved a disturbed man called Walter Callahan from two ARU rounds in the chest, and guilt that he'd failed to see the bastard who'd caused it all banged up in Addiewell for his last few, rotten years on the planet.

'Ach, it happens, Julie. Right?'

Julie knew better than to discuss details, particularly in front of a Person Of Interest in a whole new ongoing case.

'So, you both confirm that Fairbairn has been offered the opportunity to press charges against the assailant but has declined?'

Julie nodded. 'Correct, boss. We've advised him against it, but he insists.'

'So, has he said who did this to him?'

Julie tipped her head to one side, as if to say *you'll like this*. 'Neighbours called it in when they heard a loud argument and objects being smashed. These new-build homes don't offer much sound insulation. When we first arrived, we found Mr Fairbairn raging, covered in blood and swearing he would "kill the fucking bitch", like he recognised his assailant, but he refused to name her. Of course he's not been under caution, so that's only hearsay on our part. When we arrived and the paramedics calmed him down to treat him, he seemed to chew over something in his mind really hard. Then, when we were allowed to question him, he denied he'd mentioned a woman, refused to confirm what we both heard him say minutes before. Claimed he must have been concussed.'

'Fuck's sake, another wrinkle in an already messed-up night.'

'Pardon, boss?' Julie looked confused.

'Nothing, Julie. Just a lot of questions have come out of tonight – the fire that Fairbairn and other firefighters attended earlier this evening.'

Malkie returned to the living room and sat in an armchair. 'Mr Fairbairn, do you have any idea where Sian Wilson might be now?'

Fairbairn scowled at him, then at the Uniforms. 'I never said her name. I told your colleague – didn't recognise the person, happened too quick. I opened my front door and got a tequila bottle smashed in my face. I couldn't see much after that.'

Malkie scanned the carpet between the sofa and the hall-way. 'I'm confused, Mr Fairbairn. Why is there what looks like shards from a broken bottle on the carpet in this room if your assailant attacked you at your front door? And how do you interpret a surprise attack on your doorstep as "an argument that got out of hand"?'

Fairbairn looked troubled for only a second before he recovered. 'She must have followed me in here. I don't remember, I might have been concussed.'

'Yes, you said that. So, definitely a woman, then?'

Fairbairn scowled at him.

'You said "she" must have followed you into this room, Mr Fairbairn. So, you saw her clearly enough to confirm her gender but not clearly enough to identify her, is that right?'

Fairbairn closed his eyes and leaned back in his sofa. 'I'm starting to get a really bad headache, Detective. Probably from the concussion.'

'You'll be fine. If you were concussed, you'd be throwing up and making no sense.'

'I need to sleep. I can give you a full statement tomorrow, but I need to sleep now.'

Malkie stared at him until he opened his eyes. He knew he had no grounds to pull Fairbairn in for formal questioning, not for his behaviour at the scene of the fire, nor for his apparent flaky memory now.

'I and my colleague, Detective Constable Lang, will be attending the briefing tomorrow morning. Your colleague Don McCallum said he'd arrange for both squads to be there for formal statements. We can continue this conversation tomorrow, OK?'

Fairbairn closed his eyes and leaned his head back again. 'Aye, whatever.'

Malkie considered educating Fairbairn that his attendance

would not be optional, but decided to do what he still could to keep an open mind.

He dismissed the Uniforms, sent them off to write up the half a dozen or so forms even a refusal to press charges would generate.

He knew he should go home to the cabin, get what sleep he could before morning briefing at 8:00, but – as usual – his inner idiot won over his better judgement. He sent his dad a message to say he needed to pull an all-nighter, then flattened his driver's seat back and closed his eyes. Without any rational reason, something in his uptight mind made him want to be the first to know if Fairbairn left home in the middle of the night, and why.

Doing a Columbo, Steph called it. It had got him into trouble too many times before, but he knew he couldn't do otherwise if he tried.

FOURTEEN

After a crap hour of sleep in his car, Malkie called for Uniforms to do door-to-doors, waited for them to arrive, then drove back to the Livingston Civic Centre – home of the police station, the Fiscal's office, the Sheriff's Court and the SFRS offices. All the functions needed to investigate and charge bad people, decide whether to prosecute them, and try them. The second and third parts of the West Lothian justice effort were just as under-funded and understaffed as Police Scotland, which explained the *polis*'s frustration at how many bad people spent months clogging up cells on remand only to be released straight back onto the streets at the very time they should be banged up in those same cells. At least, those cases the Fiscal actually decided had a 'reasonable prospect of conviction', never enough in the eyes of every officer in J Division.

To be fair, the courts would send more bad people down if only the prison system – also on its knees – was allowed to squeeze more of them into already-overpopulated cells.

All Malkie and his colleagues could do – in-between too many hours spent at desks filling out forms – was their best to keep feeding bad people into the system, and try to ignore how many of them popped out the other side with grins on their faces and middle fingers extended.

When Steph arrived, she approached Malkie's desk, prodded him on the arm, pretended to examine his face.

'It's not even 07:30 yet. Who are you and where did you bury the real Malkie McCulloch?'

'Comedian. You're so funny I forgot to laugh.'

She grinned and sat down. After logging on and checking her email, she swivelled her chair and opened her notebook. 'Did Fairbairn admit it was Sian Wilson who lamped him with a bottle? Because as much as I hate jumping to conclusions – that's your speciality – that woman struck me as guilty as hell. Of clobbering Fairbairn, I mean. We just don't know if the guy deserved it or not.'

'Aye,' replied Malkie. 'She had some choice words for him during the aftermath of the call-out. No, Fairbairn didn't name her, but he looked busted as fuck when I piled in with whether he'd seen Wilson since the fire. Question is, why not press charges? I left some Uniforms on door-to-doors. They should be asking as a matter of course if any neighbours have motion-triggered doorbell cameras, so hopefully we'll get a hit. A woman walking about in a firefighter's uniform will be conspicuous. Then we can ask her why she attacked him, and why he refuses to have her charged for it.'

Steph flipped the cover of her notebook closed. 'What will we report at morning briefing in...' – she checked her watch – 'ten minutes?'

'Three lines of investigation. One: the fatality found in the warehouse office. Have we got anything back from the post-mortem yet? Bit too soon?'

She checked her notes. 'Aye. Fingerprints and hair follicle DNA isn't going to happen, but Lin Fraser told me she'll find some DNA if it kills her, which she seemed to find witty. She said the victim's teeth looked not to have been subject to too high a heat, so dental ID might still be possible. She said something about the state of the tooth enamel meaning she can't guarantee DNA from the pulp, but she's confident she can get a dentist to match to dental records if we can give her an ID.'

'OK. Not great, but not terrible. So, two: Duncan Duffy. I'm not sure how that will work. I need to clarify the protocols with Callum Gourlay, if his investigation indicates anything that would land it on us after all.

'Three: who smashed a booze bottle off Peter Fairbairn's head, and why are both he and Wilson being so evasive about it? Anything else you can think of?'

'No, but Graham Cormack called me to say he'll make both squads available at noon for "chats".'

'Good. Would you prefer to sit here and make phone calls or go visit the home address of the owner of the warehouse? I don't know about you, but that looked like the frame of a camp bed we saw in that office, which suggests the owner was living there. So, that might turn into an unpleasant conversation.'

'I think I need to get out of the office today, if that's OK with you?' She stifled a yawn with her hand. 'I only managed an hour of sleep. Did you get any?'

Are you going to start being economical with the facts, you idiot? Again?

'No. I sat outside Fairbairn's home for a while, just chewing things over, and fell asleep in the car, so I got an hour or so of crap sleep.'

Steph flashed him a look, one he'd learned to respect.

'I slept. What reason would I have to be watching the guy at this stage?'

'Exactly.'

'Fine. If you're sure you don't mind that it might turn into a "your husband might be dead" conversation, you head for the owner's address, but I'm happy to go too; not a job I'd wish on anyone alone. If not, I'll call Callum Gourlay and agree protocol, then we'll meet at the SFRS HQ for the briefing, OK?' He tried to keep his tone neutral but even he heard his own irritation.

Steph grabbed her jacket and stood. 'No, I'll be fine. Us chicks are supposed to be good at touchy-feely stuff, aren't we?'

He zipped his lips shut with his fingers and turned back to his desk. He could swear he felt her eyes boring into the back of his head before she did the same.

Callum Gourlay answered after only one ring. 'Scottish Fire and Rescue Service, West Lothian Fire Investigation?'

'That's a hell of a mouthful. Do you keep that written on a card, so you get it right?'

Gourlay chuckled. 'DS McCulloch. Good morning. Did you get any sleep?'

'Not much. Listen, Callum, how does this work? The fatality in the office might yet fall under our remit depending on your report. But what about Duncan Duffy's alleged comment about his BA Set? How do we coordinate between your fire investigation and any health and safety concerns about equipment and Duffy's death?'

'Our FIU techie and the equipment manufacturer will conduct their checks and we'll pass our findings on to you at the briefing, hopefully later today. There'll be an inquiry, of course, his being a sudden death. If we decide it was deliberate fire-raising arson, it'll be over to you to conduct a murder inquiry, as you say.'

'Is there anything you can tell me now? I know your full investigation will only just be getting into gear, but can you give me anything preliminary?'

Gourlay paused and Malkie heard papers shuffling. 'Subject to the usual disclaimers, all I can tell you is that the fire started in the warehouse area. Because the office was only twenty feet from it, and the fire started between the office and the entrance, there would have been no escape after the flames had ignited whichever barrels ruptured first and burning spillage poured down the corridor. So, we need to determine a few things. Who died in that office and why did he or she not escape at the first sign of fire? Why didn't the sprinkler system douse the flames at the outset? It should have delivered enough water to allow for the kind of scenario I described to you, you remember?'

'Refresh my memory, please, mate.'

'Any significant level of ethanol vapour from normal barrel seepage would have accelerated the progress of the fire but – again – we need to check the ventilation system. Anyway, once the fire gets a hold, heat expands the metal bands around the barrels. Pressure from the liquid inside forces the ethanol out through gaps that open between the staves, then you have forty per cent ethanol leaking at best, spraying at worst. After that, the sprinklers will struggle. FIU will check it all out.

'On top of all that, we need to check the fire alarm and why the victim didn't react before the fire took hold too much for them to escape.'

'Fuck's sake.'

'Indeed. The post-mortem your guys will do might tell us why they seemed not to have been aware of the fire until it was too late.'

Malkie sighed. 'Drunk or high, maybe. Or possibly some other factor rendered them unconscious or unable to escape. I'll let you know as soon as I know.'

'Thanks. I have to say, mate, I get the impression you're going to be a hell of a lot easier to work with than the last Police Scotland detective I had to deal with. Right pain in the arse, just made everyone's job harder than it needed to be.'

'Do you remember the man's name?' Malkie already had a feeling, though.

'Some guy called McLeish. You know him?'

'Aye. It's not a massive CID department in West Lothian and we all work from the same station.'

'And?'

'I couldn't possibly comment, mate. Professional etiquette, you know?'

'But he is an arse, right?'

'Aye, but you didn't hear that from me.'

Gourlay chuckled. 'You and I will get along just fine, Malkie.'

Malkie's mind prompted him to ask a question that had been lurking since he found out he'd be working with the same Fire Investigator who'd attended the aftermath of the house fire that killed his mum.

'Callum, you investigated the house fire at my parents' house. Can I ask: the cause of that fire, is it fairly common?'

Gourlay hesitated, and Malkie understood why. As well as regulations restricting what he could and could not say to civilians, he couldn't know if Malkie was psychologically OK to discuss the fire, and especially any details he might hear directly that he hadn't picked up from the report.

'It's all in the FDR1. The fire investigation report you got a copy of. But candles? Aye. Placed too close to curtains or other flammable materials. Often it's a cat that knocks it over, or it's stuck in the neck of a bottle and the top falls off when it melts down to the glass, but unless it comes into contact with something flammable, usually they just melt and burn out. Your parents' house...'

Gourlay paused. Malkie gave him the assurance he guessed he needed. 'I'm fine to talk about it, mate. I really am.'

Another pause, then, 'Your parents' house was old, wasn't

it? And a lot of the contents were old stuff too, if I remember correctly?'

'Aye. Ancient. Stuff they bought when they married. They didn't like modern home styles. Why?'

'Some of the furnishings may have been bought before fire safety laws became as strict as they are now. Everything is low-flammability and fire-retardant these days, except some really cheap rubbish from China that shouldn't even be sold in this country, although who knows any more after bloody Brexit, right?'

Malkie's mind itched. 'But the candle I gave her was a big fat thing, about five inches wide and about the same tall, and the fire happened within a couple of hours of me leaving the house. Even sitting on her bedside table, next to her bedclothes, how could a candle like that possibly fall over or burn down? They didn't have a bloody cat.'

Gourlay fell silent. For so long Malkie dreaded to ask his next question.

'Callum, what are you thinking?'

Another long silence, pregnant with dread. Malkie hated moments like this, when not seeing a person face to face could mask all kinds of non-verbal communication that could change everything.

'Nothing. Really. I just... I just find it difficult talking about a person whose death I investigated with a close relative, you know? Anyway, I shouldn't be talking to you about a past case, certainly not one so personally relevant to you; and I need to go, got a meeting. Please don't ask me about it again. It's all in the report. I'll be in touch, DS McCulloch.' A click, and the line went dead.

Malkie placed his phone on his desk and suppressed an urge to fold his hands together beside it and rest his forehead. Not with the CID room as full as it was now.

What are you not saying, Mr Gourlay?

As much as he dreaded the thought, he needed to read the Fire Investigation Report. He'd barely read beyond the word 'candle' in the management summary on the front page when he first received it. Now, he couldn't shake a rotten feeling that worse waited beyond those first few paragraphs. On the pages he hadn't had the guts to read the first time.

FIFTEEN

Steph felt her phone buzz in her pocket, fished it out and wished she hadn't.

Her stepdad. Calling her. Not an email or a text, the usual channels by which they communicated the bare minimum necessary without having to hear each other's voices.

A call.

She pressed the button to reject it and replaced the phone in her pocket.

It buzzed again, and she rejected it again.

Another buzz, a different one, a text message.

We need to talk.

Steph's heart sank into her guts. Could she? Talk to her stepdad about how his best mate raped her mum?

She switched her phone to completely silent and pocketed it again. She returned to the case notes she'd been studying, interview notes from door-to-doors and footage from three video doorbells belonging to neighbours of Peter Fairbairn. She'd already checked for updates from the SOCOs and the autopsy but, as expected, too soon. Until she and Malkie attended the briefing, she needed to fill her time with something. Any other low-level at-home assault she would have handed off to DC Louisa Gooch or DC Rab Lundy, but she couldn't forget Sian Wilson's comments at the fire scene. 'Where is that fucker?' That and the look of naked fury she'd turned on Fairbairn when he rejoined the gathered firefighters constituted more than enough reason to spend time on this herself.

It took only minutes. A camera on the doorbell of the house opposite Fairbairn's had captured someone short and slim get out of a car, charge down his driveway and bang on the door.

The person had a bottle clutched in their right hand.

She noted the time stamp. Fairbairn's drive sloped down behind what had to be his own car, a huge SUV which blocked the view of the door.

It took a few minutes for the woman to reappear, still stomping, still looking furious, but without the bottle. Steph noted this time stamp too.

Her mind had already started working not to assume that the figure looked like a woman, as Fairbairn had claimed then retracted, a woman built like Sian Wilson. She had to be about five foot nine or ten, and Steph remembered another member of the crews – Steve Grayson – was of a similar height and build. The other crew members, all male, had been taller and bulkier.

Satisfied she'd at least attempted to avoid any immediate bias, she wrote down, 'Sian Wilson at Peter Fairbairn's home' next to the two time stamps. She added a question mark as an afterthought.

She removed her jacket before settling in to trawl the door-to-door statements. Out of habit, she removed both her personal and police-issue mobiles from her pocket and set them on her desk. The display on her personal mobile showed a text from her stepdad.

She figured she could maybe handle a text from the bastard.

Hearing his voice, even on a phone, might set her off in ways she'd worked very hard to suppress over many years, if only to avoid speculation at the ever-frosty Steph Lang losing her temper at anything.

She risked it.

> I know. I didn't, but I do now. We need to talk.

She raged inside. How could he not have known? Even if he genuinely hadn't, even that could never be acceptable. Steph learned later in life that her mum and her real dad – or rather, the man of whom she had distant memories of being her real dad – had sped through the honeymoon period of their relationship into the 'any company is better than being alone' dead-end she'd since seen so many of her school friends settle for, so she'd always assumed her birth had been the result of a rare – and probably ugly – attack of amorousness from her 'real' father after a night's drinking. She'd often imagined her mum putting up with him all over her just so she could get the one thing she'd always said made her otherwise brutal life bearable: a child.

Steph's mum had loved her beyond any doubt. Her husband had never been a violent man, but her mum had protected Steph from him anyway, determined Steph would never grow into the same desperate and dependent kind of specimen she remembered him being. Pissed every night, never a good word to say about her mum, barely reacted to the many A-pluses Steph brought home from a sink-estate school that considered itself successful to suffer only one stabbing per term. When he'd disappeared one day, Steph had never bothered to ask where he'd gone, happy just to have him out of both her and her mum's life.

When her mum had remarried, she'd thought Dean might prove to be OK. Although every bit as much of a substance addict as her mum had become to endure the apathy of Steph's real dad, Dean seemed to care for both Steph and her mum to begin with. It took only a few years after her mum made the mistake of marrying him for his true nature to become evident, and Steph's mum became trapped in a self-inflicted and miserable existence of drugs and alcohol and dependency.

That ended the day she got shivved during a stretch in Cornton Vale for assault and wounding after one of Dean's suppliers had called at their home looking to settle an unpaid bill.

And through all of this, Steph had hung on to the rock that she'd thought Barry to be. Her stepdad Dean's best mate and a seemingly great guy – funny, caring, always making time for Steph and her mum, always seeming to grow fonder and fonder of them both as the years passed. Steph had never noticed the moment her mum started to distance herself from Barry. At the age she'd been, Steph couldn't have had any idea why two adults who seemed close for years might suddenly drift apart. Or shut off all feelings and civility in the space of days. She'd had more to worry about – exams, being bullied at school, avoiding the attentions of hormonal males intent on 'defrosting' her.

She unlocked her phone and typed a reply typical of her communications with her stepdad:

> Tonight. Sometime after eight.

She didn't bother suggesting a neutral meeting place because her innate feelings about the waste of space her stepdad had always been made her loath to be seen in public with him, even by people who would have no clue about their shared past.

She dropped the phone on her desk again and returned to scanning the door-to-door statements. One neighbour had reported seeing someone in some kind of 'big, bulky uniform' come out of Fairbairn's home after hearing shouts and banging from inside, but couldn't make out any details beyond that they looked 'skinny'.

Another neighbour had claimed she clearly heard the words 'kill you' as the unknown visitor left.

A third had seen nothing, but proclaimed that someone like Peter Fairbairn deserved whatever happened because he'd always been 'that kind of man'.

The dreariness and small-world self-importance of other statements drove Steph to grab her jacket and her phones and head for the canteen. She needed a coffee and a sandwich to set her up for a long afternoon taking statements.

She'd probably want a drink before her other engagement later in the evening, but she also knew she'd never lean on that particular crutch anywhere but in the safety of her own home. But she wouldn't shy away from it. Wouldn't let it lie long enough to fester and sour her.

She and her stepdad needed a long – and frank – conversation about his best mate – Steph's biological dad, the rapist.

SIXTEEN

When Steph had finished watching the last of the doorbell videos from Peter Fairbairn's neighbours, she looked up the owner of the warehouse and scribbled his address in her notebook, grabbed a Uniform – Richard Martin, she reminded herself – then headed for the car park.

As she drove, she prepared herself for a potentially brutal conversation. If the body in the warehouse office proved to be the owner, she wouldn't – except under exceptional circumstances for exceptional kinds of people – expect them to have raised any kind of alarm, yet. So, she might well be walking into – as Malkie had warned her – one of *those* situations.

She knew that some of the Uniforms used to sing stupid and incredibly insensitive songs on doorsteps, trying to make their colleagues laugh. Some called it a coping mechanism, a last nudge to themselves into detached and compartmentalised mode. As much as every officer knew the devastation one of *those* calls caused, they had to do all they could to not let it touch them too deeply, or they'd not be able to function for long in the job.

Steph considered it a good thing that the practice had died

out, ironically because of the increasing popularity of doorbell video cameras. Officers now knew their antics were recorded in full-colour HD from the moment they approached the door. She didn't doubt it still went on if officers saw no camera, but never in her presence.

William Galbraith's address turned out to be a massive luxury new-build villa in a swanky private development nestled in dense woods down a dead-end lane south of Armadale. Each property boasted huge lawns, double garages but cars parked out on driveways to make sure the neighbours couldn't miss the top-of-the-range, prestige vehicles changing every two years, even if the personalised number plates never did.

The door opened to reveal the tallest, thinnest, most elegant and attractive woman Steph could remember meeting, despite her being red in the face, dressed in running gear and soaked with sweat, which she wiped from her face with a towel over her shoulder. Normally, such a thing wouldn't influence Steph in the slightest, but she realised now that learning the identity of her biological father and how the bastard impregnated her mother made her feel like a drab and ugly duckling grown into an even drabber and uglier excuse for a swan.

She roused herself from her pity party.

The woman pressed some buttons on her smart watch, nodded to herself and smiled, then faced Steph. 'These damned things never let you get away with anything, do they?'

She spoke in a refined tone, her voice silky and husky, but Steph detected no hint of superiority. She'd always loathed men and women who thought their shit smelled sweeter because their partner raked in stupid amounts of money and bought them their perceived status. This woman exhibited none of that, so far. The concern in her eyes seemed genuine.

Steph held up her warrant card. 'Can we have a word with Mr William Galbraith, please?'

A moment of fear flashed across the woman's face, then she opened the door wide and ushered Steph inside.

'I'm Anna Galbraith. William's wife. You'll want to talk to me about the fire in the warehouse, I presume?'

Steph half-expected her to scan the street to make sure none of the neighbours had seen an obvious police officer calling at her home, but Galbraith seemed unconcerned, only fearful that police officers wanted to speak to her husband.

Steph nodded towards the inside of the property. 'Might be better to talk inside, Mrs Galbraith?'

Galbraith stood aside to reveal a hallway wider than Steph's bathroom, and a staircase almost as grand rising to the upper floor, the wall beside it a mass of framed photos, all showing Anna and William Galbraith in various exotic locations and engaged in various expensive activities. It looked like they were the kind of couple that enjoyed pushing themselves and each other. Steph saw photos of them holding medals at the finish line of the London Marathon, and others of them in action on a racing yacht, Anna at the wheel while William and three others hung out the side of the boat on ropes as it pitched nearly vertical, seawater spraying all of them, grinning like loons. She also noticed the conspicuous absence of even a single picture of the couple with children. The pair looked as happy as any couple could be, and Steph had to assume they'd made conscious decisions that they were enough for each other. For a brief moment she envied them their contentment and their obvious adoration of each other, before reminding herself she might be about to tear Anna Galbraith's happiness apart with the most brutal of questions.

Galbraith walked through to a lounge that Steph thought might well be bigger than her whole flat. She felt another touch of envy and choked it down. Not for the size and obvious luxury of the house, but because she couldn't forget the faces in the photographs. She wondered if any of them might be rape babies, then gave herself an internal kicking for a second pity party in five minutes.

They sat, Anna Galbraith in a huge wing-backed chair with her hands clasped in her lap and her legs crossed at the ankles, Steph perched on the front edge of a matching sofa, big enough to stretch out two of her head to toe.

'I've let my husband know about the fire. He's away on business but he should come home right away. He'll need to talk to our insurers, and the staff. The fire service called our home number as the registered key-holder address, but they said the keys wouldn't be necessary and that they were only calling to inform me, and to ask if anyone was likely to have been inside the building at that time of night. I told them no, never.' Again, no hint of superiority or arrogance. Steph noticed Galbraith's fingers, laced together, had turned white.

'Sorry. Your husband *should* come home?'

'I left him a voicemail. He's probably put his phone on silent again. He never sleeps well when he goes away on business.'

Steph's mental alarm went off, loud and insistent. If her husband was away on business, whose body did they find in the warehouse office?

'And you haven't heard from him today, either?'

'No. He called me yesterday from the train to Inverness, but he must be in back-to-back meetings all day today. Quite normal for him.' She smiled, but Steph detected a hesitancy about it. Did Galbraith have nothing to do with the warehouse and wanted her husband here to handle the situation? She dismissed that thought, berated herself for even suspecting herself of unconscious bias; maybe she managed the business matters and he ran the warehouse.

'My husband runs the warehouse. I'm a consultant surgeon at St John's. He and I were set up by interfering friends twenty-three years ago and have been together ever since.'

Again, Steph had to choke down a stubborn lump of envy;

not for the woman's apparent domestic bliss, but because of a sense of shame she couldn't shake. A rapist's blood ran in her veins, but to be effective in her job, she couldn't allow that to distract her.

'Are you sure you're OK, Detective?'

Steph roused herself again. This had to stop.

'Sorry, yes.' She braced herself for what had to come next. 'Ms Galbraith...'

'I'm fine with Mrs, Detective.' Again, a self-confident smile; this woman seemed more centred than many Steph could remember meeting.

'Mrs Galbraith, I'm sorry to have to tell you that firefighters found a body in the office at the back of the warehouse. We haven't identified the person yet so there's no reason to assume it could be him, but is there anyone other than your husband who might have had cause to be in the premises after dark last night?'

Panic flashed across Galbraith's face, but only for a second. 'No.' She considered for a few seconds. 'Could it have been arson? Could the dead person be someone who started the fire? There's just no one else who would have reason to be in the building overnight.'

Steph resisted the temptation to read too much into Galbraith's early question about arson. Insurance jobs lay behind a fair proportion of the fires that Police Scotland were called to investigate, but she reminded herself to remain as objective as she could for as long as she could.

Something seemed to occur to Galbraith. She produced a mobile phone from a pocket in her skirt and quick-dialled a number. After a few seconds, alarm crossed her face again.

'Now it's saying the number is unobtainable.' She scowled, started chewing on a fingernail, her other arm folded around her. 'He must have let the battery die.' Her eyes betrayed her own lack of confidence in that theory.

'Is he in the habit of letting that happen?'

Galbraith's mouth opened, then closed again. She slumped, seemed to crumble in on herself. 'No. Never.'

Steph's heart ached for the woman. She couldn't imagine the prospect of losing the depth of happiness Galbraith's photographs indicated she and her husband enjoyed. She needed to push on, but hated herself as she did.

'Mrs Galbraith, we found what looked like the burned remains of a camp bed and a sleeping bag in the office. Can you explain that?' She laced her question with as much tenderness and sympathy as she could, which never came easy to her, but her own current problems had shaken her normal unassailable sense of emotional solidity.

Galbraith collapsed backwards into her chair, seemed to shrink before Steph's eyes. She drew her legs up under her and wrapped her arms around her, as if trying to stop herself from falling apart. She lowered her head and rocked in her chair. She muttered, 'No, Bill. No,' and Steph felt no urgency to ask what she meant. Steph sat, as awkward as a child at a funeral, knowing that the normal thing, the human thing, to do would be to approach the woman, make some kind of contact, even just a hand on an arm. But she couldn't move, felt no right to intrude on her grief.

She waited. Galbraith's crisis passed, in time, and she looked up at Steph, her eyes red and glassy, any trace of embarrassment at her loss of composure forgotten or ignored.

She glanced at her phone again. Her fingers went slack and the phone fell to the carpet. 'Bill never – and I mean never – let his phone battery die, and he kept a business phone too, and I've tried both. He's the only person who could possibly have any legitimate reason to be in the office late at night, and he never, ever, let himself be completely uncontactable.'

Steph waited, gave the woman time to cross a line.

'Also... We've been having...' Tears overwhelmed her again and her voice broke. 'Yes. It could be my husband.'

She fell apart, her last words barely coherent. Steph thought she heard the word 'why', but she was in no state for further questions.

Steph watched the woman's life and hopes and any future she'd looked forward to crumble in front of her. Against her better professional opinion, Steph found strength, from some inner reserve she never knew she had, to cross the room and wrap an arm around the sobbing woman's shoulders.

SEVENTEEN

When Malkie met Steph outside the SFRS headquarters at Cambuslang to attend the briefing, she related her experience at Anna Galbraith's home.

Malkie found himself feeling both guilty at letting Steph deal with it by herself, but also relieved he hadn't put himself through that.

Sorry, Steph. I'm an idiot.

'So, odds are that's William Galbraith's body going under Lin Fraser's scalpel today?'

'Mrs Galbraith seemed to think it more than possible.'

'Fuck's sake. Poor woman. Did she have any idea why he would have been there at that time of night? Or why a camp bed in the office?'

'No, I didn't get much more out of her after she decided it might be her husband after all. I called a friend of hers to sit with her and said I'd return tomorrow morning. Until we get a definitive ID there's limited usefulness in questioning her any more today. I did manage to get the name of their dentist, but if Lin has to rely on dental ID, that could take a day or two, depending on how quickly the dentist checks their records.'

'See what you can do to expedite that, obviously. And Sian Wilson? She's more than just Duncan Duffy's bestie, isn't she?'

Steph stared at him, appraised him. 'Aye. You picked up on that?'

'I'm not a completely insensitive clod. You ready?'

Malkie looked up at the massive horizontal slats that made the building look more like a designer shopping centre than the seat of the SFRS. It made him think of a Japanese pagoda, the way the roof curved up ever so slightly at the sides. 'I have a feeling we're going to get a bit of a runaround in there. They all seemed cagey already last night, and I think they'll be very protective of Wilson. We need to be careful not to come across as interviewing them formally – we're only allowed to do that with the IC, Jeremy Lees, and the Entry Control bloke, Fairbairn. I think for today, all we're allowed to do is listen and record and ask for clarifications where needed. Until – if – either the FIU investigation or Lin Fraser's post-mortem on the body turns up something suspicious, we might still end up handing this all over to a Fatal Accident Inquiry.'

Steph considered this for a moment. 'I'm starting to think I wouldn't mind if we got to hand this one off. Got a bad feeling about it, and that's not like me.'

'Aye. I'm going to keep it shut today. All ears.'

They headed inside.

Steph pulled her notebook out. 'What's the date today?'

'Why?'

'I want to record the event.'

'What event?' He noticed the gleam in her eye too late.

She grinned. 'You exhibited a rare outburst of self-awareness.'

He opened his mouth to retaliate but she lifted a hand and called out a 'Hello' to Graham Cormack, who had appeared from inside the building.

Cormack smiled at them both and shook their hands. 'Hi.

Most of both crews are here waiting for you. You know you can't...'

Malkie sighed. 'Aye. We're just here to listen, for now. Why only most of them?'

'Peter Fairbairn called in sick, said he has a migraine after his attack last night. Also, our station commander, Flora Beattie, sends her apologies. She's also ill, has been for several months, and she's just not up to travelling to the station. She asked me to apologise on her behalf and tell you she's happy for you to call on her at home.'

Malkie detected more to come. 'Thanks. So, everyone else is here?'

'No. No one's been able to contact Sian Wilson all morning. I drove to her address last night to check on her, but if she was there she refused to come to the door. I'm very worried about her. She's not answering her mobile, either.'

Malkie and Steph shared a glance.

Here we go...

'OK. Thanks, Mr Cormack. Let's get on with this, then.'

Cormack signed them in then took them to a meeting room where most of both Red and Blue Livi Watches they'd met the previous night, or rather earlier that day, sat in their SFRS uniforms. Jeremy Lees looked about as uncomfortable as a man could. Three others, two women and a man, sat at the head of the table, in suits. Malkie guessed them to be a lawyer, a union rep and a Health and Safety rep.

Malkie's next two hours passed in a bored but frustrated cloud of SFRS technical speak and analysis of incident logs and statements and draft reports. Steph nudged him and nodded to the head of the table as one of the suits stood.

'Thank you all for your attendance. Detectives McCulloch and Lang, the FIU will email a copy of the initial first draft of their preliminary findings. Please contact us if anything needs clarified, otherwise we'll next contact you when the FIU findings and the reports from the manufacturers of the SFRS equipment on Mr Duffy's BA Set and cylinder and related equipment have been signed off. If anything in any of these reports suggests any irregularity, you will be the first to be notified, of course. You can talk to the members of both Red and Blue Watches, but please remember that only the IC and BAECO, Mr Lees and Mr Cormack, can be interviewed formally.'

'BAECO?'

'BA Entry Control Officer."

After a few more drawn-out comments that Malkie felt achieved nothing but wasting another five minutes, the meeting was adjourned.

McCallum showed Malkie and Steph to separate interview rooms where the members of both watches were to be interviewed, each accompanied by Jeremy Lees or Graham Cormack in place of the missing Peter Fairbairn, plus a rep from the Fire Brigade Union.

McCallum indicated two separate rooms with his hand. 'There's a table and chairs in the gym room and you can use the canteen, too. Can you do blue watch first? They're not on shift this week so they made an effort to come in for this.'

Malkie glanced at Steph, who shrugged. 'Aye, OK.' Steph nodded her acceptance. Neither would want to enforce Malkie's theory at the risk of alienating anyone at this early stage in the investigation.

McCallum led them between two massive, gleaming, red fire appliances, to a short corridor at the back of the vehicle bay. At the end lay a canteen, to the left a smaller room containing gym equipment; to the right, what looked like a common room. The seven firefighters sat around a table with coffee mugs and sour expressions.

McCallum closed the door to the common room. 'I'll go

first, and I suggest Kenny Donaldson, too? He's the most senior member of both squads.'

'Why not Jeremy Lees first? He's a squad chief, isn't he?'

'Sure. Any order you want them, but Kenny and I are the most senior in terms of experience, so I thought we'd be a good first choice?'

'Aye, OK. Won't make much difference.'

McCallum headed into another room on the right and closed the door.

Malkie indicated towards the door to the canteen. 'I'll take McCallum, you do Donaldson?'

'OK with me. You do have a pen, aye?' He caught a gleam in her eye and refused to dignify her with an answer.

They headed into their respective interview rooms. Malkie took the gym room, found a table and chairs he assumed had been dragged in from the canteen.

He sat, laid his warrant card and notebook on the table, checked he did have a pen on him and breathed a sigh of relief. She'd have been unbearable if he'd had to ask her for one, after all.

Two hours later, they returned to Malkie's pool car. Neither said anything for a while. Malkie broke the silence first. 'What a bloody waste of time.'

'Yep. You go first?'

'I might as well. How did you manage to sleep through most of that with your eyes open and without snoring?'

'I wasn't sleeping. I was absorbing and considering.'

She smirked at him. 'Bollocks. Anyway, Graham Cormack. I can see why the rest of them look up to him. He's just turned fifty-five, which is apparently getting into retirement territory for these guys, and he seems quite happy about the prospect. Said he has no idea where Sian Wilson is and why she might have gone missing, but admitted to being worried about her, completely out of character for her not to keep her colleagues informed. His explanation for her remarks about Fairbairn last night amounted to "something personal between them". Said he only knew they didn't get along, and never had. Said they'll never be pals but insisted that both maintained a professional working relationship. He also considered the idea of Wilson attacking Fairbairn out of character – a phrase he fell back on several times in just the half hour – but conceded her behaviour and her obvious anger at him for something did make him wonder. He had no idea why Fairbairn might have shown a particular interest in Duncan Duffy's BA Set. He claimed not to have noticed that and that he'd been briefed not to discuss any equipment-related topics until the full report is published.'

Malkie flipped to a new page in his notebook, took a deep breath before continuing.

'Stuart Simpson. Called Beaky because of his unfortunate habit of picking his nose without realising he's doing it, apparently.'

'Lovely.'

'He's young. Anyway, I got nothing out of him. Well, nothing about his colleagues or what happened last night, or Wilson and Fairbairn. Every question I asked him about the others he claimed he had no knowledge of what kind of personal dynamics went on, too new to the crews. I believed him. Poor sod looked like a rabbit caught in a car's headlights. I did find out he's had a rough upbringing, and he's passionate about making a success of his career in the SFRS. Said he thinks the rest of the squad don't quite trust him yet, so he keeps hoping for a big shout so he'll get a chance to prove himself to them. Had nothing but good to say about Wilson. Might be a wee crush going on there, or maybe just normal late-teen hormonal stuff. And complete ignorance about Fairbairn, same as Cormack, claimed he didn't notice Fairbairn examine Duffy's

BA Set and also repeated that he wasn't allowed to discuss anything other than Fairbairn's alleged assault and the deceased in the office. Pattern developing there. And again, claimed he didn't hear Wilson's comments.'

He flipped another page. 'Jeremy Lees. Again, got virtually nothing out of him. No idea where Wilson is. No idea why Wilson might attack Fairbairn. I asked him about Fairbairn's particular interest in Duncan Duffy's BA Set. Lees would make a lousy poker player. He stared at me for several seconds, opened his mouth and closed it again, then tried to claim Fairbairn might just have been worried about Duffy's comment about his BA Set over the open radio channel before he collapsed. Again, I didn't believe a word of it, but unlike Cormack, Lees looked terrified I'd push the point.'

He closed his notebook. 'That's what I got. Not much, except that there's a shitload more going on than anyone's admitting, and I have no idea how to get the truth out of them if we can't interview them properly.'

Steph let out a long breath and raised her eyebrows as if to share Malkie's assessment. She opened her own notebook.

'Cormack. He seemed more genuine than the others I talked to. He openly admitted to being aware of tension between Wilson and Fairbairn. He told me that Fairbairn is not a well-liked man. He wouldn't go into specifics, said only that the man could do with some lessons in people management. Waffled on about all sorts of nonsense related to poor communication skills, poor empathy skills, poor mentoring, that sort of thing. Then he mentioned unconscious bias. You know, like that bloody regular reading we have to do every half-year? Then, when I asked him what kind of specific biases Fairbairn might need to brush up on, Cormack held his hands up and claimed he didn't mean anything in particular, and – like you – I knew shite when I heard it.'

Fruity language from you again, Steph? Really?

'Anyway, bearing in mind that both squads are composed mostly of white, adult males, I formed the obvious conclusion.'

Malkie raised his eyebrows at her.

'Well, a working hypothesis.' She shrugged as if to accept his correction. 'Fairbairn and Wilson had obvious issues with each other, so I'm guessing the man might be a bit of a misogynist?'

Malkie chewed this over. 'I wonder if Fairbairn had suspicions about Wilson and Duffy. I'm starting to wonder if most of them did. But Cormack was adamant that no firefighter would break the rule about relationships between station colleagues.'

Steph continued. 'Paul Turner. Whole Time. I had to coax information out of him and even then, I didn't get much. He said he wasn't aware of Duffy's difficulties at first. I asked him why he didn't notice. He got decidedly defensive, asked me if I know what it's like being in the middle of a raging fire with barrels of whisky stacked around you that could explode any time, and your vision is limited by a face mask. Then he repeated the same line about not being allowed to talk about anything related to Duffy, only about the first victim and about whether Wilson might have had something to do with Fairbairn's assault. Same old, same old. But he was sensitive about Duffy. Maybe understandably given that he was supposed to be looking after him.'

'You think he fucked up? Let Duffy down, somehow?'

'If he did, proving it might be hard. And, again, not our business, for now.'

She flipped another page, and now her posture changed. She sat up, turned half towards Malkie, even held a finger out as if to say, 'Wait until you hear this.'

Malkie prayed to a god he'd never believe in, for something more than the little they had so far.

'Steve Grayson. You remember he's their equipment and safety guy? Well, after making me tell him three times that

anything he said would be confidential and he'd deny everything, he opened up. He wouldn't be drawn on where Wilson
might be or her comments at the fire scene or what she said to
me at her home, but he seemed more than happy – well, not
happy, but determined – to talk about Fairbairn grabbing
Duffy's BA Set like he did.'

She paused. She did this often, and only ever to him. Made
him wait. Wee shite.

'Grayson told me he raised a formal complaint three months
ago with the station commander, Flora Beattie, about Fairbairn.
One of the others has, too, but Grayson wouldn't name that
person.'

Malkie perked up but reminded himself not to grab at the
first decent possible lead to come their way. 'About his rotten
attitude? I mean his tendency towards unconscious bias?'

'Nope. He told me Stuart Simpson had asked Fairbairn
about what he thought might be a slightly degraded rubber face
seal, but Fairbairn had told him it was fine and not to say
anything more about it. Grayson told me that if any firefighter
expressed any doubt about a piece of equipment, then it has to
be taken out of service until checked. Simpson, being the
newbie, did what Fairbairn said, kept his mouth shut, but told
Grayson about it later.

'Then he reminded me that if I repeated a single word he'd
said, he'd deny it. Said he was close enough to being able to
afford retirement that he'd leave the service if anything came
back to bite him.'

Malkie blew a breath out as he considered the implications.
'He's really sticking his neck out, isn't he? He must be seriously
pissed off at Fairbairn to risk putting his own arse on the line.'

Steph's eyes narrowed. 'Or terrified someone might get
hurt.'

EIGHTEEN

Steph agreed to start a search for Sian Wilson, worried about her welfare as much as her possible involvement in Fairbairn's assault. Malkie returned to Fairbairn's home. The man had questions to answer.

Fairbairn's face fell when he found Malkie and a Uniform on his doorstep again. He ushered Malkie in, and they sat in his living room, on his IKEA single-bloke special furniture. Three crushed lager cans sat on the coffee table, and Fairbairn returned a defiant stare when Malkie looked at them, then his watch, then Fairbairn.

'Last night's.'

Malkie shrugged as if to say none of his business, but the room didn't smell of hours-old stale lager.

'How's your head, Mr Fairbairn?'

Fairbairn raised his fingers to the dressing wrapped around his forehead. 'Hurts like a bastard.'

'Did you manage to sleep?'

'Aye, after a couple of sleeping tablets and lagers.' He nodded at the cans on the coffee table.

'Good, good. Happy to hear that. Looked like a hell of a wallop you got. I don't suppose anything's come back to you about the incident? Even some small detail you might think inconsequential could prove significant.'

Malkie smiled his best friendly smile, despite knowing how shite he could be at pretending to be friendly.

Fairbairn heaved a more obvious sigh than necessary. 'No. I told you. It all happened so fast. I answered the door. Someone clobbered me over the head with a bottle. After that I couldn't see much because I had blood in my eyes and I was close to passing out.'

Something seemed to occur to Fairbairn, but the man would never earn awards for his acting abilities. 'Now I come to think of it, I don't remember the bottle breaking on the doorstep. It broke after I staggered through here and my attacker cracked me another blow on the head. It broke then, which explains why I can see glass in here but not in the hallway.'

Malkie nodded. 'Aye, that would explain it. So, you got hit on the front *and* the back of your head, then? And the blow to the back of your head must have been hard enough to break the bottle? Is that right?'

Fairbairn stared at him. Malkie watched the man's mind work, watched him come to the only possible conclusion – Malkie was having none of it.

'That's all I remember after I got hit the first time.' His eyes wandered, anywhere but meeting Malkie's.

Malkie gave him a few seconds to stew, to let Fairbairn know he could smell shite as much as the next man, without actually calling him out on it right now: too soon.

'Why didn't you attend the briefing this morning as we requested? Only you and Sian Wilson were missing.' He didn't get a reaction to Wilson's name, so he pushed his luck.

'And Duncan Duffy, of course.'

The look Fairbairn flashed Malkie reeked of guilt. For

allowing Duffy to go in on air for his first time? No, something else.

Malkie's temper started to fray, and he found himself asking the burning question before he could remind himself of the lines he should be making damned sure he didn't cross. 'Can you explain to me your particular interest in Mr Duffy's BA Set last night? I saw you take it from the paramedics, then examine it very closely before heading off to – I believe – give it to Jeremy Lees to put into evidence bags?'

Fairbairn thought for a second. The man would never earn any awards for quick thinking either. 'That's not within your purview, but since you've got the gall to ask me such a pointed question, Duffy said something over the open channel about his BA Set, so I wanted to see it for myself. If there's anything wrong with any of the equipment our boys rely on, I want to know about it. Duty of care, like. I just looked at it, then I watched Lees bag it and tag it, and it's now in the hands of the appropriate BA engineers at a BA workshop for testing. Don't ask me about it again, or I'll be forced to notify the SFRS and FBU and see how you like explaining it to their lawyers.'

Malkie realised he'd stepped onto the thinnest ice possible, but Fairbairn's attitude, his arrogance, had riled him beyond stopping his mouth from doing him any more damage.

'Your *people*, you mean. I doubt Wilson would react well to being called a boy, would she?'

Fairbairn glared at him. 'Figure of speech, OK? I didn't mean anything by it.'

No, your bias is completely subconscious, isn't it?

'And?'

Fairbairn frowned. 'And what?'

'Your opinion on the condition of Duncan Duffy's BA Set?'

'It looked fine. The neck seal was getting close to needing replaced but I saw no damage to the integrity of the neoprene.'

'And where is it now?'

'With the FIU. Callum Gourlay has it.'

'Hang on. I'm confused. Mr Gourlay attended last night, before you left the scene, I believe, but he only got it later, via Lees. Would it not have been more correct to hand the BA Set to Gourlay right away? When us *polis* investigate a crime scene, we have strict chain of custody processes that record who has handled a piece of evidence and when. But Mr Duffy's BA Set was taken away by you before Lees could bag and tag it, is that right?'

A look came over Fairbairn's face that Malkie knew well. The feeling that – possibly, he reminded himself – one lie or omission was unravelling and the subject felt their ability to maintain their story slipping.

Malkie waited. Silence often worked so much better than pressuring an interviewee.

'Look, I don't know, OK? I did what I thought best.' Fairbairn's voice was now plaintive, as if trying to appeal to Malkie's better nature. The man couldn't know that although Malkie tried, always, to see some good in everyone, once someone started pissing him about, his willingness to reserve judgement could evaporate really bloody quickly.

'So, why did you disappear with it?'

'I don't know. I just knew I needed to keep it safe for the FIU. I gave it to Lees, he bagged it and the FIU took it away with him after letting Steve Grayson look at it.'

'OK, I'll catch up with Gourlay later.'

'You do that. Until then, leave me the fuck alone or I'm on the phone to SFRS HQ and my union rep. Fuck's sake.'

Fairbairn slumped. If he thought he'd got through the worst of this...

'Fine. No more questions about Duffy and his BA Set. What did Wilson mean last night when she said, quote "Where is that fucker?" unquote, and why did she seem to have such a problem with you?'

Fairbairn took long seconds to respond.

'Sian has never liked me. Nothing specific, just one of those personality clashes that can happen in any team. I offered to move her to Jeremy Lees's team, but she refused, said something about her being professional enough to rise above our issues with each other.'

'Issues?' Malkie sat forward, his interest piqued, and he didn't give a damn if Fairbairn knew it.

'Like I said. Nothing specific. She can be very emotional at times, you know?'

Fuck's sake, here we go.

'Emotional?'

'You know? Temperamental. I mean, women are much more sensitive than men are, you know? What you can get away with saying to a bloke can upset a woman, especially if she's already a bit uptight, you know?'

Should I take his shovel off him now or let him dig himself even deeper? Fuck it – more rope, too, please...

'Uptight? Is Sian prone to stress at work? Does she give cause for concern about her psychological suitability for the job?'

'No, no, nothing like that. Fuck's sake, all I mean is she can have a short fuse and sense of humour failures sometimes, that's all. You work with women, don't you? I have nothing against them but they're different to us and sometimes that needs to be worked around, you know?'

'"Us" being men?'

'Aye.' Said triumphantly as if Malkie had finally got his point.

Malkie took a breath, held it, let it go slow, willed himself to compartmentalise.

'Have you heard from Wilson since the end of your initial debrief?'

Fairbairn snorted, a mix of disgust and disbelief. 'Seriously?

Last night you implied Wilson attacked me even though I said nothing of the kind, and now you're asking about when I last saw her. You think I'm stupid or something?'

Malkie smiled at him. Patient, indulging. 'I wasn't drawing a direct connection between your attack and Wilson, but you seem to think there's some reason for me to do just that. Is that the case, Mr Fairbairn?'

'I don't believe this. No. You mentioned her earlier, not me. You drew that inference. Not me, mate.' He sat back and folded his arms, every inch the petulant child caught out in a fib.

Malkie held his hands out, palms down, and indicated Fairbairn should calm down. 'Let's put your attack on one side then, shall we, since you seem to be particularly sensitive about it. I'm only asking you now where Wilson might be, because no one has been able to contact her, and she didn't attend the Cambuslang briefing this morning.'

A feral gleam appeared in Fairbairn's eyes. 'You know, maybe it *was* her that attacked me. I wrote the idea off because I couldn't think of a bad enough reason I might have given her to do such a stupid thing. I mean, no, we're never going to be buddies, but we operate fine professionally. It's only when we're in the station, during downtime, that she treats me like shit. And even then, never openly, just sleekit wee looks, you know? Turning her nose up at comments I make. Staring at me like I'm shite on her shoe or something.'

Fairbairn snapped his fingers. 'Got it.' He held his hands out as if to demonstrate how slow he'd been. 'Duffy.'

'What about him?'

'They were obviously close, maybe they had a thing for each other, even though that's against regulations. Duffy went in first, with Paul Turner, last night. It's always two in and usually with BA Sets if needed. He's only Retained. That means part-time, on-call only.'

'I know what it means.'

'Aye, OK. Anyway, Duffy made no secret of the fact that he wanted to go Whole Time. That means – sorry, aye, you know. He wanted to be Whole Time and feel like a full firefighter, wanted it for months. So, he kept asking to be first in on a decent shout, something bigger than just a poxy wee house fire, you know?'

Breathe, mate. Breathe. Compartmentalise.

'Last night, Jeremy Lees got there first so he assumed IC, Incident Command, and he put me on entry control. I told Duffy he could go in this time. With Turner's experience I thought he'd be in good hands. I couldn't know how bad it would go, could I?'

Fairbairn thought on, his hands fidgeting as if trying to work out where a piece of a jigsaw needed to go.

'Fuck. That'll be it. She blames me for letting Duncan go in first. She thinks if I hadn't let him go in first, he'd be alive today.' Now Fairbairn's features changed. 'Poor cow. No wonder she's pissed off at me. She must have been shagging him after all. Stupid cow.'

Malkie gave him time, and more metaphorical rope.

Fairbairn nodded. 'Aye, that has to be it. She's blaming me for Duncan's death. No wonder she came looking for blood last night. I told you – she can be volatile, jump to snap judgements.'

Malkie resisted an urge to sneer at the man, to communicate his disgust at the sight of him more excited at finding a decent excuse for Wilson's hatred than appalled at his possible – albeit circumstantial – culpability in Duffy's death.

Irony flooded Malkie's mind. Even eight months after it happened, and despite Callum Gourlay's clear findings that a knocked-over candle caused the fire that killed his mum, Malkie still refused to let go of an irrational and unjustifiable mantle of guilt. This man, Fairbairn, sent a man into a burning warehouse that took his life, and even given he'd been obligated to send someone into that building, seemed to feel not a shred of guilt, not a scrap of culpability.

I don't know whether to despise you or envy you, Fairbairn.

NINETEEN

Steph only had to say the words 'Sian Wilson, the usual, please' to DCs Louisa Gucci Gooch and Rab Lundy to set them off on what they already knew to be the standard checks. Many coppers hated that scene in TV dramas where the DI seems to need to tell experienced officers to start CCTV searches, add the car registration to ANPR alert lists, check electoral rolls and credit agencies, and myriad other standard checks they carried out on most investigations.

They turned back to their desks to get started and Steph checked various national databases for any criminal history, Wilson's previous addresses, known family members, and emailed a request to the SFRS for her – and the other squad members' – HR records. Then she did the same for William Galbraith and his wife Anna.

She remembered Anna Galbraith's comment that she'd left unfinished. 'We've been having...' What? What had they been having? Personal issues? Marital problems? That didn't chime with the way the woman had talked about her husband or the genuine worry already evident in her before she found a police officer at her door.

Were they having financial troubles? After relationship issues, 'money troubles' most often followed the phrase 'we've been having'. Most coppers knew that many residents of swanky and impressive properties with flash cars parked on the drives were nothing like as solvent as they liked to appear. In Glasgow they called such neighbourhoods 'Spam Valleys', because the inhabitants spent so much on outdoing the neighbours and running the newest and most expensive cars and – more often now than ever before – paying overambitious mortgages and keeping their heads above financial water, they could only afford to eat tinned meat.

Whenever arson was suspected, attention always focused initially on the owner and their financial situation. Callum Gourlay hadn't submitted his investigation report yet, might not for days, and the fact that William Galbraith – assuming the body from the warehouse office turned out to be him – died in his own premises, tended to make that usual suspicion less likely, but she asked DI Thompson to OK Gucci and Lundy to run a financial check on him.

She checked in with Lin Fraser at the morgue. Fraser confirmed that she'd managed to extract viable tissue from the pulp in the victim's teeth. She also confirmed that the heat inflicted on the body, while enough to destroy all outer soft tissue, had not damaged any dental structure, and both knew that a dental comparison would take far less time than waiting for a DNA comparison by the ever-overworked forensics lab.

She checked in with Callum Gourlay, who advised his report would – as she had feared – take a few days. When pushed and assured twice that no one would quote him, he confirmed that although checks on the warehouse's alarms, sprinklers and ventilation would take longer, he could be certain the fire did start in the storage area where up to a hundred barrels of whisky had sat on pallets stacked to the ceiling. He told Steph his current working theory, that faulty electrics in a combined environmental heating and cooling system had ignited some leakage from very old barrels in the rear of the area, but he insisted again that this theory could change.

Steph recorded the information, but marked it as not signed off and provisional only.

A couple of Uniforms called in that they'd revisited Sian Wilson's home, and found she'd obviously packed in a hurry and scarpered. They found her passport in a kitchen drawer, but an inability to leave the country did nothing to narrow the search for her. Steph could think of no reason to assume any connection between Wilson and the Galbraiths, but it would be checked. Which begged the question: had Wilson gone missing because she'd attacked Peter Fairbairn?

Or, possibly, the poor woman had crawled off somewhere to mourn her closest friend, and to indulge herself in a well-deserved breakdown.

Steph left Gucci and Lundy to their checks and headed for Wilson's home.

As she'd been told, Steph found clear evidence that Wilson had packed in a hurry. Drawers and wardrobe doors hung open and a kitchen drawer holding bills and batteries and various coins and keys hadn't been fully closed.

Steph saw no signs of a struggle or forced entry. She sat on Wilson's sofa and studied the room. Her eyes stopped on the photo she'd seen earlier. Wilson and Duffy at some seaside camp site, a static caravan behind them, a table holding food and a wine bottle in front of them, glasses in their hands and smiles on their faces. She stood, removed the photo from its frame but found nothing written on the back. She bagged it to check out later. Where better for the woman to fall apart than somewhere she considered a happy place?

Steph locked up and returned to her car.

Time for a conversation she could never be ready for, so she decided to get it over with quickly.

She swallowed bile, along with a stubborn lump of shame for the loathsome genes that she now knew formed half of her.

Time to confront her stepfather, to find out what and when he knew about her rapist pig of a biological father.

TWENTY

Malkie returned to the station just in time to catch Gucci and Rab Lundy trying to leg it out the door for the day. Gucci offered to stay to cover both of their notes so Rab could get away to the pub.

She logged on again, opened the case file and navigated to the records they'd both entered previously.

'Eight of them are full time, two of them part time. Or rather, seven are full time plus the deceased. All are on the electoral role. No police records, any of them, although Stuart Simpson had been suspended from school a few times for low-level nonsense and general misbehaviour. No drugs or drink offences or cautions on record, couple of minor disciplinaries against Sian Wilson for scuffles with colleagues, although I didn't see any other names. No driving arrests on any of them, but Stuart Simpson got three points on his licence two years ago, a week after buying his first car. He's not had any since, so he must have learned his lesson.'

She scanned down the notes. 'Ah. Paul Turner has had credit problems going back a few years. Apart from that and Stuart Simpson's juvenile record, neither of us found any red flags of note. As for Duffy...' – she switched to a different file – 'Preliminary report says he just suffocated, believe it or not.'

'Seriously?'

'Yep. Starved of oxygen plus smoke inhalation. I guess that's why he tried to pull his mask off?'

Malkie's mind flashed back to how Peter Fairbairn had grabbed Duncan Duffy's BA Set and examined it himself, before handing it over to Lees.

'Something stinks here, Gucci.'

'Doesn't it always, boss?'

'What level were Stuart Simpson's juvenile issues?'

'Minor vandalism, graffiti, that sort of thing. Apparently he had a bit of a word with himself when he turned eighteen and nearly got sent to Chateau Saughton for his first adult screw-up. He joined the SFRS and by all accounts, he's keen as anyone could be, eager to make a name for himself, leave his past behind.'

'I wonder if that's why he always seems terrified of us coppers.'

'Could be.'

Malkie paced forward and back, his hand massaging the back of his neck as if that might somehow loosen something his brain just wasn't seeing.

He stopped. 'You get home, Gucci. Thanks for staying, I appreciate it.'

Gucci grabbed her coat and bag but stopped short of the exit from the CID room.

'I forgot to say, there's a message from the desk sergeant for you. Someone called at reception and asked for you. When I told her you weren't available, she asked to leave a message.'

Malkie's guts sank. Only one person had taken to asking for him at reception recently, because she didn't have his mobile number and never would. He asked the question, his heart in his mouth. 'Any name?'

'Sandra Morton? You know her?'

Yes, I bloody do.

'Thanks, Gucci. Get yourself home now.'

She left, but only after a look that told Malkie she hadn't missed his reaction to the name.

Malkie sat at his desk, hoped Gucci had got the name wrong until he read it on the message. Sandra Morton, the most ill-advised school romance he could have possibly got himself into, turned toxic and nearly lethal when her knuckle-dragging brothers had taken umbrage at him for dumping their sister and stabbed him. She'd called on him twice recently, both times to drop bombshells on him. First, that she'd been pregnant by him, more than twenty years ago. The second that she'd lost the baby. Malkie had gone from dreading having to take on responsibility for a daughter to not knowing whether to be gutted or relieved to hear the child hadn't survived.

He considered ignoring the message. Nothing Sandra wanted to say could be of any interest to him. But then, if he ignored this one, how long until she ambushed him in reception again? Better to get it over with, maybe get the message through once and for all? He dialled the number on the message.

'Sandra Morton?'

Malkie took long seconds to push words out. 'It's me. Malkie. What do you want?'

Silence. He considered hanging up but knew he needed to see this through and make sure this became their last conversation.

'I'm sorry to call you again, Malkie. I really am. But I need to talk to you. It's important.'

'About what? You already let me think I'd been a father then told me I never was. What other mind-fuck do you have planned for me?'

'I deserved that. I'm sorry. I got confused, didn't know how you'd react.'

'Did you care how I reacted? Why would you or I care anything about each other after what you and your brothers put me through? Please enlighten me, Sandra, because I'm one wrong word away from hanging up.'

'I can't talk about it over the phone. We need to meet.'

'No. You can just fuck off, Sandra. I'm sorry you miscarried, I really am, and I'm sorry I reacted so badly when you first let me think I might be a father, but if you're still carrying around baggage from that after more than twenty years, that's your problem to deal with, not mine.'

'One coffee. Thirty minutes. You name the place. After that, if you still feel the same, I promise you'll never hear from us again. I swear it, Malkie.'

'Us?' A shiver ran down inside his guts.

A further hesitation on her end of the line had his nerves rattling. What the fuck did she mean?

'Me and my family. My younger brother, Peter, died thirteen years ago, but my dad and my older brother, William, the one who stabbed you, they're still alive and living in Livi. Give me half an hour and I promise we'll never contact you again, none of us.'

Fuck's sake. Is it worth it? Will she keep her word when I tell her to fuck off and never talk to me again?

'I'll text you when I can make time, let you know where.' He hung up in the middle of her trying to thank him.

Malkie glanced at his watch. Nearly half past six. Sandra's call had rattled him, and he wanted nothing more than to get home, eat, sit by the reservoir for a while then crawl into his bed.

But he needed to talk to Flora Beattie too. How late would be too late to interview someone at home? Might as well follow up one shitty phone call with another shitty conversation, get them both out the way in one shitty evening.

He looked up her number and punched it into his phone.

'Hello?'

'Ms Beattie?'

'Yes?'

'This is Detective Sergeant Malcolm McCulloch of Police Scotland. Please accept my apologies for not calling you earlier today but we've been busy, first day of any investigation always a bit full-on, you know?'

She hesitated for a few seconds, then he heard her sigh. 'You're welcome to come to my home now but I'd appreciate it if you kept it short tonight. Is it that urgent?'

Malkie tossed his thoughts back and forth, weighed up what he'd heard last night and today.

'I believe it is, Ms Beattie.'

TWENTY-ONE

Flora Beattie lived in a terraced cottage on South Street in Armadale. As he walked the short distance from the gate across the tiny patch of neat, green lawn surrounded by immaculate strips of flowerbed, he saw evidence of building work piled against the front wall. It took him a few seconds to realise Flora Beattie was having a ramp installed to her front door. Did she have a husband – he caught himself, reprimanded himself – a *partner* with mobility issues? Or a child? Then he remembered Don McCallum's words that morning: 'She's ill... for several months... not up to travelling to the station.'

The door opened and Flora Beattie appeared, supporting herself on two crutches. She grinned at him and her eyes crinkled. Malkie cringed, embarrassed – privately – of his first impression of the woman being a little on the stocky side to be a firefighter, then he wondered just how long she'd been hobbling about on crutches and getting bugger-all exercise.

'Come in, Detective McCulloch. I'll put the kettle on.' She stepped aside and Malkie squeezed past her into a hallway that reminded him of his granny's house: thick patterned carpet, coat stand and shoe rack, telephone on a small table. He noticed only two pairs of shoes on the rack: a smart, black, sensible pair polished to a high shine, and a pair of white trainers, spotlessly clean.

With difficulty, and slowly, Beattie led him through to a small lounge. She'd managed to cram a lot into the small room without it seeming cluttered. Against one wall stood a dresser that looked older than him but in better nick than he'd ever be. Besides that, a glass cabinet full of all kinds of ornaments and things, also like his granny used to collect. He turned to sit on the sofa and found Beattie watching him with a twinkle in her eyes.

'My mum owned this house before me, and I grew up in it. When she passed, I couldn't bear to erase her stamp on the place after I'd known it like this my whole life.'

Malkie smiled. He appreciated how a person would want to preserve the memories of a parent rather than clean the slate, probably more now than he did eight months ago. Before...'

'I'm sorry I couldn't make it to the station for your interview, Detective McCulloch.' She indicated the crutches before resting them against the side of an armchair. She sat on it, slow and careful, then used a remote control to lean it back.

'Ach, the tea. I forgot.' She pressed another button, and the chair started another slow rise.

Malkie waved a hand at her. 'No, no. It's fine, Ms Beattie. Really. As promised, I don't mean to stop for long anyway.'

'OK. What do you need to ask me? I'm afraid I've only had a telephone update from Peter Fairbairn this morning. He promised to call back again later this evening, but I don't know much as of now. Only that we lost Duncan Duffy and that he reported some kind of problem with his BA Set before he collapsed. Paul Turner pulled him out, and an ambulance rushed Duncan to hospital but he never regained consciousness. He told me that Sian Wilson was beyond distraught and that came as a surprise to me. It suggests something more than friendship between them, and SFRS firefighters are not permitted to have close personal relationships with colleagues employed at the same station.'

She thought for a few seconds. 'Callum Gourlay told me that the fire started in a storage area full of whisky barrels on pallets? That means as well as the fire and smoke alarm and sprinkler systems, he'll need to check out the environmental control system too. The only other things he said is that he found no obvious trace of suspicious accelerant anywhere, nor any evidence of ethanol leakage from any of the barrels. But I can't comment on whether he's found anything suspicious, so you'll just have to let him complete his investigation, and if he decides anything illegal has gone on, then it'll be all yours.'

She held her hands up and flashed him a closed-mouth smile. 'And that's as much as I can tell you, for now. I've made arrangements to make sure I can get into the station tomorrow, whatever state I'm in.' She indicated her legs in explanation for her hampered mobility.

Malkie fished for something to say but came up blank.

'Multiple Sclerosis, Detective. Started eating away at me three years ago. Late onset. Obviously.' She grinned again. Malkie had to like the woman. 'I'm taking early retirement because I won't be any use to man nor beast, soon.'

Malkie's heart broke. He couldn't help thinking about Deborah Fleming. He'd met her at an ex-services outreach centre during a previous investigation, and they'd got to know each other since. A *friendship with potential*, Malkie liked to call it, but never within her earshot. Her face flashed across his mind. Half ruined in an accident during an RAF helicopter training exercise, like much of the rest of her burned and brutalised body, but with a dazzling smile that her injuries had failed to kill.

'Detective?'

Malkie roused himself from his thoughts. 'Sorry, Ms Beattie.' He opened his notebook, as much to give himself a few moments to recover as to refresh his memory.

'I'm sorry to hear about your health issues, Ms Beattie. I have a friend who has mobility issues and I know how unsympathetic society can be to—'

'Disabled people?'

A chill ran down Malkie's neck as her expression turned stern. He gaped at her, knew he had no chance of saving the moment, so he could only plough on.

'I believe Steve Grayson is responsible for assessing the safety of all the equipment your officers use, is that correct?'

Steel appeared in Flora Beattie's eyes. 'That's correct. Why?'

Malkie realised he needed to be careful, that he may already have crossed a line and dumped himself on her bad side. 'Nothing specific. Just that another of your officers seemed to take responsibility – and with some urgency – over Mr Duffy's BA Set. I would have expected something like our Police Scotland chain of custody system, where the minimum necessary number of people handle evidence, and all contacts with it are carefully logged?'

Beattie studied him for long seconds. A frown furrowed her brow then disappeared again; Don McCallum would have some explaining to do later. 'I would agree, Detective. Only the Incident Commander should have handled it, and even then only to secure it and bag it for the Fire Scene Investigator. Do you know who took Duncan's BA Set from him?'

'Peter Fairbairn. One of your two watch commanders, I believe?'

This time, Malkie felt no doubt. Recognition of something made her scowl and turn away, something that pissed the woman off but didn't surprise her.

'Ms Beattie?'

She took a second to recover. 'If any fault in Duncan

Duffy's BA Set is found to have contributed to his death, I will make sure it's fully investigated and the report passed to you immediately, Detective.' She mulled again for a spell. 'Did you see anyone from the FIU already in attendance at this point?'

'The Fire Investigation Unit? Yes. Callum Gourlay. He arrived after Fairbairn took Duffy's BA Set away.'

'Then it should have been handed straight to Callum Gourlay for what you call "chain of custody". Gourlay should have examined it, not Fairbairn. Not after Duncan's distressed comment about his BA Set over the open channel. I'll look into that tomorrow.' Her expression added a silent promise that she'd do just that.

'Thanks. I've been in touch with Callum Gourlay already and he's confirmed he'll pass his interim report to me but with caveats, rather than waiting for the final report to be published.'

'Yes, he's *good people*. Where is that BA Set now?'

'I believe it's where it should be... a BA workshop?' He paused, unsure if he recalled where, exactly, that was.

Beattie nodded as she rubbed her right leg, which had spasmed and straightened. Her grimace of pain told Malkie his welcome may already have been outstayed.

'I'll let myself out, Ms Beattie. I apologise for having had to interview you this evening, but the first forty-eight hours of any investigation—'

'I know, I know, Detective McCulloch. It's fine.' She frowned again as another spasm stretched her leg.

Malkie left and knew just who he needed to see before he returned to his dad and their cabin on the shore of Harperrig Reservoir.

TWENTY-TWO

The instant Dean, her stepfather, opened the door to his flat, Steph knew it would end badly. She'd hoped for an appearance of abject apology. She got a scowl and a hand waved to order her inside. She took a deep breath and walked into the flat she'd done most of her growing up in and escaped the first chance she'd got.

She stood, watched him take a can of beer from the fridge and shamble over to the sofa. He indicated she should sit on an armchair opposite as he dumped his arse down.

Steph remained on her feet. She studied the sorry excuse for a man. Fat, unwashed, his hair greasy and unkempt, his fingers yellow from decades of never going more than a half hour without a cigarette in his hand. He looked like he'd started shaving again, at least. Not cleanly, probably a beard trimmer on its lowest setting. The lazy bastard couldn't even be bothered looking after a beard.

'Well?' Her tone furious already, despite her best intentions to start this ordeal from the moral high ground and stay there until she returned to her car. She crossed to the window and stared down. She'd parked in a well-lit spot opposite one of the few CCTV cameras on the estate that still looked operational. So far the vehicle looked unmolested, but she intended to be out of here long before any of the hoodied animals she'd passed in the stairwell had a go at it.

She reminded herself for the millionth time how right she had been to get out of this misery when she could. Joining Police Scotland had put the wind right up him and his mates, suddenly scared they couldn't even smoke joints inside in case she decided to nick them. They never realised that even the satisfaction of arresting people like him would never be worth the experience of having to cuff them and be close enough to them for long enough to process them at the station. But she never let them know that.

He finished a long swig of his beer before speaking. 'I didn't know.'

Steph waited for more, and gaped at him, appalled, when nothing more came.

'You didn't know.' She kept her voice low and controlled, matter of fact, as if running the statement through her mind for a sanity check.

'You didn't know your best mate, the man I used to call Uncle Barry and sit on his knee all evening as he cuddled me, raped my mother. You didn't know.'

She studied the look on his face, saw no trace of regret, no indication he came anywhere near appreciating the enormity of her statement.

'I didn't know. Your mum never told me. How *could* I know?'

She hunted for words, fought for calm but failed. 'How could you *not* know, you stupid bastard?'

He jumped to his feet. 'Don't you talk to me like that. You're still my stepdaughter.'

Her temper broke, this last comment too much. 'Don't you

ever call me that. Don't you fucking dare. You stopped being *anything* to me the day my mum died in Cornton Vale, after she got done for assault because you had her so off her face on your cheap skag she didn't know what the hell she was doing.'

She caught herself, her language failure unacceptable to her, even given such extreme provocation. 'Never call me that, you pathetic excuse for a man. You hear me?' Her tone turned low and dangerous, and Dean paled.

A vicious gleam appeared in his eyes. 'I never forced the stuff on her. She lapped it up. Probably because of you.'

Steph bit down on her rising fury. She mustn't let this prick drive her to do something she couldn't walk away from. She remembered how much she wanted to push her 'Uncle' Barry off the balcony and reminded herself that nothing she could do to either of them would ever be worth throwing away her career.

'Explain that to me, Dean. How was I such a disappointment to her that she needed your junk to get over me?'

Dean floundered but managed to dredge a dose of poison from his feral little brain.

'You were so up yourself, you made her feel worthless. That's what you did.'

She waited, watched Dean as he realised he needed to back up his snide little barb with a little more detail. He probably hadn't thought this far ahead, and that came as no surprise.

'You walked around here like a wee madam, you and your fucking homework and those fucking sickening report cards, then your oh-so-fucking-impressive exam results you couldn't help waving in her face. You made her feel like shite on your shoe. She cuddled you and congratulated you every time you came home smug as fuck and bragging about another one of your pathetic achievements, but as soon as you fucked off to bed she got piled into a bottle and whatever I had handy to help her numb her pain, and cried her fucking eyes out.'

Steph reeled. She'd thought finding out she was a rape baby made her filthy enough. To think that even her own mum never meant any of the pride and adoration she claimed to burst with every time Steph climbed another step on the way to something more than she could ever offer her daughter – it was too much. She'd lived for those evenings, the days she got to tell her mum she'd impressed her teachers again, that she'd risen above her sink-estate upbringing to achieve something of worth, even just a piece of paper that proved she had a brain, and a mind, and an aptitude to use them, to push them and grow herself.

Had it all been a sham? Had her mum only pretended to encourage Steph's studies and her achievements because she thought it the only good thing she could do for her daughter? Had she pumped herself full of drugs only to numb her pain from how much her daughter shamed her? Did Steph, even from her youngest days, drive her to destroy herself from the inside out?

Steph sat, heavy and unstable, on the armchair. Dean smiled, his eyes full of malice, proud of bringing Steph low at last.

She refused to cry, refused to give him the pleasure of witnessing her breakdown.

Dean's face took on a new depth of menace, and Steph braced herself for... for what? What could be worse than everything she'd already learned about herself?

'You can come out now, mate.'

Steph's blood ran cold. Her stomach sank and she fought not to throw up. Even he wouldn't, would he?

A bedroom door opened, and 'Uncle' Barry stepped through, one hand clutching his ribs, his face bruised and his eyes wary from the last time she'd kicked the shit out of him.

Steph's world pitched around her. She stood but wobbled. Blood pounded in her ears and adrenaline tingled through her.

Barry stared at her from the other side of the sofa, looked

ready to bolt at the first sign Steph meant to finish the job. The look of dread on him, his pathetic posture reeking of fear, only enraged Steph more. Her father. Her biological father. This manky, shameful example of all that could go wrong in a man – his blood ran in her veins. The weakness and venality and complete absence of moral fibre polluted her genes and could never be unpicked. As long as she lived, she'd be a shadow of all that was wrong in him, a cheap knock-off of the worst kind of human being.

She leapt over the sofa and was on him before she realised she'd moved. He cowered and screamed, a squeal of terror. She felt Dean's hands on her shoulders and lashed out backwards with her elbow. She felt a crunch, and Dean staggered back screaming his own pain and rage.

She punched Barry. Something in her stopped her from aiming directly for his septum. As much as she wanted to hurt the man, as much as she wanted him to suffer as much as she had, and now probably always would, a steel core inside her refused to cross a line to murdering the bastard, however much he deserved it.

She landed blow after blow on him. She willed herself not to land any one punch too hard and too precise to kill him, but struggled to persuade herself why. His face became a bloody pulp. His struggles slowed to a slow and semi-conscious shake. His eyelids swelled and bloated, and she felt teeth snap off.

Dean hauled her off and threw her behind him. As she tumbled to a stop against a wall, Dean leaned over Barry, tried to open one of his eyes, yelled his name into his unresponsive face. He pulled a phone from his pocket and dialled.

'Ambulance. I need an ambulance really bloody quick.' He reeled off his address, then hung up. He checked Barry over, felt for a pulse.

'You couldn't even do this right, you stupid wee fucker.'

He sat back on his heels and turned to Steph.

'Never mind. You're really fucked now, darling stepdaughter. Completely and utterly fucked.'

Steph could never have imagined that an animal like Dean could have planned this.

But he was right. She was, indeed, fucked.

TWENTY-THREE

Malkie parked up on the long tree-lined drive leading to the Lothians Ex-Services Outreach Centre, the LESOC.

At this time of the day he fully expected Deborah to already be in bed, but having just finished a shite day and facing the prospect of finding and rereading the report on the house fire that killed his mum, he risked a detour on the off-chance.

He saw that the lights in the reception area still burned, so Dame Helen Reid, the fierce but admirable boss of the institution, must still be up and about. He drove to the front door and parked beside the wide, granite steps that led up to massive sliding doors.

Inside, he did find Dame Helen at her desk, through the reception and office area and behind a door on the right side of the mahogany, tartan-carpeted and polished-brass foyer. He knocked on the door only just loud enough to distract her from whatever papers lay on her desk. Making any more noise than he had to would seem like disturbing the stately peace and quiet of the place, like coughing in a church.

'Detective McCulloch. How lovely to see you. It's been... Oh it must be almost a week since your last visit?' A knowing twinkle in her eye threatened to embarrass him, but somehow she never made him feel anything other than a fond familiarity, despite her lofty title and her stern manner.

'I was just passing, Miss Reid. No, really. I'm heading back to Livi, and thought I'd pop in and see if she's still awake?'

She smiled at him, would believe none of it, and would know a fib when she heard it. She glanced at her watch then reached for her desk phone. She dialled a number without needing to look it up.

'Deborah, dear. Have you taken your meds yet? No? Good. Would you have time for a visitor before you take them, do you think?' She smiled as she listened, fully expected whatever response she got. 'OK, I'll send him up. Oh, it's Malcolm, by the way.'

She grinned as she replaced the phone. 'I didn't think she'd have to think long about it. Come with me, Malcolm.'

She led him up the grand staircase and along a hallway. She stopped with her hand on a doorknob. Malkie noticed that the woodwork and fittings of the doors and furniture looked decades old but well-maintained, much like Dame Helen herself.

'I wouldn't stay long, Malcolm. She won't want to send you packing herself, but she takes her meds at nine.'

Malkie nodded. 'I'll be out before lights out, I promise.'

She nodded and opened the door.

Deborah's face lit up when he walked in. She sat up in bed, a massive adjustable thing with more knobs and levers than he'd ever seen on a bed before. She grabbed a remote control and raised her backrest, then grabbed another and muted the TV. When Malkie noticed she'd been watching soaps on catch-up, she shrugged, sheepish but good-natured.

He pulled a chair to her bedside and sat. She reached out a hand to him. He took it and they held on to each other for a few seconds.

'I've missed you, dirty old man. It must have been days since you last called. People will start talking.' She grinned, and for the hundredth time he marvelled at how the flames that had burned her so badly across half her body and face had left her teeth white and gleaming and perfect. Even with only one side of her mouth able to smile, it lit her up and warmed his heart.

'I'm starting to wish I'd never said that.'

'What? "Dirty old man"? But it was the perfect cover story. Well, certainly the way you looked that day. Speaking of which, is that a new suit?' She gaped in mock disbelief.

He looked himself over, knew her compliments wouldn't last long. 'Aye. Straight from Asda. I think it might even have some real wool in it. No' bad, eh?'

He hadn't been wrong about her compliment.

'You know, with a new pair of shoes and some decent shirts and ties, a girl might find you almost sexy.'

He glowered at her. 'You took that too far, by the way.'

She laughed. 'So, to what do I owe the pleasure of a second visit in eight days? And so late in the day?'

Malkie wanted to tell her what a shite day he'd had and how shite he expected the next few days to be, too. But he'd decided weeks ago never to pollute his time with Deborah with the ugliness of his job. She didn't need to hear it, and he refused to risk her sympathy; he'd done enough thumb-sucking his whole life and needed it to stop.

'Ach, just a shitty day, you know. Frustrating. But hey, I got to see inside an actual fire engine today. A warehouse in Livi burned down and I had to attend.'

He stopped himself. She'd know enough to work out the only reason the *polis* would be called out to a building fire. She held his look for a second but didn't pry. She never did.

'Did they let you toot the horn?'

'No. I didn't ask. I have to maintain an image of professionalism and competence in front of witlesses, you know?'

'Witlesses?'

'Aye, witlesses. Some of them are, anyway.'

She laughed again, the undamaged side of her face beaming enough to eclipse the rutted and leathery scars that covered the other. She'd lost the sight in her left eye, and it still unnerved Malkie that as milky and scarred and obviously ruined as it was, it still moved around as her good eye did.

'You're doing it again, Malkie.' Her voice sounded soft and gentle but held a mild rebuke.

'I'm sorry, Deborah. Still gets to me sometimes, what they did to you.'

She sighed. 'For the tenth time, Malkie, *they* didn't do this to me. Well, not directly. Their budget cuts, yes, but I knew as much as my fellow pilots how they'd been cut, and I chose to still get in the damned thing.'

Malkie stopped talking for a few minutes. They sat in silence, and he found himself glad that – as usual – an extended lack of conversation between them felt comfortable and safe rather than awkward.

Eventually, she spoke again. 'So, what happened today that upset you so much you risked Dame Helen's wrath by calling on me when I'm in my bed?'

She always made him smile when he most needed to.

'Ach, just a couple of casualties of the fire. Then I met a lady tonight who made me have a word with myself, like you did when I first met you.'

Concern replaced amusement on Deborah's face. She said nothing, but took his hand again.

'She's one of the firefighters. Management, actually. I had to interview her at home because she's too ill to come to the fire station. Turns out she's got MS, late onset, and I got the impression it's aggressive. I had to ask her some difficult questions about her own firefighters. Felt like such an insensitive clod, so I did.' He stared at her hand, stroked the back of her fingers with his own, and was delighted to feel her respond.

'I suspect she'll be very aware that sometimes people have a job to do, and it can't wait until a better time. I doubt she thought you insensitive, Malkie. Scruffy and unfit, but not insensitive.'

'Ah, that's all right then.' He thought he might make himself sick if he smiled any more at her tonight. Which made him wonder just how much he was coming to lean on her. On a woman who had more pain and struggle to overcome than he ever would. Shouldn't she be leaning on *him*?

'Funny thing.' She waited until he looked up from their intertwined fingers.

'People think they couldn't cope with the kind of nonsense I have to deal with. But everyone has their loads to carry, don't they? One person's load might seem light to someone else carrying much heavier troubles. But to them, both their problems are as real and scary as everyone else's.'

She shook her head. 'Oh, for God's sake, listen to us. Talk about something else. How's your dad and when are you inviting me and Miss Reid to the reservoir for dinner again?'

Malkie pushed the miserable frame of mind that seemed to settle on him too easily these days to one side. 'He's OK. The cabin is keeping us both busy, getting it fit to be called a home. The roof is watertight again, and the windows, and we even got a bloke in to put some insulation in and front it with plasterboard. Means we don't get to see all that lovely wood from the inside, but it also means we don't freeze our arses off during the nights. Oh, and we have separate bedrooms, at last. I'm sick of his snoring, noisy old sod.'

She laughed and stared at him in disbelief. 'Hah! Don't you dare. Last time Miss Reid and I visited you – far too long ago, by the way – he told me that you were driving him up the wall with *your* snoring. And worse.'

Before he could answer, Deborah's bedside phone rang. She didn't reach for it, and it didn't ring again.

She put on a glum face. 'That will have been Miss Reid. Bedtime for me, I'm afraid. Sorry.'

He looked at his watch. 'Ach, I should get home to Dad, anyway. And there's something I need to do before bed.' The instant the words were out, he regretted them, finding Callum Gourlay's FIU report on his mum's death being about the last thing he could imagine wanting to look at, but he knew he had to.

He stood, buttoned up his suit jacket and straightened the knot of his tie. He held his hands out as if to invite judgement on his efforts.

She frowned in confrontation. 'Nope. Sorry. Still getting dirty old man vibes. Must try harder.'

He leaned over her bed, aimed a kiss at her forehead. At the last second, she reached up with her uninjured hand, grabbed him around the back of the neck and pulled him down. She kissed him. Only briefly, but long enough to send some kind of message he'd torture himself later deciding how to interpret.

'Visit me again, Detective Sergeant McCulloch, or I'll get you at playtime.'

He saw her good eye moisten. He touched his forehead to hers. 'Will do, Flight Lieutenant Fleming. I promise.'

He found Dame Helen waiting at the foot of the staircase. Her office door had been closed so he figured she'd waited to lock up after him.

'I do believe you two are good for each other, Malcolm.'

He thought over his response, determined to express his honesty without crossing over into a pity party.

'If I can come to believe I deserve her, Miss Reid, then yes; I think we could be.'

By the time he reached Harperrig Reservoir to find the

cabin dark and his dad already gone to bed, he knew there was no way on earth he'd look for Gourlay's report that night.

He told himself he didn't want to wake his dad, but he knew he just didn't want the last, perfect hour to be ruined.

He threw his jacket over the back of a chair and pushed his shoes off without untying the laces, set his alarm for seven, then fell into bed and got bugger-all sleep all night.

TWENTY-FOUR

Malkie gave up trying to sleep when the first glow of sunrise started to colour the orange glow from Edinburgh to the east. He showered, dressed and arrived at the CID room just as the morning briefing started. He logged on to his computer and opened his emails. He had time to see Callum Gourlay's name on the newest email in his inbox and the title 'Interim report – *work in progress*' before McLeish's loud and arrogant bellow requested his presence.

He sat beside Louisa Gooch. 'Where's Steph?' Gucci shrugged and looked at him as if to say *Don't you know?*

She leaned close. 'Something's wrong, boss. Something's very wrong. McLeish has been seen smiling.'

Malkie stared at her. 'Fuck.'

'I know, right?'

'DS McCulloch, sorry to interrupt your private little meeting but I wondered if I might ask you to pay bloody attention, please?'

Malkie sat up, nodded, every inch the professional. 'Sir.' *You prick.*

McLeish ran through some low-level incidents from the

previous night, and some stats on volume crime that the Scottish Office had a particular desire to see come down either organically or via some 'tweaks' to reporting metrics, then handed over to Susan Thompson.

'Malcolm. The Galbraith Bonded Warehouse?'

Malkie stood. 'Building has been gutted and will have to be demolished. Three appliances were called from Livi and Bathgate. One casualty found by the firefighters, already too far gone to consider rescuing by the first pair who went in to assess the situation. A further casualty when one of those firefighters, Duncan Duffy, complained about his breathing apparatus, then collapsed. Paramedics managed to restart his heart at the scene, but the gentleman then died en route to St John's and couldn't be resuscitated. Fire Investigation Unit have sent an initial report, albeit with a warning of heavy caveats until they complete their investigation. A few hours after the fire, crews were stood down apart from the Bathgate crew damping down the inside to prevent re-ignition. One of the Livi crew, Peter Fairbairn, a squad chief, was attacked at home: someone lamped him with a bottle.'

Thompson flashed him a look.

'We're looking into whether Fairbairn's attack might be connected to some harsh words we heard directed at him by another of his crew, Sian Wilson, who seemed more upset about Duncan Duffy's death than even her colleagues seemed to expect. We've visited the home address of the owner of the warehouse. DC Lang found only his wife at home. She said that her husband ran the warehouse and also, at first, that he'd gone to Inverness on business last night. After further discussion, she seemed to decide the fatality in the building might have been her husband after all. DC Lang left further questions until today.'

Malkie sat.

Thompson stood. 'When will we get ID on the fatality? The first one, I mean.'

'Lin Fraser said she'd be able to extract some viable DNA from the victim's tooth pulp, and we got the name of his dentist from his wife. DC Lang will get his dental records today.'

'OK. Thanks. What's next?'

Malkie tuned out the rest of the briefing, impatient to read Gourlay's email. When Thompson wrapped up, he rushed back to his desk before some officers had even stood up.

Malkie had hoped to see an attachment, an actual report, albeit riddled with caveats. Gourlay had only listed several bullet points. Malkie couldn't blame him; he'd had enough people promise not to quote him only to do just that, and earn him a kicking, too many times before.

1. Fire was started deliberately. *TO BE CONFIRMED*

2. Primary site of ignition appears to have been an overloaded electrical socket under a climate control unit behind the bulk of the barrels in the storage area. *TO BE CONFIRMED*

3. Said climate control unit has not been serviced since 2017, according to the sticker on it. Needs to be confirmed via whatever digital or paper records can be salvaged from fire damage. *TO BE CONFIRMED*

4. Initial accelerant *may* have been a slow leak of liquid from a barrel at the backmost edge of the lowest shelf of pallets. *TO BE CONFIRMED*

5. Victim found inside the building is as-yet unidentified, subject to post-mortem. Details to be shared with FIU.

6. BA Set issued to the deceased firefighter, Duncan Duffy, has

been secured and will be examined by FIU, with the assistance of Livingston Fire Station's accredited H&S safety equipment technician, Steve Grayson. Enquiries to be made into why squad chief Peter Fairbairn removed said BA Set before turning over to FIU. *TO BE CONFIRMED*

When Gourlay had told Malkie he'd commit to very little at such an early stage, he hadn't been kidding, but the first paragraph was all Malkie needed to see: deliberate fire setting, which made the death of the person in the office culpable homicide, at the very least. Malkie grabbed his desk phone and dialled him.

'Callum Gourlay, FIU. Can I help you?'

'Morning, Callum. Are any of your findings still "to be confirmed"?'

He meant it as an icebreaker, but it backfired.

'DS McCulloch, I made myself very clear to you from the outset. My findings can only be provisional and carry heavy caveats until—'

'Callum. Mate. I was joking. I knew anything you'd give us now could only be hypothetical; I expected that, honestly.'

Gourlay sighed down the phone. 'OK. Thanks for that, but this case is throwing up some ugly possibilities that are seriously testing my sense of humour.'

Malkie switched down a gear, couldn't afford to alienate this man. 'I get that, I promise, and I'm grateful for your candour and your willingness to trust me with your early opinions, OK?'

'Fine. What can I do for you?'

'Well, your first paragraph is a showstopper. A couple of points I'd like clarified, though. As much as you feel comfortable with,' he added, to avoid stressing Gourlay even more. 'What does a warehouse need climate control for? Is that something to do with the ageing of the whisky?'

'Aye. There are two ways of storing the barrels. Rickhouse, mostly in American distilleries, where the barrels are stored in racks with plenty of airflow. Or on more closely packed pallets. Barrels on pallets don't get as much airflow, and airflow encourages consistency of temperature which assists the gradual leakage of ethanol, what they call the "Angel's Share", so the whisky matures faster and more powerfully.'

'And you think one of these ventilation units failed, and caused the fire?'

'It's a theory.'

Malkie knew to let that one go. 'My other query's related to Duncan Duffy's BA Set.'

He heard Gourlay's sigh down the phone. 'That's not relevant to any homicide investigation you might conduct, is it?'

'It might be, Callum. Please, humour me.'

Malkie left Gourlay to continue unprompted. Open and voluntary statements very often yielded better information than closed, specific questions.

'Jeremy Lees passed it to me when he took it from Peter Fairbairn, and I took it into FIU custody for testing by us and by the manufacturer the SFRS leases its BA Sets from. Steve Grayson will be kept in the loop as Livi Station's BA engineer.'

He paused, and Malkie knew when people paused it often meant they were either trying to frame their comments carefully, or to throw caution out the window and cross a line. Usually, a combination of both. Malkie wanted to let the man continue when he felt ready, but also recognised he might need a gentle nudge.

'You want me to call you on my personal mobile, Callum?'

'Aye. Please. This is a bloody rotten situation.'

'Two minutes.' Malkie grabbed his jacket and headed for the stairwell down to the foyer and dialled Gourlay's number again as he walked into the landscaped grounds around the Livingston Civic Centre.

'OK, Callum. This is my personal mobile; it's not being recorded, and you have my word that I'll repeat nothing of what you say to me now.'

After a pause, Gourlay continued, but he sounded like he'd rather have his teeth pulled out with pliers.

'I have no reason – no earthly reason – to suspect that any of those firefighters might have anything they'd want to hide or keep quiet about, but...'

Malkie gave him the space he needed.

'Fairbairn examining Duffy's BA Set doesn't sit well with me for two reasons.'

Another pause. Gourlay might be about to stick his neck out.

'There have been complaints lodged, formally, with Flora Beattie, concerning equipment – including BA Sets – being allowed to remain in use despite concerns about their safety margins. I believe none of the equipment is ever allowed to actually become illegal, and the tolerances for safety are incredibly tight, as you would expect of equipment these guys rely on to keep them alive in some pretty horrific situations.'

Another pause, this one definitely a line being crossed.

'But allowing equipment to get so close to its safety tolerances is foolish at best, reckless at worst. If a firefighter says he or she believes a BA Set is faulty, then it has to be taken, what we call, "off the run" or "OTR" immediately. But...'

Malkie waited.

'If a firefighter were to be pressured not to formally complain about something in a BA Set, if he were perhaps reluctant to make waves... Someone might persuade themselves they were worrying needlessly under severe enough circumstances. But that would be obscene, a firefighter reluctant to put a BA Set OTR because they felt pressured to keep their mouth shut. That's just... unthinkable, to be frank.'

'Who lodged those complaints, Callum?'

'I don't know. I really don't. I only know complaints have been lodged. You'll need to ask Flora Beattie about that, but for fuck's sake do not let her know you heard that from me.'

'I won't.'

Malkie mulled over this bombshell, needed to know one more thing in order to give it the credibility he feared he needed to.

'Why are you telling me this, Callum? Don't you lot stick together, no?'

Silence for a moment, then, 'When your lot investigate a crime, if you detect the slightest whiff of corruption, don't you call in Internal Affairs, or whatever they're called here? Even on your own people if it's thought to be serious enough?'

'Professional Standards. We hate doing it, but stopping bad coppers from being bad outweighs any sense of abstract loyalty. Or at least it should.'

'And it makes you even more sick if it's people you know, right?'

'Aye, it does.'

'Then you'll understand why I bloody hate telling you these things, but... I have reasons. Reasons I can't just chase this through normal channels alone. Now, can we leave it at that for now? And can I trust you?'

'You can trust me, Callum.'

They disconnected and Malkie returned to the CID room. As he passed Thompson's desk, she stood and nodded her head towards the stairwell.

Malkie informed Gucci and Lundy that he needed to head for the mortuary. Gucci shared a sympathetic smile with him; she knew how much he hated days like today. Rab Lundy limited himself to a simple 'Have fun'.

Outside the CID room, on the stairwell, Thompson leaned on the railing in front of a window and gazed out over the same landscaped grounds Malkie had just returned from.

'You want the good news or the really bloody awful news?'

'I don't suppose I can just have the good news?'

'McLeish is leaving us. Couple of months from now.'

Malkie felt a cold lump of dread land in his guts; the bad news really would have to be awful to offset getting rid of McLeish. He waited.

Thompson turned, leaned back against the window and sighed.

'He's got himself assigned to a Major Investigation Team.'

Malkie adopted the same position. Screwed his eyes shut, willed the last five seconds to rewind and never happen again.

'Fuck.'

He headed for the canteen for coffee and a bacon roll – *fuck it, two* – before facing another day with his mood about as foul as it could get.

TWENTY-FIVE

Steph woke to late-morning sunshine blasting through her living-room window and warming her face, and a blinding headache.

She sat up, turned, lowered her feet to the floor. The coffee table beside her sofa was littered with her warrant card, baton, cuffs, notebook, packs of sterile crime-scene gloves, shoe covers, an empty Kahlua bottle and a glass half full with the last of the booze. The Kahlua had started unopened. Her mouth felt like she'd had a tongue transplant from someone twice her size; it stung as she tried to swallow and peeled away from her dried-out teeth. Her head pounded.

She reached for the remnants of the liqueur, swilled it round her mouth, and managed to swallow it without gagging.

She looked at her watch. Nearly eleven. Not good.

She stood, crossed to the kitchen sink, turned on the cold tap and felt it with her fingers until it ran about as cold as it could at this time of year, then she stuck her head under and held it there. Her headache banged even harder against the inside of her skull, and she coughed as water running down her face and across her nostrils triggered a drowning reflex, but she held her head steady until the pain became too much even for her.

She grabbed a tea towel and dried her hair, harsh and furious, then filled the kettle to make coffee.

She leaned back against the worktop and studied the carnage from the night before. The mess on the coffee table formed a stark contrast with the rest of the room. Steph kept everything tidy, everything in its established place, not compulsively, as far as she knew. More likely simply because she loved order. She'd learned discipline at an early age, learned to never wake her stepdad Dean if she came home late, never to cough or sneeze or put her feet down on flooring she knew to be loose and creaky. The slightest noise never failed to elicit a heavy and over-obvious sigh and tut from her parents' bedroom. Steph had learned from Dean that a few choice words, or even just a sound, could cause someone so much more guilt, fear and stress than even physical punishment. She'd even learned how to push down on her bedroom door handle, open the door and close it again without the mechanism making the slightest noise. She'd only realised after she left home what a tyranny of passive aggression she'd come to think of as normal.

Her self-taught discipline had matured as she progressed through primary and secondary schools, and she'd learned at a younger age than most children that escape from the kind of ugly and sordid life that Dean kept her mother trapped in depended on powering through her education and coming out of it with better grades than even her teachers had expected from the sullen and contrary wee girl her infancy had turned her into.

She'd planned to use whatever qualifications she earned herself to find lucrative employment of some kind and rescue her mum from the prison of drugs and alcohol she didn't even know she rotted away in. A shank made from a sharpened toothbrush had ended that dream while her mum had been on remand in Cornton Vale women's prison. On remand for the assault and wounding of a dealer she'd attacked out of desperation during a spell of punishment by Dean, when he denied her all but the minimum fixes she needed to not die.

After her mum did die, Steph found no reason to carry on living with Dean, and every reason to get as far away as possible from him and his rotten existence.

Thoughts of Barry dragged her tired and battered mind back to the previous evening.

She dumped her backside back on the sofa but resisted an urge to lie down and let the whole damned world just fuck off. She clutched her head in her arms and screwed her eyes shut. When had she started using language she'd worked so hard from such a young age to resist? Had she fallen so far? Had she allowed Barry and Dean and their despicable ambush to push her into a place where even her non-negotiable standards of behaviour slipped and fell by the wayside? Had they succeeded in dragging her down to a level she'd fought so hard to rise above? Oh, the bastards must have enjoyed hearing her pushed so far, infuriated so much that she used *language*.

Fuckers.

She allowed herself to use the word in her mind, and only when no other word would do, but she prided herself on never, ever, depending on the crutch of abusive language out loud. She couldn't even *think* the 'c' word, even letting it flash across her mind made her feel weak and ugly, as if she debased herself by even acknowledging the word mentally.

She stood, crossed to her window. Her flat looked down on Linlithgow high street. Riddled with damp and in need of decoration in at least half of the rooms, she loved it, and had stretched herself to be able to afford it. High ceilings, wide doorways, elaborate cornices and grand fireplaces, old and stately staircase, it epitomised everything her own childhood home had never been.

She had no illusions she was cocooning whenever she came home. She'd spent too many years thinking of home as a place to be avoided and escaped from. Now, home needed to be her safe place, her hideout.

The only grief from her former life allowed to live here with her was regret. Regret that her mother wasn't able to hang on until Steph could save her; and regret – irrational and idiotic, she knew, but no less real – that her childhood self hadn't seen her mother's plight and been a better daughter to her.

Christ, she was starting to sound like Malkie.

She opened a window and allowed cold February air and the sounds of the high street to wash over and around her. At least some, and surely the majority, of the people who lived and worked around her had to be the furthest thing from the kind of sub-species she'd grown up with.

As she turned around to make coffee, her eyes fell on the clutter on her coffee table, and a folded-over photograph. Sian Wilson and Duncan Duffy in happy times, sipping wine in bright sunshine under a caravan awning, somewhere next to a beach.

A penny dropped, and she cursed herself for not having thought of it earlier. She grabbed her phone and quick-dialled Malkie.

'Steph. Are you OK? You've got us all more than a wee bit worried here. Not even calling in.'

She told herself *enough*. This wasn't her. This wasn't the woman she'd crafted herself into.

'Sorry, Malkie. I had a rotten headache when I woke up and I'd left my phone in my car.'

Silence for a few seconds, then, 'I'm adding this to our "to be talked about later" list, OK?'

She knew he meant that he needed reassurance from her, if not an explanation. 'Aye, fair enough. I'm coming in, just needed time for some painkillers to kick in. Listen, I think

Wilson might have gone to the caravan I saw in the photo in her flat, if she still owns it, or maybe it belonged to Duffy. Anyway, the time stamp on the back dates it to only late last year, so there's a fair chance she could be there.'

'You've got the photo, aye?'

'Of course I do.'

'Aye, all right. You get some breakfast down you, then get over here. If you'll arrive any later than noon, I'll be at the mortuary. I told Lin Fraser I'd be there at lunchtime to get whatever she can give us.'

'I'll see you there, then.'

As she placed her phone back on the coffee table, she noticed the bruising to her knuckles. Malkie had noticed them yesterday, from the previous time she'd beaten the shit out of Barry. She searched her minimalist and rarely used make-up supplies and found some foundation cream. She covered the bruises the best she could, and reminded herself to keep her hands out of sight as much as she could until those healed too.

She'd been pushed beyond any reasonable limit. He'd had it coming to him.

But she'd lost control. Twice, now. And that scared the shite out of her, as Malkie might say.

TWENTY-SIX

Malkie returned to Livi Fire Station. His phone buzzed during the drive. When he parked, he checked, didn't recognise the number on the text, but feared he could guess from what it said: 'Please, Malkie'. He pulled the crumpled note that Gucci had left him from his pocket. Same number. Sandra Morton. Again.

Fuck. She's not going to let go, is she?

He stored the number in his contacts but promised himself it would be temporary.

He found both Flora Beattie and Callum Gourlay waiting for him. Flora insisted all three talk together, and Malkie hoped her intention would be to cooperate for everyone's mutual benefit rather than close ranks.

Her first comment after closing the door to her office and manoeuvring herself into her chair allayed his concerns.

'We have ourselves one hell of a mess here, don't we, gentlemen?'

She glanced from Malkie to Gourlay and back again. Nobody seemed to know who professional etiquette dictated got to go first. She put both men out of their discomfort.

'Fine. I'll start.' She opened a file on her desk and handed a sheaf of stapled papers to Malkie. 'Mr Gourlay's initial report. We'd prefer not to let you keep that yet, until he finalises some points, but we can discuss it here and now.'

Malkie opened the report, saw a lot of preliminary official guff and a paragraph of management summary followed by several pages of text, diagrams, tables and bullet points. He closed it again. 'Summarise it for me, please. Treat me like an idiot who doesn't have a clue what all this means.'

Beattie held out a hand to indicate Gourlay should continue. He sat forward and half-turned to face Malkie.

'Either Duncan Duffy's alarm whistle failed, or he didn't hear it, or the issue with his BA Set was so catastrophic that by the time he heard it go off it was already too late for him. Or he ignored it.'

'The one that should have told him the time had come for him to turn around and make his exit? No firefighter would ignore that, would they?'

'More experienced firefighters develop an instinct for how far beyond the whistle they can push their luck, but they still don't take chances. Ever. For some reason, Duffy ran out of air in about half the time he should have. For some other reason, even though his cylinder gauge was accurate, either his whistle didn't sound, or he didn't hear it, or...'

Malkie waited, as always.

'Or he heard it but he'd already suffered too much respiratory distress for it to make any difference. Have you got the results of his post-mortem yet?'

Malkie's turn to wriggle in discomfort. 'Aye, but the report's not finalised yet, so...'

Both Beattie and Gourlay raised their eyebrows as they glanced at Gourlay's initial, but as-yet unfinalised, fire investigation report. 'Aye, fair enough. The post-mortem findings are consistent with Mr Duffy running out of air before he expected to, then trying to remove his face mask which allowed smoke inside, and hydrogen cyanide accelerated his respiratory distress. Our coroner says he'd have fallen unconscious in seconds. What we can't comment on is why his air ran out early and why he panicked and caused all that to happen in such a short space of time. That's your area of expertise.'

Beattie and Gourlay shared a brief look.

Beattie sat forward now, looked troubled. 'If there had been more air left in his cylinder, positive pressure would have stopped smoke ingress, so he must have pulled it away from his face and been trying to breathe in environmental air, which would have been just stupid given the thick smoke in there.' He seemed to realise what he'd just inferred and cast an apologetic look at Flora Beattie, before continuing. 'Callum has examined Duncan's entire BA Set. The mask, neck seal, hoses, cylinder, fastenings, everything, are fine. Even the low-pressure alarm whistle.'

'Had his cylinder pressure fallen low enough to have caused him problems?'

'Aye. It was nearly empty. When full, positive pressure would have stopped smoke from entering his mask. When empty, the BA Set gets sucked onto the face, and he'd have suffocated. But it should never have got that empty without his whistle going off. In fact, he should have been checking his gauge often enough to get far more warning. He must have lost pressure quickly, which means something had to have damaged the integrity of his air supply. But he would have checked out his own BA Set and all the other equipment – his cylinder pressure, his valves, the neoprene seal, positive-pressure test, everything – both when he picked it up at the station and before he entered the building. It's standard and mandatory procedure.'

Malkie fished for a way to ask his next question without causing friction. 'Could he have been... Too stressed to remember all his training? Could he have missed something?'

Gourlay turned a hard look on him.

Beattie caught it. 'Callum?'

'Possibly. I've heard of only one case in all my years in FIU of a warning whistle getting so clogged with ash and other matter that its sound had been muted, but not silenced. And yes, if Duffy had already succumbed to severe stress, he might have been breathing hard and fast, and become too focused on his surroundings. He could have forgotten to check his gauge. Then – theoretically – when he first got a low-pressure point, he might have started breathing even more aggressively.'

All three fell silent. The last thing any of them wanted was for a blame game to start.

Malkie decided to bend some rules. 'The post-mortem found that Duffy had a heart condition. Were you aware of that?'

They looked at each other; they hadn't been. Beattie recovered first. 'Duncan passed his assessment during recruitment without any apparent fitness issues. And...' – she opened another file on her desk and turned a few pages – 'He's passed every regular fitness and medical test, again without issues.'

Malkie held his hands up to head off a defensive tone in her voice. 'He had something called cardiomyopathy. It can lie dormant and asymptomatic for years, decades even, without problems, but can then flare up later in life and has been known to make even elite athletes drop dead without warning.'

Beattie couldn't hide how much this troubled her. 'Our screening processes don't always detect conditions like that. It's something that's changing, though. Screening is being improved.'

'It's only a suspicion at the moment. The post-mortem report hasn't been finalised yet.'

Beattie turned to a different page in her copy of the FIU report. She glanced at Gourlay, whose face told Malkie he knew exactly which page she'd turned to. Beattie sat back and sighed, took a moment before she could look back up at Malkie.

'Telemetry readings from Duncan's BA Set show his respiration rate had indeed spiked heavily from the moment he entered the building. Heavily enough to throw out our standard air-time calculations.' She hesitated a moment more, and Malkie felt a bombshell coming. 'And from five minutes before he raised a BA alarm, his breathing became even more intense. Then he suffered some catastrophic loss of pressure for some reason. No wonder he tried to rip his mask off despite the density of smoke in there.'

She seemed to slump in her seat. Gourlay looked guilty, despite his only part in this having been to accurately report established SFRS safety protocols and findings. Malkie thought it must feel similar to when police officers have to inform some poor mother that her teenage son has killed himself a week after getting his motorbike licence.

'I think Callum and I need time to go through the report in more detail. I only got a chance to skim it when I arrived at lunchtime.'

Malkie nodded. 'Of course. Shall I check in with you again at close of business today? Will that give you enough time to agree your joint findings?' *And get your stories straight?*

'Yes. That'll be fine, as long as Mr Gourlay can hang on here for an hour or two this afternoon?'

Gourlay nodded, solemn and looking far from happy at the prospect.

As Malkie opened Beattie's office door to leave, he turned back. 'Is it normal for an FIU investigator and the commander of the station being investigated to confer on the report?'

Beattie nodded at Gourlay to answer.

'Absolutely, Mr McCulloch. Normal procedure.'

Malkie hadn't missed the return to formality during the course of the conversation, which he could only hope didn't indicate some piss-taking on the horizon.

As he reached his car, he heard Gourlay calling him. He

turned to find the man approach him but then walk past him and nod towards Malkie's car. Malkie unlocked the doors and Gourlay got in on the passenger side. Malkie got in too, his curiosity meter maxed out.

It took Gourlay a few seconds. He stared out the window so long Malkie wondered what the hell he had to say, and how significant it might turn out to be.

He pulled a folded sheaf of papers from inside his jacket and handed it to Malkie.

'I thought Beattie said she didn't want me to get a copy of this yet?'

Gourlay stared at him. The level of dread in his eyes rattled Malkie, made him almost afraid to read the damned thing.

He unfolded the papers, found it to be an FIU report, but not regarding the warehouse fire. It concerned the house fire that killed his mother.

He looked to Gourlay for an explanation, knew he must look bewildered, even frightened.

What the fuck am I about to find out? Proof of my culpability, after all? Isn't that what I've been looking for all these months?

Gourlay nodded at the report. 'Page seven.' Then, after a pause and a hard swallow, 'And I'm sorry, Malkie.'

Malkie turned to page seven, his fingers shaking and his palms sweaty, and he didn't give a toss that Gourlay could see the state of him.

Page seven had the usual dense chunks of dry, technical text, above and below a diagram. It showed his mum's bedroom: bed, TV stand, other furniture, doorway and windows. A large red cross in a circle grabbed his eye. He checked the legend beneath the diagram, but he already knew with a sickening certainty what the symbol indicated.

Source of the fire. Candle which set light to old, pre-Furniture and Furnishings (Fire) (Safety) Regulations 1988 curtains.

He swallowed, to work some moisture into his mouth, then turned to Gourlay. He couldn't find words to articulate the inevitable conclusion. Or rather, he could find words but couldn't utter them for fear of making them real.

Gourlay's face turned grim. 'You said "Even sitting on her bedside table, next to her bedclothes" or something like that.'

Malkie felt his gorge rise, the implications both liberating and damning at the same time. His mum and dad never had a cat and she never lit the candles on her windowsill because she always slept with the windows open. Unlike the one he gave her eight months ago, unaware it would be her last birthday gift from him, even without the fire.

He hadn't bought her the candle that had killed her. He hadn't let her die because he'd been too weak and couldn't deny her pleading to light it on her bedside table.

The candle that killed her had been sitting on the windowsill for years, under old curtains, and his dad would never light one so close to them.

Someone else had to have lit that candle.

Only one theory found room in his troubled mind.

Did some fucker kill his mum?

TWENTY-SEVEN

As Gourlay climbed out of the car, Malkie spotted one of the firefighters sitting on a chair outside the open vehicle bay doors, his elbows on his knees, his head down, a cigarette in one hand.

He trawled his mind for the verbal clues he'd tried to lodge in his brain the night of the fire. Bald. Strange, haunted look. Paul Turner. The man who had gone in with Duncan Duffy and brought him out already near-dead. How the hell could he have forgotten the man's name already, given his role in the events? He shook his head as if to wake his brain up.

Fuck's sake. Do better.

As he approached Turner, the man looked up at him, and Malkie almost recoiled from his bleak and haunted expression. He didn't bother trying to hide it, just stared at Malkie as if he'd been waiting for him.

'Good morning, Detective McCulloch.'

Malkie wanted nothing more than to keep walking. The privacy and quiet of his car beckoned, but he couldn't walk away from a man so clearly in pain. He sat next to Turner. 'Call me Malkie, mate. At least until you piss me off or I have to arrest you for something, OK?'

He meant it as an icebreaker, even hoped for a smile, but Turner's eyes took on a desperate look, as if that prospect scared the shit out of him for some reason Malkie suddenly wanted to get to the bottom of.

OK. Maybe a bit early to be giving this guy permission to use my first name. When will I ever learn?

'Are you OK, Mr Turner? You look... preoccupied?'

Turner looked behind him, towards the inside of the vehicle bay, then faced Malkie again. He seemed to struggle to find words, or – as Malkie had seen too many times before – decide what might be safe to say.

'It's just that I took responsibility for him, you know? That was his first time into anything serious wearing BA and under air, and...' He tailed off, stared at the ground again.

'Under air. That means...'

'BA Set, aye.'

'He'd have done all the necessary training, wouldn't he? You all would? So, he should have been completely familiar with BA Set protocols? Can I ask why you feel responsible? Any specific reason, mate?'

Turner's head snapped up. Malkie saw fear there. Bewilderment. Why did the man seem to carry so much guilt?

Why do I? Stop it. Focus.

'Aye, of course. He'd done all the training. He'd not done it before, him only being Retained for six months, not in a live situation. He as good as begged Fairbairn to let him go in with me. We agreed since the warehouse looked to be a small building with only a single floor and a limited number of compartments. We thought it would be a good one for him to cut his BA Set teeth on, kind of thing.'

His voice faltered again. 'We thought he was ready, or we wouldn't have let him go in. *I* thought he was ready. But...'

Malkie sat on the chair beside him and waited. He found himself needing to listen to Turner, despite his own troubles.

He waited, his favoured technique when questioning someone being never to try too hard to drag it out of them.

Turner struggled with some argument with himself, before speaking again. 'I think he panicked, Detective. Well, not panicked, but I think he let himself get more stressed than us more seasoned old boys would, and I think he must have been breathing harder than the BA duration tables allowed for. Much harder.'

Malkie raised his eyebrows, more and more feeling like an out-of-depth schoolboy.

'Sorry, calculations we do based on cylinder volume and pressure, and typical respiration rates of each person who uses one. We set an alarm so a whistle goes off when the remaining air drops to what's needed to return to the entry control point without needing to go into the safety margin, usually about twelve minutes. Two go in for the initial assessment and a third stays at the door as BA entry control officer and records time of entry, cylinder pressure, takes their tallies and maintains the board.'

Malkie stared at him again.

'The BA entry control board, the entry control officer uses it to record who goes in and when and how much time they can stay safe on air until they have to start their exit. If Duncan's time had been calculated as per the usual formulas, that would have assumed measured breathing. None of us heard him actually hyperventilating on the open radio channel, but I think he must have gone through his supply faster than the calculations allowed.' Turner frowned.

'But?'

'But his whistle should have sounded to tell him he'd reached his turnaround pressure, and he should still have had time to get out before running out of air. The place had only three main compartments and wasn't nearly big enough for one of us to get lost even in the kind of thick smoke we encountered.

A lot of firefighters have died because they got "lost", but that couldn't have happened here or I'd have known about it. I'm sure I did keep a close eye on him. Only thing is, I can't be certain he was checking his gauge every five minutes, as he should have been.'

'His gauge? On his air supply?'

'Aye. We're supposed to monitor it so the whistle never comes as a surprise. Or in case it's too noisy inside a building for us to be sure we'll hear it.' He scowled again and shook his head.

'Could his BA Set have been faulty? Can that happen?'

Malkie couldn't miss it. Turner's hand stopped halfway to his mouth as he raised his cigarette. Only for a second, but even that brief hesitation told Malkie enough.

'Mr Turner? Could it have been faulty?'

'No. They're checked on a strict schedule by Steve, by each firefighter before relying on them in a live situation, and again by the BAECO.'

'The entry control officer.'

'Aye. So, the chances that we allowed Duncan to go into that building with a faulty BA Set are... minimal.'

'Has it happened before? To other firefighters in other stations?'

'Aye. Seals degrade over time, valves stick, whistles get fouled, screws and washers work loose, that sort of thing.' He seemed to realise what he might be admitting to. 'But Steve Grayson wouldn't miss anything like that. No chance.'

'OK, OK. I believe you. But it does happen.'

'It *can* happen.'

'And could something like that explain why Mr Duffy might have run out of air before he should have?'

Turner took on a defensive posture, dropped the butt end of his cigarette on the ground, folded his arms and sat back. 'Yes, but there would have been warnings. He would have been made aware.'

'Even if he did panic?'

'I retracted that word. None of our boys would panic, not after the training we've had, and not when he knew I had his back.'

'You were behind him? So, you saw this all happen?'

'I didn't mean literally. I meant figuratively. I led. Letting him go in first would have been pushing our luck for his first time. The first I knew he'd got himself in trouble was when he alerted us all on the open channel to some kind of problem with his BA Set. We think he panicked because we're supposed to call out a BA emergency, but Duncan just started yelling.'

Malkie left him alone, decided he'd just gained an embarrassment of information riches, more than he could have hoped for when he first sat down with the man.

He stood. 'Thanks for your candour, Mr Turner. And for the crash course on firefighting protocols.' He turned to leave, but one further thought occurred to him.

'You said no one saw anything wrong with his BA Set. How do you know that? For certain, I mean?'

Turner looked suspicious again, as if Malkie thanking him for so much information had him reviewing every word he'd said. 'The checks that the individual firefighters and the entry control officer do immediately before entry should find any last-minute problems. And Callum Gourlay allowed Steve Grayson to examine Duncan's BA Set when we all returned to the station. He wouldn't let Steve handle it, but he let him look at it. I thought it weird, almost like he felt a need to get a second opinion.'

'And why would he be doing that? Any idea?'

Turner seemed to realise he'd talked himself into some kind of corner. Malkie watched him weigh things in his mind. Whether to risk dumping a colleague in it? Or to avoid revealing something he'd only now realised he might be in danger of doing? Malkie couldn't guess.

'Because Duncan's BA Set should have been bagged and tagged the minute we took it off him, but Callum Gourlay only got it thirty minutes later, after Jeremy Lees got it from Pete Fairbairn.'

'Thanks. Appreciate the info. There's something I need to ask you though, Mr Turner.'

Turner's face returned to the same miserable expression he'd been wearing when Malkie spotted him.

'We have to run background checks on every Person Of Interest in a serious investigation like this.'

'OK...'

'And that includes financial checks.'

Turner's posture turned defensive again. 'Aw, fuck's sake, no. Me? I'm not that desperate for money, Detective. The SFRS is my life. I would never jeopardise that for anything. I wouldn't get the same money in any other job at my age and the pension is far too good to risk.'

'You understand my interest though, right?'

'Well, aye, we heard Callum Gourlay thinks it might have been deliberate, but I don't. Not sure what else I can say to convince you.'

'OK. Calm down, Mr. Turner. For your own good, tell me where you were on the night the warehouse fire started. Were your crew on duty that night?'

He smiled. 'Aye, I was in the station. Along with the rest of my crew – me, Beadle, Duffer, Steve and Dimples.'

Malkie frowned at him.

'Sorry. Me, Jeremy Lees, Duncan Duffy, Steve Grayson and Graham Cormack. And we were there or out on shouts from the start of our shift. Does that answer your questions?'

Malkie held his hands up: Turner's tone had started to turn strident. 'That's fine, Mr Turner. I had to ask.'

'OK. Fine. I can vouch for everyone in my crew, but not for Fairbairn's. They were off duty until Jeremy called them in.'

Malkie assured Turner he'd follow up on all they'd discussed, which had him grimacing and sighing all over again, but he seemed more relieved to have given himself a solid alibi than anything else.

Malkie returned to his car. He needed to check in with Lin Fraser at the morgue, then he had some hard questions for Peter Fairbairn about why he delayed getting Duffy's BA Set to Lees for bagging.

He knew he was diverting his mind from facing up to Gourlay's revelation, but he'd become a master, over many years, at putting off the most painful of his responsibilities until he couldn't deny them any longer.

He headed for the morgue, and another painful responsibility.

TWENTY-EIGHT

Steph showered and dressed in record time. She wanted at least a half hour at the station before meeting Malkie at the mortuary.

On top of her regular outfit – black jeans, white blouse, brogues and her favourite jacket – she thought about the icy blast of air that had hit her when she opened her window, grabbed a scarf and a pair of fingerless woollen gloves, and hated herself for the real reason she did so.

She filled a beaker with coffee, grabbed a scone from the bakery a hundred yards from her flat and drove to Livi Civic Centre and the station in ten minutes less than she should have. One more creeping sense of losing control of herself? Or just giving in to a reckless streak she never realised she had?

At her desk, she dived straight into the collection of national databases that Police Scotland used to dig out information during the course of their investigations. All offered a wealth of information that the public would never get their hands on. Even detectives like her needed a solid reason to access certain kinds of records, and everything got recorded, audited and checked by some automated Big Brother in a server somewhere to make sure none of them went poking about in stuff they had no legitimate cause to. She always laughed when some bad TV cop drama had someone poking about in the DVLA's database without permission to help a mate find someone that the police themselves might not even have recorded as a Person Of Interest.

She found no trace of Sian Wilson owning a caravan, according to CRiS, the DVLA of caravan ownership. She tried Duncan Duffy's name, too, and again found nothing. She'd obtained clearance to examine Wilson's financial and phone records on the basis that her alleged – and then denied – attack on Peter Fairbairn might be repeated and possibly even escalated given her obvious fury at the man. Phone records showed no calls to or from her mobile since the night of the warehouse fire. Financial records showed no credit card transactions which might identify where she'd gone or whether she'd checked into a caravan site somewhere. She did find a large cash withdrawal the morning after the attack on Peter Fairbairn, which could – *could*, she reminded herself – suggest she'd planned her disappearance in advance.

She checked whether Wilson's father, mother or sister might own a caravan and again turned up nothing. She did the same with Duncan Duffy's parents. Again, nothing. She then checked for every member of both Livi SFRS squads and their immediate family members. She found not one of them owned a caravan, but Don McCallum owned a mobile home. She looked up the model on the manufacturer's website and saw no chance that what they thought could be a caravan in Wilson's photo could possibly be the same model as McCallum's motor home.

She scanned Wilson's photo and added it to the case file, then viewed it at high resolution and zoomed into every square inch. She saw a couple of dark-grey smudges against the grey-blue water of the Firth of Forth, but not distinctive enough to provide a reliable fix on the location, the whole background having been artistically thrown out of focus, probably using some smartphone filter.

In the top right corner of the blurred background, almost out of the frame, she spotted a larger light-grey smudge on the sea. She zoomed in but got nothing but more grey blob. Again, she thought about how bad movies had wizard techies zooming in to ridiculous levels with software that could invent pixels the camera never had a chance of capturing. She zoomed out again, and in that odd way that a more distant look at something with less detail can seem clearer than a closer view, she recognised it. The Bass Rock, an island a mile off the East Lothian coastline, forty-seven miles to the east of Livi, around the other side of Edinburgh and a few miles past North Berwick. Next, she searched for all caravan and camping parks along that stretch of the Lothians coastline as a starting point, and found a half dozen. She printed off a list, then did a manual scan of satellite map views for beaches backed by areas of grass which could possibly match the location in the photo. She ended up with four locations, including two which looked further from the sea than in Wilson's photo, but she kept them on her list. She couldn't be sure Thompson would authorise the time and travel to drive to the other side of Edinburgh to check them all; Wilson had only been accused of an assault, and an assault claim that had since been withdrawn. Priority had to be the burnt corpse and dead firefighter in the morgue.

That reminded her. She checked her watch: a quarter to noon. She folded and pocketed the papers and stuffed them in one of the many pockets inside her jacket. Malkie always expressed amazement at how she could produce gloves and shoe covers at any crime scene from deep in its recesses. She'd never told him she had a large extra pocket stitched in by a seamstress. It also explained why she wore a jacket until it was threadbare and falling apart before she'd buy a new one and have to pay again for the work. She knew she'd get the piss ripped out of her by every officer in J Division CID if word got out about it, so she'd never even told Malkie, and meant to keep it that way.

She headed for her car and the short drive to St John's and the mortuary.

She found Malkie on a bench outside Lin Fraser's office. He had that look on his face, the one that told her he was 'doing a Columbo', exploring theories devoid of relevant supporting facts. He called it keeping an open mind and examining all possibilities, but she knew that as much as he always tried to see some good in everyone, he could never shake his natural tendency to catastrophise everything.

'How did it go at the fire station?'

He jumped, scowled at her. 'Do you put bloody felt pads on the soles of your shoes or something?'

'Nope. You were just doing your thing. Where were you, Columbo?'

Malkie frowned as he looked her up and down. 'Why are you wearing a scarf? And gloves?'

'Because it's bloody freezing out there, that's why. Anyway, did they let you play on one of their fire engines?' Her grin disappeared when Malkie failed to react to her hilarious question. 'Not good?'

He seemed to need to make an immense effort to sit himself up and start talking. 'They think Duncan Duffy just panicked. Well, not panicked, but he had to have been breathing too hard and too fast if he used up a full cylinder in half the time he should have. Jury's still out on whether an equipment failure might have contributed, though. It was his first time "on air", operationally.'

Steph watched him lean forward again and his head dip. 'Anything else?'

He opened his mouth, but then closed it again. He shook his head, and the absence of even a one-word answer told Steph she was being lied to. Another conversation for later.

She let it go. For now. 'I assume "on air" means on a BA Set. Surely these guys have multiple alarms for things like that?'

'Aye, he said that, too. A whistle should go off when they hit a predetermined time or cylinder pressure or something, so they have time to retrace their steps and get out before they even get close to running out of air.'

'And nobody heard a whistle from Duffy's BA Set, no?'

'Not as far as Turner remembers. I read somewhere that they have some kind of telemetry thing that's supposed to monitor stuff like that, too. Oh, and Turner admitted he went in first, so Duffy would have been out of sight behind him, and he admitted that he wasn't making sure Duffy checked his pressure gauge every five minutes, as he's supposed to. Not much of a stretch to wonder if he allowed Duffy to fall behind him, too.'

'So, faulty BA Set, then?'

'Turner said it can happen, but he also said Steve Grayson's far too good at his job to let it happen to their gear.'

She opened her mouth to ask what Malkie had found so noteworthy in Turner's version of events, when Lin Fraser's door opened.

A late-middle-aged couple stepped out, their faces pale but their eyes red, their lips pursed tight as if letting air in might also let grief out. She and Malkie both knew the look of people called in to identify a deceased, and it never got any easier to know how to react. She settled for standing with her hands clasped in front of her and lowering her gaze. Malkie followed her lead.

When they had disappeared through to the exit, Lin Fraser turned to them.

'I'll never, as long as my arse points south, get used to this bit of the job. Hate it. Duncan Duffy's parents. Positive ID but we knew that would be a no-brainer. Unlike the other poor sod you sent me yesterday.'

They followed her back into her office. A second door at the rear of the room led, they knew, to a short corridor with a viewing window, and a further door into the area where the messy stuff happened.

'You want to come through?'

Malkie sighed. 'Not really, but I always feel we owe it to the poor sods.'

Lin led them first to Duncan Duffy. 'Not much to this one. Hydrogen cyanide poisoning from smoke inhalation caused him severe respiratory distress. He would have passed out in seconds, then not been able to get any clean air into him until he went into full cardiac arrest. He had undiagnosed hypertrophic cardiomyopathy. Most people never suffer any symptoms but in rare cases it can trigger sudden death in the fittest of individuals. Even in today's age of furniture and fabric fire-resistance standards, too many of our building structures and materials give off far too many toxic fumes far too quickly for safety. I've found no other signs of injury except some bruising around his neck consistent with the poor man trying to rip his own breathing mask off.'

Apart from the disturbing colour of Duffy's skin – a blue tinge from oxygen starvation on top of the usual pale-grey cast that dulled the man's natural skin colour – he looked undamaged. Steph always hated people on TV saying a dead person 'could just be sleeping'. Dead people looked anything but at peace, in her opinion. The total relaxing of all musculature rendered them slack and unreal, even after an undertaker had done their best. The thing that never failed to unsettle her at post-mortems were the eyes. The eyes of sudden-death victims tended to stay open, and Steph never quite learned to handle the 'thousand-yard stare'. That or the complete lack of shine in them. Without regular lubrication from their tear ducts and blinking, their eyes dried out, took on a matt texture, with little reflection. When TV programmes used actors to depict dead people, their eyes always, always, still glittered with moisture, and she wondered if adjusting the picture to remove shine and reflection would simply be too disturbing to the delicate sensitivities of viewers who wanted to experience the thrill and gruesome details but would lose their lunches if they saw the real thing.

'Steph?' Lin touched her arm, her face frowning in concern. 'I asked if you're ready to see the other customer?'

She nodded, but knew she'd be as far from ready as Malkie to turn to the adjacent table.

'Blood type matches that of the suspected victim. I did manage to extract some viable DNA from his tooth pulp, but the results will take a while, of course.'

Steph pulled her notebook from one of her many pockets. 'I got the name of Mr Galbraith's dentist from his wife.'

Malkie frowned at her, for only a second so Lin Fraser wouldn't see it, and she realised she should have visited the practice already.

She berated herself. She needed to get her act together. This wasn't her, and Malkie obviously thought the same.

She saw Lin flash Malkie a concerned look, then gazed down at her customer. Steph never failed to be impressed at how Lin could look on the worst of atrocities that one human being could inflict on another, but see past it to the person that had been, regardless of the extent of the damage. She'd remarked on more than one occasion that her real 'customers' were the family and other loved ones; they were the ones she needed to find answers for. Answers and that horrible but accurate word 'closure'.

'This man died of smoke inhalation. His burns were all

post-mortem. But the good news, if there can be any, is that he wouldn't have known a thing about it, wouldn't have felt a thing.

'When I opened him up, as well as smoke damage to the lining of his lungs, I found his stomach and blood to be as full of alcohol as I think I've ever seen one human body hold before. And his liver was on its way to fatal cirrhosis. If he hadn't been killed in that fire, I doubt he would have survived another month if he kept drinking as much as he had on the night he died.'

'Whisky?' Steph already knew the answer to the question.

'Yes. Most of a 700ml bottle of forty per cent proof whisky in only a few hours, I'd estimate.'

'OK. Let me have a copy of his dental diagram, Lin. I'll call ahead then go over there now.'

Steph pulled her phone from her pocket and headed for the corridor beyond Lin's office, more to escape their scrutiny than anything else.

TWENTY-NINE

Malkie waited in the car while Steph asked William Galbraith's dentist personally to expedite a dental comparison.

He craved Deborah's company, but two visits in two days would be pushing it, and besides, he couldn't share this with her, wouldn't be fair. Deborah possessed an incredible inner strength, and a non-negotiable determination to face her appalling injuries head-on. How could he moan about finding out he hadn't killed his own mum after all? More, she mustn't be the first person to hear about the possibility – as obscene and horrific as he found it – that his mum's death might not be the result of a blameless accident after all. The man who needed to hear that first waited for him at home, in their ramshackle wee cabin on the shore of Harperrig Reservoir, once a happy place and a place of refuge for Malkie and his dad, now a last resort, their hope for a future together following the trauma they'd both endured.

He felt like a trip to Monty's Bar, where he kept hoping to find some kind of alcoholic drink he didn't find too disgusting for him to get pissed on and enjoy the numbness he imagined his so-called drinking buddies found in their glasses. It was also the only place where he didn't feel like a complete loser. He'd learned after only a few visits just what the few regulars at the dank and sticky pub had achieved in their own lives before being brought low and dragged into their cups by life and its many cruelties. He'd since castigated himself for assuming every drunk he encountered elevated his own sorry life in comparison, and had learned to enjoy their company as fellow casualties of brutal reality. 'The Bungled and the Botched', as he'd heard it called in one of his favourite films, unsurprisingly about a man who hits lower than bottom through his own hubris, but then manages to redeem himself. He always wondered, at the end of every viewing of that film, if he dared to hope for the same to happen for him.

He had a word with himself, shook off another pang of catastrophising. He did love that word.

Steph returned to the car, and they headed for the station.

The instant he and Steph entered the Civic Centre, she grabbed him by the elbow.

'Canteen. Now.'

He didn't argue. Didn't dare.

The Livi Civic Centre coffee shop had one table favoured by many for its privacy. Tucked behind a partition wall at one end of the serving area and barely narrow enough for one small table and two chairs, it offered as safe a place as any inside the building to converse in private.

Steph bought two coffees and two muffins. Lemon and white chocolate this time. Both, he suspected, were likely to remain untouched.

She sat, pointed at him. 'You first. Spill, old man.'

Malkie slumped. Could he tell her? Would his dad mind being the second person he related his most recent calamitous revelation to? Would he mind if that person was Steph, the one person he'd know Malkie leaned on more than anyone or anything else? He decided Steph looked to be in one of her moods when refusing to spill would not be an option.

'At the fire station, Callum Gourlay dropped something on me that's more than I can process. Can I share it with you before I have to break it to my dad? Maybe you can help me make sense of it because I bloody can't.' He felt tears well, wiped them away. He didn't mind Steph seeing them, but he feared if he let them out, they wouldn't stop.

Steph, ever more sensitive and compassionate than she'd let most people know, leaned forward and covered his hand with hers. She said nothing, also a proponent of Malkie's belief in letting people say what they want when they want.

'Remember I told you I bought Mum a scented candle for her birthday, and remember I told you I left in a huff because she knew it would be the last birthday present she'd ever receive from me and as good as emotionally blackmailed me into lighting it on her bedside table? You remember all that?'

'Aye, and I also remember telling you how I could give my pig of a stepdad a hedge-trimmer for his Xmas and wouldn't lose a wink of sleep if he lopped his own fingers off with it. You have to separate out the act from any unforeseeable consequences resulting from it.'

He smiled, remembered how she'd given him a lecture based on her stepdad and gardening tools even though he lived seven floors up in a tower block.

'Well... Thing is... Fuck's sake, this is too much.'

She waited.

'Gourlay's report says that the candle that started the fire that killed her was on the windowsill, nowhere near her bedside table.'

Malkie saw the same fear he'd experienced flash across Steph's eyes, but she gave him more space before commenting.

'I'll check with Dad tonight, but I already know there's no way he'd light any of the dusty old candles she'd collected on that windowsill over the years. Not so close to curtains he knew predated flame-retardant fabrics by a decade or more.'

She still said nothing, and Malkie knew she wanted him to voice the same question she'd already be asking herself. The question that might turn Malkie's life – and his dad's – upside down and rake up all the pain and hurt and guilt she'd tried to help him through since the night it happened.

'Someone else had to have lit that candle, Steph. Dad wouldn't light it or if he did, he'd have moved it somewhere safe. Mum couldn't have because by that time – and unknown to me – the cancer had her so weak she could barely stand.'

He lowered his head, swallowed, had to work up to asking the question.

'Did someone murder my mum, Steph?'

Steph's phone buzzed, but she ignored it. She took a moment. Malkie knew she'd be tempering her usual no-bullshit manner of communication with her undoubted care for him.

'Oh, Malkie. What can I say? Possibly. Sorry, that's as far as I can go. It's not a ridiculous theory.'

'OK. I'll talk to Dad tonight. We need to decide whether I need to report this. I know Thompson will support me, but I won't be allowed within a mile of it. You neither, probably.'

'True. We just have to hope it doesn't fall to Pamela Ballantyne's legendary powers of tact and sensitivity.'

He smiled at Steph's concise and perfect summation of DI Gavin McLeish's protégée and fellow career ladder climber. As he thought of McLeish, Thompson's bombshell came back to him.

'Aw, bollocks. I forgot to tell you. McLeish has got himself a new position. In a Major Investigation Team.'

Steph's appalled look told him she thought the prospect of McLeish and an MIT team descending on them and running any serious cases would go down with everyone except Pam like a shit-sandwich.

'I know, right? He fucks up twice and causes a massive stooshie, but Senior Damagement let him join an MIT. Who knows what kind of embarrassment that idiot could cause to the Force in an MIT? I mean to our division. We're not allowed to call it a Force any more, are we?'

'Not since everything changed on April Fool's Day 2013, mate.'

Malkie chuckled but wasn't about to be distracted.

'Anyway, young lady. I need to know how you're coping with developments in your own personal life. How are you knuckles after your uncle Barry carelessly smashed his face into them repeatedly?'

As he asked, he glanced at her hands and noticed, again, the fingerless woollen gloves he'd never seen her wear before. A penny dropped and his heart sank.

'Aw no, Steph. Again?' He looked at her in horror, terrified of hearing just how bad a shitshow she might be getting herself into.

She pulled her gloves off. Fresh bruises on all eight knuckles, cuts on two of them.

Malkie grimaced in helpless frustration. 'When?'

'Last night. I went to talk to Dean, my stepdad. He pushed my buttons, got me good and riled, really piled it on. I refused to give him the satisfaction until Barry stepped out of the bedroom. Dean had set me up, ambushed me. And he'd done such a good job of winding me up. I went for Barry like I've never wanted to hurt anyone before.'

She removed her hand from Malkie's.

'Dean gave me enough time to make sure the damage I did would constitute Grievous rather than just Actual Bodily Harm, then pulled me off him and called 999. Ambulance only, though. I suspect he means to hang it over my head, knows what such a serious assault charge will do to my career.'

She banged her fist on the table. Malkie had his back to the rest of the coffee shop, but he didn't give a damn who might have reacted.

'I'm such a bloody idiot. I let that bastard play me like a bloody fiddle.'

Malkie hunted for something to say that might come close to reassuring her, but came up blank.

'It's fine, Malkie. There's nothing you can say, is there? Short of paying one of our less savoury professional acquaintances a wodge of cash to hurt him, all I can do is wait and see what he means to do with this. If he bothered to set up a phone to record it, I really am screwed.'

Malkie tried again to find something to say that wouldn't insult her intelligence or the depth of their friendship.

She laughed. 'Oh, stop that. There's nothing you can say to help, and you might burst a blood vessel trying to think of something. I feel better for having "shared", though. Even though I'm about as ashamed of myself as it's probably possible for me to be. I'm just glad it's only you I've told, so I don't feel as much of a disaster-zone.'

She grinned, but not for long.

'Cheeky mare.'

They sat in companionable silence for a while. Malkie even managed to eat his muffin. Then hers, too. 'Fuck my waistline. I need sugar.'

As happens so often that many coppers wonder if there's a God of Pissing the *Polis* Off, his mobile rang.

'Malkie? Louisa.'

'Are you about to ruin my day, Gucci?'

'Probably. Peter Fairbairn's had a brick through his window and his tyres slashed.'

'OK. I'm with Steph. We'll head over to his house.'

He informed Steph and they headed for the car park to grab a pool car. As they walked out of the front door, she stopped him.

'I forgot to say: I got William Galbraith's dental records and emailed them to Lin. But I came away with something else a bit juicy. The practice's receptionist obviously hadn't brushed up on her GDPR for a while and had no clue about what she's allowed to share about their patients, even with us *polis*. It took me only a minute of leaning close and fishing for her rather colourful opinions of Galbraith. She enjoyed confiding in me that he's not paid his bills in six months.'

They reached the car and Malkie spoke over the roof before getting in. 'Money troubles? Insurance job? But then why would he get drunk as a skunk in the same place he'd set his own fire?'

'Unless he paid someone else to do it and they got the date wrong?' As ridiculous as that sounded, both knew more idiotic errors get made by amateurs all the time.

'Sian Wilson? I can't believe that.'

The lack of any further comment from Steph told Malkie they were, for once, singing from the same hymn sheet.

Steph checked her phone. 'Positive ID. William Galbraith.'

Malkie sighed. 'Let's get it over with, shall we?'

THIRTY

They parked a hundred yards from Anna Galbraith's home to wait for a Police Scotland Liaison Officer to join them. Malkie watched Steph reassume her professional game face. When she switched the car engine off, she asked him if he was good to go and he knew all trace of her previous fragile state of mind had evaporated, leaving nothing behind but cool, functional Steph.

Malkie allowed her to stand in front as she rang the doorbell, the Family Liaison Officer – PC Theresa Carmichael – bringing up the rear. When Galbraith opened the door, she took only the briefest look at Steph's face and crumpled. Steph caught her, and Galbraith sobbed into her chest. The woman's arms flailed as if she'd lost control of them, as if she sought something to hang on to.

They got her onto her sofa and gave her all the time she needed. The FLO headed for the kitchen on autopilot to make coffee. By the time Galbraith sat up, her face begged Steph not to say the words, but she had to.

'I'm sorry to inform you, Mrs Galbraith, that we've identified the deceased from the warehouse fire as your husband.'

Galbraith folded in on herself, her arms wrapped around

her stomach, and rocked in place. Malkie sat in the armchair opposite and Steph took up position beside Galbraith.

When Galbraith looked up again, the inevitable question, the one both dreaded, came.

'Can I see him?'

Steph waited for Galbraith to look at her, then, 'I'd advise against that, Mrs Galbraith.'

Galbraith took a second to get the meaning behind Steph's words, then lost it again. She tipped sideways and Steph had no choice but to support her with an arm around her shoulder; she had to hold her upright and hope she didn't topple the other way, but Malkie knew Steph would find such closeness uncomfortable.

Carmichael appeared with a tray holding three steaming mugs, sugar and milk. She placed it on the coffee table then retreated until the time came for her to play her part. Galbraith sat up, pulled a handkerchief from a box beside the tea tray, wiped her eyes and blew her nose.

Malkie reached for the tray.

'No.' Galbraith pushed his hand away. 'Detective Lang. Milk and sugar?' Her voice trembled and broke on the last word.

'Just milk, please.'

Galbraith turned to Malkie and raised her eyebrows.

'Not for me, thanks, Mrs Galbraith. I'm Detective Sergeant Malcolm McCulloch, Detective Constable Lang's colleague. And this' – he indicated over his shoulder – 'is Constable Carmichael. She's a trained Family Liaison Officer and I would strongly recommend you allow her to remain here until you can arrange for family or a friend to stay with you. Do you have parents or siblings or grown children you can call?'

Galbraith glanced at Carmichael, who returned a smile that Malkie and Steph knew to be more than just a result of her training; only a particular sort of person lasted long as an FLO.

Galbraith returned her smile, seemed comforted by
Carmichael's manner, as all good FLOs were trained for.

'We have no one, Detective. Only each other. William has a
sister but she lives in Hong Kong, and I have no siblings. Our
parents all passed some time ago. And no, we never had
children.'

Steph could swear she heard a tinge of regret in Galbraith's
words and had to wonder how lonely and empty the woman's
life would be now.

'Was my husband very badly wounded?'

Malkie watched Steph's eyes turn gentle and kind, something few people ever saw. 'Severely. I'm sorry.'

Galbraith nodded. 'Did he...'

'No. The circumstances of his death mean that he's
extremely unlikely to have known anything about it.'

Galbraith scowled at her, then something seemed to click in
her. 'Had he been drinking?'

Steph nodded.

'And you're sure he wouldn't have suffered?'

'As sure as we can be.'

They gave her a few moments to digest everything. As
much as Malkie hated breaking this kind of news to people, he
hated even more having to then interview them. Some crumbled so completely that only sedatives and rest were possible.
Galbraith didn't.

'You'll have questions for me.'

Malkie couldn't help but admire the woman.

Steph opened her notebook. 'Only if you're sure you're up
to it. We can come back later if you prefer.'

Galbraith managed a wry smile. 'No. Let's get this over with
so I can fall apart in peace after you're finished.'

Even Steph stared at her with something like admiration on
her face.

Malkie sat forward; as much as he'd said he'd leave the

talking to Steph, now that Galbraith knew him to be the ranking officer, he needed to start building his own rapport with her.

'We appreciate that, Mrs Galbraith, we really do. The quicker we can leave you to...' And he dried up, damage done with only his first full sentence. 'I mean...'

Galbraith smiled at him. 'Ask me your questions please, Detective.'

'Call me Malkie. Please.' He turned to FLO Carmichael and asked her to wait outside. Carmichael would understand; questions were coming that Malkie needed to ask, but no one but him or Steph needed to hear Galbraith answer. For now, anyway.

'I'm sorry we have to ask, but you told my colleague, DC Lang, that your husband had gone to Inverness on business?'

Galbraith stared down at her hands clutching her paper tissue. 'I thought he had. He told me he had. But I couldn't contact him when DC Lang came here yesterday... That's unheard of. He always kept both a personal and business phone on him, and replacement batteries.' She swallowed, took a moment. 'I think I knew yesterday, but seeing you both on my doorstep now...'

'I can imagine, Mrs Galbraith. Can you think why he might have been in the warehouse at that time of night?'

'No. Unless...'

'Mrs Galbraith?'

She took another moment, seemed to face a crisis in her own mind. 'Did my husband start the fire, Detective McCulloch?'

'Malkie, please.' He smiled again. 'Why do you ask?'

She flashed a look of fear at him, as if his responding to her question with another confirmed some deep fear.

'Did he?' She held his gaze.

Malkie refreshed his memory from the management summary he'd read in Callum Gourlay's report. Fire started in the storage area at the front of the building, in a tight space behind ceiling-high pallets, Galbraith on the floor of the office at the back of the building.

'I can't say for sure until the Fire Investigation Report is finalised, but there's no obvious evidence so far to support your husband having started the fire, no.'

She wilted, looked relieved, or as relieved as any woman in her situation could.

'Why did you ask me that, Mrs Galbraith?' He – and Steph, he felt sure – already knew the answer. He remembered what Steph had reported her saying the previous day: 'We've been having...'

Galbraith visibly took a hold of herself, faced him as if ready to unburden herself.

'The warehouse has been operating at a loss for two years. We have to charge more than the big names because we just don't get enough business to match their margins.' She paused, braced herself. 'William told me he had meetings set up with a big distillery on the Black Isle to sell it all, the stock and the building. It's not a family business. William built it from nothing so although it broke his heart to feel he'd failed, he cared more about the jobs of our staff than he did about his pride. He said we would make enough out of the deal to retire comfortably for life, said he might even like to slow down, spend more time on our boat.'

She leaned forward again, seemed to fight off another break-down, then straightened again. 'He said the sale would also ensure we could afford healthy redundancy payments for our staff.'

She turned desperate and desolate eyes on Steph. 'He's been lying to me, hasn't he?'

Even Steph wriggled a bit. 'We'll look into that in the course of our investigation, Anna.'

'What do you mean, your investigation? You just said the evidence suggests he didn't start the fire himself.'

Steph held her gaze, waited for her to reach the ugly conclusion by herself.

'Someone else started it? Someone murdered my husband?' They both saw another crisis threaten to break the poor woman.

Malkie reeled under a sudden image of some fucker reaching into his mum's bedroom window and lighting a candle.

He stood. Steph's head snapped up, a question on her face.

'Mrs Galbraith, you now know about as much as we do, and I'm truly sorry that's all we can give you at this time. I promise you that DC Lang and myself will keep you as fully informed as our investigation allows us to, but right now we need to put all our energy into finding out if someone did deliberately burn down your warehouse. I hope you understand.'

He called for Carmichael, who appeared in a second. She sat beside Galbraith and Steph stood.

Galbraith looked to be slipping into shock. Carmichael nodded at him: *I've got this.*

He doubted Anna Galbraith even noticed them leave, and Malkie found himself ashamed of his relief when he stepped out into the front garden.

Steph joined him. He recognised the look on her face. If – when – they caught the fucker who started the fire, he promised himself he'd let Steph spend five minutes alone with him before they arrested him.

Or her.

THIRTY-ONE

Malkie headed for Peter Fairbairn's house again. He sent Steph back to the station for some desk time and some food.

When Fairbairn opened his door, Malkie knew this could only go badly.

'What are you doing here? Why aren't you out looking for that fucking psycho? Fucking bitch nearly cracked my skull this time. Fucking brick through my window! And my tyres. Not just one, all four slashed. And I can't replace them until the insurance pays out, so I'm going to have to take the fucking bus to work.'

Malkie stood, calm and patient, until Fairbairn exhausted his inner supply of indignity and expletives. He was familiar with receiving the 'hairdryer treatment' from McLeish – and once from Thompson – but most frequently from witnesses and suspects savvy enough to know how much abuse they could hurl at an officer of the law before getting themselves banged up.

Malkie waited until Fairbairn's breathing slowed and he leaned a shoulder on the doorframe.

'Who, Mr Fairbairn?'

He gaped at Malkie as if despairing of some kind of idiot. 'Wilson. Who else?'

Malkie took a breath; he meant to enjoy this. 'Sorry. Now you're sure it *was* her, Mr Fairbairn?'

'Yes.' His volume started to rise again. Malkie held his gaze until he seemed to sag. He'd learned the look from Steph but even he shat himself when she turned one of her looks on him, and he counted himself a friend of hers.

'And how can you be so sure, Mr Fairbairn?'

'Because I watched her slash my tyres. When she'd done all four, she saw me standing in the window, picked up a loose brick from my lawn edging and lobbed it at me through the window.'

He fished a piece of paper from his trouser pocket. 'And I found this stuck through my letter box. I'm telling you that fucking bitch is unhinged.'

Malkie reached over his shoulder before remembering Steph wasn't there to supply him with nitrile gloves. He found a plastic evidence bag in his inside jacket pocket – although how long it had been there, he had no idea – opened it and indicated for Fairbairn to drop the paper into it and sealed the ziplock.

In blue ballpoint pen it read 'Tell them or I will.'

Malkie raised his eyebrows at Fairbairn.

'No fucking idea, mate.'

Malkie decided he'd shown the man enough latitude. 'One more expletive, F-bomb or any other swear word from you, directed at me, and we are going to seriously fucking fall out with each other. Understand?'

'You're having a go at me? That fu... that bitch slashed my tyres and put my window in and nearly concussed me again and you're threatening me?' Fairbairn threw his hands in the air, turned around and stomped into his living room.

Malkie released a long-suffering sigh before following him. He sat on the sofa opposite Fairbairn in his armchair.

'So, Mr Fairbairn, please tell us what Ms Wilson, if it was her, meant by "Tell them".'

Fairbairn didn't answer immediately, and Malkie recognised – for what felt like the millionth time in his career – someone who thought they could outsmart a seasoned copper with shite concocted on the hoof.

'I've got no idea. You'll need to ask her.'

'Which way did she drive off and was she in her own car?'

'How the... hell would I know if it was her car or not?' He took less than a second to buckle in the face of Malkie's increasingly dangerous expression. 'Could have been. Funnily enough, I never pay that much attention to the make and model of every firefighter's vehicle in my station.'

Malkie scribbled the registration number in his notebook. 'We'll put out a BOLO and notify ANPR.'

Fairbairn stared at him, blank.

How do you *like it, mate?*

'Patrol cars and automatic number-plate recognition. She made a mistake driving her own car, if she did, into town. Her home address is rural, isn't it? Fewer cameras outside of town but we should get a hit on her now. Which reminds me – are you aware of Wilson or Duffy having owned a caravan?'

Fairbairn looked about ready to erupt again, but he bit his tongue with an obvious effort. 'No. At the moment I'm more concerned with where she is rather than where she and Duncan might have gone on holiday, but no, I'm not aware of either of them owning a caravan. Don McCallum owns a motor home, I think.'

'Yes, we know. We have reason to believe Wilson and Duffy had the use of a caravan – or rented one – only last year, so we're trying to locate where it might have been.'

Fairbairn seemed to rack his memory, happy to exercise his brain in the interests of helping Malkie catch her.

'No. I can't think of anyone else. Not on our squads, anyway, but that's no surprise.'

'Why?'

'Because they don't share their personal crap with me. Jeremy Lees wants so much to be everyone's buddy he's far too over-familiar with his squad, but I keep my distance. We're colleagues, not pals.'

Malkie couldn't help comparing Fairbairn's professed attitude to that of Gavin McLeish; other officers were resources to be used to achieve his own personal ambitions, and the idea of forming any kind of social bond with his underlings would be anathema to him. The corporate culture that had polluted the Force over the past ten years seemed to value impersonal management, with a utilitarian focus and both eyes always on performance, with the welfare of the Force's 'most valued resources' no more than a box to tick called Duty of Care.

'Now, back to the note.' He raised his eyebrows in question again.

'I already told you. She probably thinks I shouldn't have allowed Duffy to go in on air. She must have thought it too big an incident for his first time. That'll be it. She blames me for his death. I told you all this before.'

Malkie feigned mutual realisation, watched Fairbairn relax as he probably considered job done, before going for him, again.

'Odd, though.'

Fairbairn's face fell.

'You seeming to remember that all over again after telling me exactly the same thing less than forty-eight hours ago.'

Malkie waited. Fairbairn swallowed.

'I forgot. I'd been hit on the head, remember?'

Malkie held his gaze for long seconds. Fairbairn tried to stare him down, but a momentary double-blink betrayed him.

'And other than you believing she blames you for letting Duncan Duffy enter with Paul Turner and on air for his first time that night, you can think of no other reason Wilson might want to hurt you, twice, and demand that you "Tell them", no?'

'No.' His voice small and devoid of conviction.

'Are you sure about that?'

Fairbairn's eyes took on the same suspicious, almost feral cast he'd noticed the first time he interviewed him. 'What else are you thinking about?'

Malkie couldn't help himself, his patience with the poor excuse for a man in front of him near exhausted. 'I'm talking about complaints made about you concerning allowing critical safety equipment being left in service despite – in Mr Grayson's expert opinion – being too close to their legal manufacturer tolerances.'

Fairbairn exploded. 'I knew it. Did Grayson tell you that himself, or was it that bitch Beattie?'

Malkie couldn't help but raise his eyebrows at the outburst, and Fairbairn seemed to realise what he'd said.

'I didn't mean that.'

Yes you did, you misogynistic fucking disgrace of a man.

'Flora's never liked me. Well, not as much as her teddy bear Jeremy Lees. That man isn't fit to be a crew chief. Let alone—'

'Let alone what, Mr Fairbairn?'

'Doesn't matter. She's always favoured Lees over me, purely because I run my crew far tighter than Lees does. He's weak, and soft, and that's how people get hurt.'

Malkie stood before his temper broke completely. 'Do you need further medical attention, Mr Fairbairn?'

'No.'

'Have you anything else to say to me about what you claim to have been another assault on your person by Wilson, Mr Fairbairn?'

'No. Sian Wilson attacked me and I have no doubt about it, now.'

'I'll now go and ask the same neighbours again, to check

their doorbell cameras. Is there anything else you want to ask me, Mr Fairbairn?'

'No. Nothing. Just find her. Please.'

Back outside Fairbairn's garden gate, Malkie stopped to calm himself.

Is Fairbairn full of shit? Fuck, yes.

He spent a fruitless half hour checking every house on the same street that had a doorbell camera. Nobody managed to find anything more than feet walking past on the pavements, their cameras being focused on their own drives rather than the street. One man, though – Sidney Baxter, grizzled and toothless but with a sharp gleam in his eyes – said he'd seen someone running away at the time Fairbairn claimed Wilson had been there.

She'd been gone by the time he found his spectacles on top of his head.

But Sidney was adamant; the person he'd seen had been a tall, slim woman.

THIRTY-TWO

It took Steph only a minute to get Thompson to agree they now had enough motive, opportunity and means to at least arrest Sian Wilson for the attack on Peter Fairbairn, if not quite enough to charge her. Wilson had seemed furious beyond reason at Fairbairn the night Duncan Duffy died, which Fairbairn put down to the misguided blaming of him for allowing Duffy to be first in before – she seemed to believe – he was ready for his first time on air. Clear motive. Nobody had a clue where she'd hidden herself, so they had to assume an opportunity would be no problem for her, until they learned otherwise. And who better to burn someone to death but leave the building relatively untouched than a firefighter? Thompson initiated the request for a warrant, while Steph – given their confirmation of Wilson as a prime suspect – began scouring internet mapping sites to narrow down a location for the caravan site in Wilson's photograph.

She rechecked the photograph at various zoom levels and decided she wasn't imagining a vertical sliver of near-white against the light-grey rock on the right edge of the island as seen from the angle in the photograph. Had to be the lighthouse on the historic fort and prison. She plotted a line from the island back to the coastline that would put the lighthouse on the far right of the rock in any viewpoint. She narrowed it down to a small site with only a dozen pitches, above the beach at Canty Bay. She pulled up the website, scanned the photograph gallery and found it: one photograph showed the view from the caravan pitches out into the Forth, with Bass Rock about the same distance out and showing the lighthouse on its right-hand side.

She slapped her hand on the desk and muttered, 'Ya dancer.' More loudly than she meant to. Gucci smiled at her. Pamela Ballantyne scowled, but not for long. Even the threat of a hard look from Steph was enough to shut most people down.

She scribbled the name and location in her notebook, screwed up the sheet of paper with four sites on it and tossed it in her waste bin, then headed for Thompson's desk to secure her permission for a trip to the seaside.

Thompson listened and checked what Steph showed her on her own screen, then told her to 'Go get her. But first, tell me what's been troubling you. Even Pam Ballantyne expressed something that could – at a push – be interpreted as concern.'

Steph considered opening up to her boss but couldn't find a way to admit she'd nearly beaten her 'uncle' to death – twice – without getting herself put on enforced leave.

'I'm fine. Personal stuff. It'll pass.' But she felt tears form on her eyelashes and she knew Thompson couldn't miss them.

'Bollocks. You're not focused, Steph. Take a Uniform in the morning to check out those caravan parks. Tonight, order a pizza or something. Watch crap TV. Take a bath. Whatever. Just leave the job behind for at least a few hours. And that's an order.'

Steph lifted three fingers to her forehead in what she believed was a Girl Guide salute. 'Yes, ma'am.'

'Steph, I hope you know you can talk to me any time. And stop that "ma'am" shite.'

Steph returned to her desk to grab her jacket. She tried to fix her mind on the past hour of solid police work. She'd almost felt good, until Thompson's mention of her apparently obvious preoccupation reminded her of a day long in her past and early in her childhood. It had been a rare family day out, at an East Lothian beach, before her mum became too dependent and money became too short.

'Uncle' Barry had taken her for a wade in the sea when she'd been no more than an infant. She remembered stepping off a steep drop-off in the sand under the water. She remembered the world going dark and muffled and salty and smothering, until Barry pulled her out of the surf by her ponytail. She remembered everyone laughing at her because she cared only about the ice-cream cone she'd lost.

She remembered Barry cuddling her, but laughing with the others as he did it, and she knew she wouldn't be eating much for the rest of the evening.

THIRTY-THREE

Back in the car, Malkie checked his emails on his police-issue phone. Still nothing from Callum Gourlay. He tried not to think the worst of the man, but he couldn't be sure if that came from a belief in Gourlay's good nature, or because Malkie feared he'd need him if his bombshell on page seven turned into a whole new shitshow.

He called the station.

'Police Scotland. DC Robert Lundy.'

'Rab? Malkie. Have you or Gucci turned up anything noteworthy on any of the firefighters?'

A moment's silence, then Gucci's voice; Rab would never be as industrious, or as effective, as Gucci.

'Hi, boss. Apart from Paul Turner's bad credit and Stuart Simpson's juvenile record, both of which I think you already know about, nothing. Sorry.'

'OK. Thanks, Lou. Keep looking, aye? Oh, and if digital forensics can get into Wilson's social media accounts, look for photos of her or Duncan Duffy at a caravan somewhere.' He glanced at his watch. 'It can wait until morning.'

'Will do.' They disconnected.

A Uniform drove him back to the station. He considered wasting more time at his desk, but instead headed straight to his car. He'd rather pull his own fingernails out than face his dad right now, but he knew that wasn't an option.

When he pulled up outside the cabin, his dad appeared on the deck, a tea towel in his hand.

'I went ahead and ate. Wasn't sure when you'd be home.'

Malkie kicked his own arse, internally. 'Ach. Sorry, Dad. I should have called you. Been full-on, yesterday and today.'

'Sit. I'll bring you some chili.'

He heard the microwave run for two minutes and plates rattling, and dad appeared with a steaming bowl, a pack of crackers and a glass of water.

'Thanks, Dad.' He realised he'd eaten nothing but two muffins all day. He polished off half the bowl before coming up for air.

'Hungry?' His dad's smile and the twinkle in his eyes couldn't fail to lighten Malkie's mood.

He finished the rest of his meal then took a long swig of water. He stretched back in his chair and burped.

'Pig.'

'Yep. Sorry.'

They sat in silence for a while. Malkie watched for bats fluttering past in the gloom of the approaching sunset, saw a few, marvelled as he always did at the complete absence of sound from their wings. He heard a splash from the shore of the reservoir and saw ripples spread out in concentric circles; something had just turned into supper for one of the trout that the nearby angling club stocked the water with.

He waited. And waited. When his dad stood with a concerned frown and said he needed his bed, Malkie gave him a half hour then headed for his own room. He pulled one of three document boxes out from under the bed, opened it, scanned the tabs on the tops of the files hanging from rails on either side.

When he found the one he'd been looking for, he pushed the box back under the bed and returned to the deck. He lit a citronella candle on the table in a vain effort at banishing the hordes of insects he knew would see the porch light as their call to torment him.

It took him another five minutes until he could force himself to open the file. His copy of Callum Gourlay's FIU report into the fire that killed his mum. He glanced over his shoulder as if his dad might sneak up behind him and see the document. He mustn't, not until Malkie had made his own mind up first. The poor old sod had suffered more grief, pain and suffering in the past year than any decent person should have to, and Malkie was fucked if he would add to that without being damned sure he had no option.

He started reading. Every word. Unlike the time he'd received it in the mail while his dad still languished alone and neglected in St John's for six months. During that one reading, he'd made it as far as the words 'candle on a windowsill' and had to stop. On a later reading, which he made himself suffer only because he felt he owed his dad as full an explanation as possible, he again made it as far as page six, and the official summary statement and Callum Gourlay's signature. He must have read the words 'candle on a windowsill' on both readings but had managed to ignore them. Had he been so intent on clinging to a belief in his own guilt that he'd skimmed over the words without allowing his brain to register the discrepancy?

His candle, the one he'd bought for her birthday, had melted long before the wick burned down. It had never been his candle that killed her. It had never been his fault. He tried to cling to the fact that he'd slammed her door closed as he stomped out, a door they never closed precisely because his dad needed to hear her if she called for him. The fact that his dad admitted he'd put earbuds in to crank up the rugby at Murrayfield without disturbing her, and so hadn't heard her screams for help, did nothing to persuade Malkie to let go of his need for culpability.

He had to have contributed somehow, needed to believe that in order to keep suffering for her, but Gourlay's report did all it could to deny him that indulgence.

He threw the report on the table.

Bats fluttered past him, as soundless and erratic as ever. Birds called out from their roosts as they settled for the night. No wind disturbed the reservoir, its surface smooth and black and immense. He tried to draw comfort from it all, from its timelessness, its ancient and peaceful calm, as still and clear and pure as he could ever remember it.

He woke with a start when his feet slipped off the chair he'd propped them on. His back ached. His mind, foggy and tired, reminded him to pick the report up from the deck and carry it through to his room. He collapsed into bed fully clothed for the second time in two days.

He slept through sheer exhaustion, the strain from a shit-show of a day after getting no sleep the previous night. But dreams haunted him. Nightmares half-remembered that woke him, sweating and panicking, through the worst night's sleep he could remember.

The scraps he could remember all featured candles and windows and curtains, all ablaze. He thought he remembered a brutal glimmer of awareness in those dreams of being afraid to turn around, and now he realised what he'd been terrified of seeing. Mum, in her bed, dead or dying, and him standing staring at the candle, preoccupied more with who lit the fucking thing.

The final time he was ripped from sleep, the admission he'd been fighting in his mind – and losing to – hit him with pitiless violence.

Even the sickest bastards he'd ever put away wouldn't set fire to an old woman's bedroom without one hell of a reason. He nearly threw up as he finally allowed himself to follow the thought through to its logical conclusion.

Someone he'd put away.

Even if he didn't bring the cause of her death into her bedroom. Even though he'd slammed her door shut. Even though – if, he insisted to himself – his dad had compounded their joint duty of care by listening to his rugby game through earbuds.

His career choice, his hunting and bringing down the worst kind of sub-human animals, had led to his mum's death.

He staggered to the shore of the reservoir, to his favourite rock; flat and high enough to sit on in comfort. He held back wave after wave of fury and revulsion at himself. He told himself he just clung to whatever scrap of culpability he could, because he feared that if he ever absolved himself of blame completely, it would somehow desecrate his memories of her. The day he felt no guilt for her death would be the day he started to move past the event, and he felt certain he'd never forgive himself enough for that to happen.

His self-flogging was interrupted by his phone, still in his trouser pocket when he'd collapsed, fully clothed, into bed.

'DS McCulloch?'

'Malkie. Susan.'

FFS, what now? Early morning calls from the boss never turned out to be good.

'It's Peter Fairbairn. He's been murdered.'

'Aw Christ on a bike. How? Who?' He dreaded hearing the very answer he got.

'Burned to death in his home. I think we have a strong candidate for the who. I sent Steph home last night. I'm worried about her. She'll look for Sian Wilson today, after you attend at Fairbairn's house.'

THIRTY-FOUR

Malkie called Steph and told her not to bother attending Peter Fairbairn's home, but to get an extra couple of hours sleep then concentrate on finding Sian Wilson.

Livi SFRS Red Watch stood outside, rolling hoses and packing away equipment. A blue tarp had been hung over the front window, and a forensics van parked outside told him the SOCOs had already got started. Lin Fraser came out of the front door and waved to Malkie while she signed herself out of the scene.

'Nasty way to go. Really bloody painful. Someone cracked him over the head with something blunt and heavy and he ended up on the floor. If he regained consciousness, he'll have suffered excruciating pain from the intense heat before the flames even touched him. I'll know that when I dissect his lungs, see if the tissue's burned.'

Fuck's sake, Sian. Could you do this? Did even he *deserve this?*

He caught himself, reminded himself how Steph always helped him stay on the right side of confirmation bias; Sian Wilson might have put herself firmly in the frame for all three of the attacks on Fairbairn, but coppers had fallen on their arses before by fixating on the obvious to the exclusion of small details that didn't fit their theories.

'I mean, we're looking for a specific suspect.'

She turned to head back to her car. 'I'll try to expedite, get you an initial report later today.'

'What time did the fire get reported?'

'Shortly after four a.m., I believe. No alarm was heard, which is idiotic in a firefighter's home, but neighbours heard the front windows blowing out.'

'Thanks, Lin. I last saw him at six thirty last night if that helps.'

'Not really, so much damage done to him, but I'll bear it in mind. Oh, by the way, that Callum Gourlay guy is inside. Scene manager OK'd him to have a look given that he's FIU. He's fully suited so no risk to the scene integrity.'

Malkie signed himself into the scene then approached the SOCO van. As he got himself suited and booted, gloved and masked, he asked the usual questions.

'Anything you can give me so far?'

'You'll need to—'

'Wait for the initial report. I know, but it's always worth asking, isn't it?'

The female SOCO gave him a look that suggested he have a word with himself.

'Is he identifiable?'

'Yes, but not pretty.'

Fuck.

'Any printable surfaces still viable?'

'Aye, we think so, but there's a hell of a lot of burn damage. Only in this room: the door was closed and the SFRS got here before it burned through to the hallway.'

'Any chance of DNA transfer?'

'Maybe in the hallway or the kitchen but not in the living room, too much damage.'

'Anything noteworthy on the deceased?'

'Wallet and keys on the kitchen table. Wallet is Peter Fairbairn's, the owner of the property, I believe?'

'Aye, that's him. Anything else? Broken tequila bottle maybe? No. Scratch that. What about his phone?'

She reached into a plastic crate in the back of the van and produced an evidence bag containing a blackened metal skeleton of a mobile phone, melted plastic and circuit board that even Malkie could tell looked fucked beyond saving.

'Damn it. Sim card? Memory chip?'

'Doubt it but you might be lucky. But...' She held a finger up and grinned. She pulled a second evidence bag from the crate containing another mobile phone, this one intact and undamaged. 'Found this in a kitchen drawer.'

Malkie took it from her. The first device looked to have been a smartphone from the size of it and the remains of the multiple camera lenses on the back. This one looked simpler, less sophisticated. Exactly what he'd expect from a pay-as-you-go burner phone: cheap, functional and disposable.

'I'll get DI Thompson to escalate but you can ask digital forensics to prioritise the number and the call record, aye?'

She looked at him. 'Really, super, urgent?'

'You have no idea. Thanks, I really, super, appreciate it.'

'No problem.' She took the evidence bag from his fingers and dropped it back into the crate, and Malkie headed inside.

The hallway looked undamaged but for smoke stains. Nothing had been burned, or even charred. The living room, though, had been gutted. The remains of what he assumed to be Peter Fairbairn lay on the floor. Black and charred, Malkie couldn't make out much detail.

He saw someone in a white SOCO suit step into his peripheral vision.

'Malkie.'

Malkie looked sideways at him, could only see his eyes above the face mask. 'Callum?'

'Aye.'

'Well?'

'This wasn't her. It wasn't Sian. Or if she did do it, she doesn't care a whit about us knowing she did it.'

'Care to explain to the ignorant, here?'

Callum indicated various areas on the walls. Malkie saw nothing different, but noted he didn't point anywhere on the floor, or on the body.

'Accelerant. Everywhere. Spread all over the walls but none on him or on the floor. Only the walls.'

Malkie didn't miss an ominous emphasis on his last few words. 'Unless, as you say, she or he didn't care any more, maybe didn't care about anything any more?'

'True, if *he* or *she* really is that far gone. Possibly.'

They stayed silent for long seconds, allowed the moment to pass.

Gourlay crouched down, looked more closely at Fairbairn's body. Malkie had to swallow a gag reflex; nothing on earth would get him any closer to the blackened, blistered and peeling corpse. The smell alone threatened to send him packing.

Gourlay stood again. 'Whoever did this wanted the poor bastard to suffer. Accelerant sprayed all over the walls so that the place would go up quickly and the flames would generate intense heat before they actually reached him. It would have been like being baked alive in an oven, bloody awful way to die. No firefighter I know would do that to someone.'

Malkie touched Gourlay's arm and nodded towards the hallway. Gourlay took one last look then followed Malkie into the hallway, and then out to the street. They gave their scene suits, shoe covers and face masks to a SOCO to dispose of and stepped outside the scene tape.

'OK, Callum. I'm confused. You say no firefighter would want anyone to die like that, but the way he died sounds – to me – like something only a firefighter would know how to do? To make him suffer, I mean?'

'No, no. Any half-intelligent person can do some internet research and find out how a fire develops from high to low in a small compartment like a living room. The door had been closed to contain it, so it didn't spread to the rest of the house or the adjoining properties. The smoke would have stayed high longer than the flames, which would have super-heated the air and radiated downwards. Fairbairn could well have been dead before the smoke or flames took him. Poor bugger.'

'I'm still not convinced. We're bringing Wilson in for questioning as soon as we find her.'

Gourlay shook his head as if disappointed in Malkie. 'Sian Wilson didn't do this. I don't know many of them very well, but nothing I've heard about her makes me think she'd be capable of this.'

'Then who, Callum? Some unidentified arsonist? Why risk killing Fairbairn, considering it seems obvious the warehouse had been the main target? Unless you think Fairbairn might have known who did it? Might that explain his interest in Duncan Duffy's BA Set immediately after they brought him out? He seemed to care more about the equipment than the man.'

Gourlay opened his mouth but closed it again. 'I don't know.'

Malkie's temper broke. 'Oh, come on, Callum. You've already told me – in front of Flora Beattie, even – that complaints have been lodged against Fairbairn, but you wouldn't tell me by whom. Beattie is going to have to tell me now that this is a murder investigation. Why don't you save me some time, no?'

Gourlay stared at him like a rabbit caught in a car's headlights. His mouth opened and closed again. He frowned, paced away and back again. Eventually, he seemed to persuade himself to cross a line.

'There were two complaints. Steve Grayson, the guy who does all the Livi Station's safety inspections on the equipment before sending it off to the company we lease it from...' He needed a moment to continue. 'And Sian Wilson.'

'Fuck's sake. And you never thought to tell me this earlier, mate?'

'I couldn't. Not my place. Flora needed to tell you this. I'm not even supposed to know until she escalates it up the SFRS chain.'

Malkie walked away a few paces, stopped, turned, glared at Callum as he fought to control his temper. 'And when would she do that, do you think?'

Gourlay shrugged. 'Up to her. For all I know she'd already spoken to Fairbairn about it, or she may have sent it up her management line already. You need to ask her.'

Malkie willed himself to calm down. How often had he ached to pass information on to someone to ease their worries or confirm their worst fears, but couldn't, because strict rules dictated how much officers can say to Persons Of Interest or witnesses or family, and when.

He walked back to Gourlay and placed a hand on his arm for a second. 'I'll talk to her. I don't want to take my frustrations out on you if you're bound by your own rules.'

'Thanks. Even now, I only know Grayson and Wilson's names from hearsay. I couldn't pass chat off the grapevine to you officially.'

'It's fine. Really.' Malkie stretched and twisted his neck, yawned and groaned as aches and kinks from a shite night's sleep worked themselves out of his vertebrae.

'Not sleeping?'

Malkie heard the unspoken remainder of Gourlay's question. 'No, not after your wee bombshell yesterday.'

'Sorry.'

'Not your fault. Mine. I should have read your report properly when I first got it. That bloody page seven doesn't leave much room for doubt, does it?'

Gourlay looked embarrassed for having done his own job well, eight months ago.

'Ach, I appreciate you putting me straight, Callum, even if you've set a hell of a lot of really fucking ugly hares running.'

They stood in respectful silence as a mortuary van pulled up. Two SOCOs exited the front door with Fairbairn, bagged and tagged on a gurney, and loaded him into the vehicle, then returned inside. The van drove off, and Malkie turned back to Gourlay.

'Do you know if Flora Beattie is expected at the station today?'

'Not sure, but I heard she suffered a mild relapse. Apparently, stress is one of the worst things for MS.'

'Well, I need to talk to her again, but I'll go as easy as I can on her.'

THIRTY-FIVE

The Canty Bay caravan site was a sorry sight. Twelve caravans, all of which had seen better days, lined up along a grassy bank above the beach, no office, no shop, no toilet or shower block.

In the early morning light, Steph could make out the Bass Rock a mile offshore but only faintly. She saw no lights burning in the windows of any of the caravans, but people sat outside one eating what smelled like bacon rolls at a table strewn with lager cans and takeaway food wrappers. She wound her window down a few inches and – no surprise – caught a whiff of the musty sweet smell of cannabis for breakfast.

She stopped the car. Every one of them hid one hand under the table and waved the other in the air as if shooing away insects. She flashed her warrant card at them and showed them an SFRS photograph of Wilson. They confirmed that they'd seen a 'moody wee cow that looked like her' staying in a caravan further down the line. When she asked about Wilson's comings and goings, all they could tell her was that they saw her drive out to the A198 shortly after eleven the previous night.

As Steph walked down the line of caravans, she looked

through each gap towards the Bass Rock. At the last one she got what she wanted. She took her phone out and opened Wilson's photograph. The angle of the island to the camera, the colouring and design on the side of the caravan, the awning, all matched.

A hundred yards further on, she turned right and strolled down to the beach, then worked her way back along the foot of the grassy bank until she arrived behind what she hoped would turn out to be Wilson's hiding place. She clambered up the banking and tucked herself out of sight at the back. She put one foot on top of a gas canister and pulled herself up to a window at the rear. She saw only vague details through a manky window. An unmade bed, clothes strewn everywhere, a magazine. Further into the interior she could see what looked like a kitchen area on the right and a door opposite on the left. Beyond that, gloom and what could be a sitting area.

She saw no movement. No sign of anyone.

She made her way to the side facing away from the other caravans and again pulled herself up to peer inside a side window. Again, she saw nothing clearly, only a U-shaped banquette of seats, foam cushions that could be converted into beds.

She peered to her left, towards what was indeed a small kitchen area. On a worktop sat tins of soup, bread rolls, a box of breakfast cereal, bottles of water, other bottles of some clear alcohol, and another ashtray and packet of cigarettes. She couldn't make out if the bread had any mould on it.

She returned to her car via a road that ran along the southern edge of the park. She drove past the mob smoking weed and parked up at the head of a track marked 'private road' that led from the A198 to other properties she could just make out in the gloom to the east of the fork. She turned her car, lowered her seat back, and waited.

Her mind wandered, despite her attempts not to let it, to Dean and Barry. She scoffed in disgust but didn't know whether her scorn belonged to Dean or Barry or herself. Her stepdad and a man she'd thought of as an uncle through most of her childhood, but turned out to be her real dad. She slammed her hand into the side panel of the door. She wanted to be furious at them, more for what they'd put her mum through than for what they did to her, so many years later. But her fury came, she knew, from the knowledge that she would always carry Barry's manky genes. As rationally as she tried to dismiss any clichéd and dated idea that blood ran deep, she couldn't deny that DNA inherited from a scumbag like Barry could only taint her. Barry had lived his life the way he'd wanted, disgraced himself as he chose to, but that didn't mean she'd inherited any of his weakness or his complete lack of moral fibre.

She'd had no say in who had contributed fifty per cent of her genetics, but she'd had complete control over how she used those genetics, how she identified the strengths they had gifted her and made the most of her aptitudes to rise above the rotten existence that her birth could have meant for her.

She remembered Dean's other comments, his claims that far from making her mum truly proud, Steph's repeated academic achievements had shamed her, driven her to the very alcohol and drugs that had given Dean such total control over her life, her daughter, and their mutual humiliation.

No. She found herself unable to believe that. She cast her mind back to that day on the beach, to her whole manky family laughing at her for crying because she'd lost her ice cream. She closed her eyes and willed herself into a calm and meditative state, played what she could remember back on a screen in her mind. She could see no clear, specific memories of her mum's reactions to her near drowning, but neither did she remember any trace of anger at her or disappointment in her. If her mum had laughed like the others had, she'd remember a far worse and more total sense of betrayal.

No. Her mum had been weak, but had loved her daughter, her only child, and no number of vicious, poisonous claims from Dean could have changed that certainty. She simply could not have grown up to miss her mum as much as she did if she'd ever been given cause to feel so let down by her.

She opened her eyes as she felt a tear roll down her cheek. She caught it in her fingertips and studied it, a rare occurrence, one which she couldn't imagine anyone except Malkie ever being allowed to witness.

Eventually, exhaustion overcame her, and she slept.

At a quarter to ten, she woke with a fright when a car drove past the front of hers and headed towards the caravan park. Steph waited until it passed, then opened her door, eased it closed, and followed.

She found the newly arrived vehicle parked at the back of the last caravan in the row, as she'd hoped. This time, she walked along the road beside the site to hide from the gang who still sat around their table, smoking so much weed she feared even she might fail a drugs test while driving home.

She approached the caravan from the far side and peered through a window.

Wilson sat, a bottle in one hand and her head in the other, weeping.

Steph suppressed a pang of sympathy for this woman who'd lost her oldest friend, would likely lose her career, and may well lose her liberty for fifteen years or more. Would she be any less furious and any less intent on revenge if she found someone had caused her mum's death? It hit her like a freight train, exactly what Dean, her nominal stepfather, had done. Barry had played his part, giving Steph's mum the best thing that ever happened to her at the same time as robbing her of any scrap of self-respect she might still have to clung to before the bastard raped her. And Steph had nearly killed him for it, more than twenty years after the event.

If Wilson had killed Peter Fairbairn, Steph wouldn't sleep well for months if the poor woman went down for it. Against every fibre of her professional being, it occurred to her to just return to the station, claim she hadn't found her. It wouldn't prevent her eventual capture, trial and incarceration, but it might give her a few months more liberty.

To do what? To mourn? To drink herself to death?

She knew she should call for uniformed backup, should have brought a Uniform with her as Thompson had instructed, but the thought of Wilson being led away in cuffs didn't sit well with her.

What was happening to her, to her non-negotiable adherence to the job and all its rules and regulations? If she started even contemplating allowing a major suspect in a homicide to disappear again, how much further would she need to fall to consider ending Barry's repellent existence? And Dean's, for that matter. Might as well be hung for a Dean as a Barry?

She went to the door on the other side of the caravan and knocked. It opened.

'I told you before. I don't want your...' She swayed, stared at Steph, her eyes struggling to focus. 'Who the fuck are you?'

Steph stepped up, took Wilson by one arm and led her gently but firmly back inside, before any of the weed brigade further up the park noticed and came to enjoy the show.

Wilson tried to resist, but Steph could smell so much – she glanced at the bottle in her hand – tequila on her breath, she'd been lucky to have driven here without killing herself or someone else. Steph sat her on the sofa, made sure she didn't mean to resist, fetched her a bottle of water, then sat beside her.

'Sian? Sian, look at me. Please.'

Wilson did, her eyes glassy, and recognition crept into them. 'You're a police officer. You were at the warehouse the other night. The fire that killed my Duncan.' Tears spilled but she kept talking. 'My beautiful, beautiful Duncan.'

'Yes, I am, Sian. I need to take you in, we need to ask you some questions. And we need to make sure you don't hurt yourself.' She nodded at Wilson's near-empty tequila bottle.

Wilson glanced down at it, then back at Steph. She handed the bottle over and accepted the bottle of water in return. Steph decided her instincts had been correct; she might get to arrest her without further degrading her dignity.

'Will you come with me, Sian? Back to Livingston?'

'I didn't mean to do it. I just wanted to punish him.'

Steph ached to ask what Wilson wanted to punish Fairbairn for but knew she could use nothing she learned from the woman in this state. She cautioned her, but knew she'd need to do it again after getting her sobered up. Cautioned, arrested, and with a brief beside her. Only then could she and Malkie question her.

She stood, took Wilson by one arm and lifted her to her feet. 'Let's go a for a drive, Sian. Let me take you home.'

She found Wilson's keys, locked up her car and the caravan and switched off the valve to the gas canister, then walked her to her car via the road, happy to see that the party animals had retired inside their own caravans.

Wilson made no effort to resist. She allowed herself to be guided into the passenger seat, lifted her arms like a child as Steph fastened her seatbelt. By the time Steph got in on the driver side, Wilson had propped her head against the window, her eyes closed.

Steph called Malkie, got his voicemail, so she left a message advising him of the development and asking him to attend the station immediately. Then she called the East Lothian division to advise she'd taken a suspect into custody on their patch and promise she'd do the paperwork as soon as possible.

As she started the engine, she heard Wilson speak just once

more, her voice small and broken. 'My Duncan loves this place. His sister owns it. We're going to spend our honeymoon here.' She smiled, as she slipped into sleep. 'Mr and Mrs Duncan Duffy.'

Steph had to fight back tears of her own so she could see clearly enough to drive both of their battered souls home safely.

THIRTY-SIX

Malkie pulled up outside Flora Beattie's home for a second time and braced himself for confrontation.

He'd detected a steel core in the woman during his last visit, a force not be fucked with and not just because of her senior role in the SFRS. He would need to watch his mouth to keep her onside, to stop her from withdrawing all professional good-will completely. He needed to tell her one of her crew had just been murdered, the second of those under her care to die in less than a week; then he needed to as good as accuse the second of those of professional negligence.

How wrong could it go?

When he rang the doorbell this time, a nurse answered.

'Can I help you?'

Malkie showed her his warrant card. 'I'm Detective Sergeant Malcolm McCulloch from Police Scotland. I need to talk to Flora Beattie, please.'

'No, sorry.'

'I beg your pardon?'

'I said no. She's too—'

From inside the house, Beattie's voice called, barely audible, weak and exhausted. 'Let him in, Linda. I need to talk to him, too.'

The nurse stood aside with bad grace and Malkie stepped in. He entered the living room to find Flora Beattie looking like death warmed up.

'Good grief. Are you OK, Ms Beattie? I can't interview you if you're not completely capable, for my sake as well as yours.'

'No, I'm really not, but I need an update from you. Jeremy Lees, bless him, he's a sweetie but he says he doesn't want me worrying too much and isn't keeping me updated. And anyway, unless you caution me this won't be an interview at all, just a chat, right?'

Malkie sat, waited until the nurse finished a final few tasks, signed what he assumed to be an attendance log, extracted an assurance from Beattie that she wouldn't stay up too much longer, flashed a warning look at Malkie, then left.

Malkie watched her struggle to push herself further upright in her chair. He wanted to help but couldn't know whether his offer would be welcomed or dismissed.

She settled herself with a heavy groan, closed her eyes and drew a long breath, then returned her attention to Malkie.

'So, Detective. What progress?'

Malkie hadn't expected to have to provide a recap of four days' worth of investigation, and he needed to be careful he revealed only the appropriate and minimum necessary information.

He decided to rip the bastard sticking plaster right off, as Rab Lundy was fond of saying.

'I'm sorry to have to tell you that Peter Fairbairn is dead, Ms Beattie.'

She closed her eyes again, laid her head back on the headrest of her armchair, but said nothing for long moments. When she looked at him again, he saw only exhaustion.

'How, Mr McCulloch?'

Rip the bastard thing right off.

'He died in a fire in his home.'

She stared at him. 'Accidental?'

He longed to give her an answer that wouldn't just make her ongoing troubles much worse, but knew he owed her the professional courtesy of candour.

'Doubtful. But that must go no further for now, however much you might want to keep your other crew members appraised. Please. Not until we progress our investigation.'

Beattie's eyes bored into Malkie's, promised nothing but demanded more.

'We have one main avenue of investigation we're pursuing.'

'Sian Wilson.' She said it as a statement rather than a question.

'Yes.'

'No.'

'I'm sorry?'

'She wouldn't. She hated Peter Fairbairn with a passion, but she's too smart to ruin her career – and a very promising career, at that – because...'

She stopped herself, reconsidered. 'Because they didn't get on with each other.'

Malkie's turn to stare her down, but she didn't break. 'Why? What happened between them?'

'Peter Fairbairn might have been an excellent firefighter, but I've never met a more opinionated, misogynistic, intolerant and downright nasty little man, Mr McCulloch. And Sian was the only woman other than myself employed in Livingston SFRS. He and I have had words, and I've needed to slap him down a few times, but...'

Malkie gave her time.

'He's reputed to have treated Sian like a second-rate fire-fighter. Never overtly, never in any way that could trigger official sanction, but Sian had confided in me several times that she feared to find herself alone in the same room with him. She never went into details, but I know anything he tried would have been rebuffed with menaces; Sian is no delicate little wallflower.'

Malkie took this in, added it to Wilson's growing list of motivations to have killed the man, but found himself unhappy to have to do so. It didn't feel right, regardless of the circumstantial evidence piling up against her.

It's bloody Walter Callahan all over again.

'But she wouldn't go that far. I'm positive about that. Not just because Fairbairn was a pig.'

'Why wasn't something done about him? Why didn't you discipline him?'

'Because he was clever as well as vicious. He never went so far that he gave me or anyone else concrete cause to raise a grievance, always managed to stay well inside the "her word against mine" defence so beloved of toxic males the world over. I've warned him to watch his behaviour on several occasions, but he just threatened to complain about *me* bullying *him* in the workplace.'

'What a fucking creep.' The words came out before he could stop them. He looked at Beattie, feared he'd just fucked up any chance he had of securing her cooperation, but her expression told him she thought the same, although he couldn't imagine her ever using such language.

'What about complaints I've heard of, about him pressuring Steve Grayson to push the limits on safety equipment right up to legal tolerances?'

Her head snapped up, her eyes furious. 'Who told you that?'

'It doesn't matter who told me, Ms Beattie. That, along with the way Fairbairn snatched Duncan Duffy's BA Set from a paramedic, then examined it very closely before handing it to

Jeremy Lees – and I observed this myself – tends to lend credence to the statements, doesn't it?'

'Damn it. You should not have heard that. If I find out—'

'Ms Beattie, can we remember our priorities here, please? We have a line of investigation running into who we found dead inside the building – no, I can't tell you anything about that – and we're working with you and the FIU to investigate any technical failure that may have contributed to Duffy's death, but our priority, right now, is to determine who killed Peter Fairbairn and William Galbraith and why, in case that person decides someone else needs to die.'

He took a breath. 'Can I put it any more clearly than that?'

She sagged in her chair. 'Fair point, Detective. Fair point. I just...'

He waited. His phone buzzed in his pocket, but he ignored it.

'I'm close to being forced to retire on health grounds, as you can see. I've worked at that station for three decades since I first joined the SFRS, and I'm not embarrassed to say that apart from Fairbairn, I'm well-liked and well-respected by every member of both crews. And that respect and affection goes two ways. I'm immensely proud of them, every one of them, including Sian, and it's been my highest priority to hand over to a successor that I can be sure will do them justice. I found out that Peter Fairbairn told Steve Grayson on multiple occasions to stretch the regulations to their limits in order to save money. Nothing more than that. He wanted to build a case for him replacing me, so he stacked up lots of little achievements and other arguments in support of his belief that he would be my natural successor.'

She paused to take a drink from a beaker of water. Malkie decided he needed to wrap this up and leave her to rest.

'I wanted Jeremy Lees to replace me when the time comes, but Fairbairn never held anything but contempt for him. He's a bit soft on people and hates confrontation, but he's a superb fire-fighter, popular with the troops, has more experience than any of them apart from Don McCallum and Kenny Donaldson, who have both made it very clear they want nothing to do with a management role.

'Add to that the fact that just about every other member of both crews has, at some time or another, expressed displeasure with Fairbairn and in some cases even a desire to transfer out of the station if he replaces me, and you have, I'm afraid, several people who had good reason to loathe Peter Fairbairn. Granted, Sian believes she has the most immediate and compelling reason to want to hurt him, but the man was universally unpopular and the last person anyone wanted to see take my place when I'm forced to leave.'

Malkie saw where she meant to take this and he dreaded it.

'In fact, you could argue that even I had a motive to kill the man, rather than see him ruin all I've built over three decades.'

'Agreed, Ms Beattie, but...' He glanced at her legs and her crutches leaning on the side of her chair.

She managed a small, sad and weary smile.

'I had nothing to do with it, Mr McCulloch, but neither – I'm beyond certain – did Sian.'

Malkie left her to her suffering. She managed a weak smile and a shake of his hand, and Malkie chose to believe she harboured no ill-feeling; both had only been doing their jobs.

Back in his pool car, he checked his phone. A voicemail from Steph. She'd found Wilson. Malkie headed for the station, and possibly one of the most conflicted interviews he could imagine.

THIRTY-SEVEN

Malkie and Steph stopped at the door to interview room one, Malkie's hand on the handle, but loath to push down on it and open the door. Sian Wilson had been cautioned again now that she'd been sobered up, but Malkie couldn't shake a feeling that – yet again – the wrong person might be waiting for him in that interview room.

During the standard interview strategy meeting they'd held with Thompson beforehand, all had agreed that Wilson had ample motivation – at least in her own mind – for killing Fairbairn, knew too well the means by which he'd died, and they couldn't write off her having had plenty of opportunity, since no one could confirm her whereabouts for four days. They decided that motive could prove to be her weak spot, so they'd focus on her apparent hatred of Fairbairn to begin with.

Gucci and Lundy were currently going blind requesting and watching every piece of CCTV footage from every camera they could identify along the A198 from a mile before, to a mile after, the turn-off for the caravan site. Wilson's own car had been flagged for ANPR but not her cousin's, flagging every car owned by any friend or family of hers simply not feasible until proven necessary.

Steph punched him on the arm. 'Come on. The sooner we start...'

He opened the door. Wilson sat at a table, her head in her hands, just as Steph had found her in the caravan. She looked up as they entered but no recognition or other feeling either way played in her expression. She looked too exhausted and broken to care.

Malkie nodded to her brief and to the Uniform posted to watch over her. He noticed she'd already been given a plastic tumbler of water. He and Steph sat. Malkie suppressed his usual naive instinct to offer the woman a comforting smile; this was a Person Of Interest strongly suspected of having tied a man up and burned him to death in the most painful way possible.

Steph started the recorder and stated the date, time and the names of all present. All too soon the time came for Malkie to start his questioning.

'Ms Wilson, you're being interviewed in connection with the death of Mr Peter Fairbairn, who—'

She exploded out of her chair, backed up against the wall, her eyes wild and dangerous like a cornered cat. 'What? No. I didn't. What? How...'

She glanced from Malkie to Steph and back again, and Malkie got a horribly familiar feeling he'd experienced too many times, that her reaction might be genuine. He felt Steph stiffen in her chair next to him, either because she felt the same or in preparation to encourage Wilson back into her chair. Probably both.

'Sian, please, sit down.'

She looked around the room like the same cornered cat looking for any escape despite knowing she had nowhere to go.

She shook her head. Tears welled. Her mouth opened and closed.

After a few seconds, she calmed herself with an obvious effort, seemed to realise she wasn't doing herself any favours by kicking off. She sat, clasped her shaking hands on the table in front of her, her knuckles white.

'I didn't kill Peter Fairbairn. I didn't even know he was dead until you told me.'

She hesitated before continuing.

'How did he die?'

Malkie felt like a fraud already. His gut screamed at him that this woman knew nothing about Fairbairn's death. Two months ago, he'd felt the same certainty about Walter Callahan. He needed to get it right this time.

'You don't know?'

She held her hands out, seemed frustrated and helpless. 'How can I know? I didn't fucking kill him.' She glanced at the recorder. 'Sorry. This is distressing. Actually, it's horrible. I hated the man, yes. Actually, I didn't hate him. I never wished personal harm to him. I loathed him. Despised him. But I wouldn't let a rotten wee shite like him make me ruin my own career.' She looked from Malkie to Steph and back again as if not believing her statement could be anything but self-evident.

She broke down. Tears poured. Steph grabbed a handful of tissues from a box on the table and handed them to her. Wilson said thank you in between sobs that racked her.

Malkie waited for her to regain control of herself. 'Sian, you've given us ample reason, witnessed by several people, to believe you were furious enough at the man to want to hurt him. You've done so twice already, and we can't rule out you having had opportunity for his murder because we're unable to account for your movements over the past four days. It's looking bad for you, Sian. You must see that?'

She nodded, miserable as anyone could be. 'I accept it looks bad, but I... Did not. Kill him.'

'Where have you been since the night of the warehouse fire?'

'I went to Fairbairn's address to wait for him to get home, to confront him with it, then I went home. After you' – she nodded at Steph – 'came to my house, I packed and went to the caravan. My head was splitting open.'

'Confront him with what, Sian?'

She stared at them like they were idiots. 'He caused Duncan's death. It's bloody obvious.'

Malkie waited.

Wilson sat forward. 'Fairbairn told Stuart Simpson to keep a BA Set in use even though Stuart had doubts about the face seal on it.'

And there it was. The reason Sian hated Fairbairn. The reason Stuart Simpson always looked terrified to speak to a copper. The reason Steve Grayson had complained about Fairbairn to Beattie. Safety of firefighters was non-negotiable, always, but Peter Fairbairn had forced a young man to go out on a shout knowing he might have to put his life at risk with equipment he had no faith in.

Wilson interrupted Malkie's thoughts. 'Are you listening? I asked Fairbairn why he took Duncan's BA Set away so quickly, and if he'd found any failures in it. He said no and tried to close the door. I pushed inside and into his living room. He started on at me, calling me everything he wanted to in the station but never could for fear of losing his job. He pushed me up against a wall, pressed himself against me, then...'

She had to take a second. 'He leaned into me. He put his face in my neck, and his hands... He groped me.' She looked like she might throw up. Malkie believed her based on Flora Beattie's reluctant description of Fairbairn, and he wished he could go back and rip the fucker's head off himself.

'Anyway...' She swallowed, took some water, gathered herself and sat straighter in her chair. 'Duncan should never have been allowed into that building for his first time on air. He was only Retained, not Whole Time. Damned good at his job but he got called out to half as many shouts as the rest of us, so he had nothing like our hard experience. And that warehouse fire was too big a shout for him. Whisky barrels in an enclosed space and only one available entry control point. Duncan shouldn't have been anywhere near that one.'

'And who made the decision to allow that?' Malkie already knew the answer.

Wilson glared at him.

'I need you to answer for the recording, Sian.'

She glanced at it and nodded. 'Peter Fairbairn made the decision to allow Duncan Duffy to go in on air for his first time during SFRS attendance at the William Galbraith warehouse fire.'

Having stated this apparently crucial piece of evidence as clearly as she felt able, she sat back in her chair as if she thought the job done.

'Paul Turner is Whole Time, aye?'

She nodded.

'Good man?'

'He's good. He can be a bit gobby sometimes but he knows what he's doing. He's had two decades of experience, so he performs on instinct a lot, but he's as sound as any of us.'

Malkie suspected she already knew where he wanted to go next. 'He would have gone in ahead of Duncan, correct?'

'Aye, he'd have led.'

'And what would Paul's responsibilities have been with respect to Duncan being on air for his first time?'

'He'd have made sure Duncan stayed close, checked his gauge regularly, watched to make sure he followed all the protocols, generally looked after Duncan's safety.'

'Do you all do that? Check your gauges regularly?'

She hesitated. 'Mostly.'

'Mostly, Sian?'

'After years on the job, you develop an instinct for how long a particular capacity of cylinder under a specific pressure will last you. But even experienced firefighters – especially experienced ones – still check their gauges in case of equipment faults.'

'Would Paul have made Duncan check his gauge every time he checked his own?'

'Yes. It's one of the most critical safety checks while on air.'

'Is there any chance he might have assumed Duncan would know that and not consider it necessary to remind him?'

She chewed her lower lip as she shot Malkie a poisonous look. 'It's possible. But Duncan wouldn't have needed to be reminded. It's fundamental BA Set safety.'

'And I believe there are other measures taken to warn a firefighter of problems with their BA Set, yes?'

'The whistle. It goes off if the gauge detects low pressure from the cylinder.'

'And it's loud, I would imagine. No chance a firefighter wouldn't hear it if it sounded, no?'

Her eyes turned suspicious again. 'Why are you asking me this?'

Malkie sat back now, a subconscious signal to Wilson that he intended not to answer that question.

'Did Steve Grayson ever mention any issues with these warning whistles?'

Wilson's temper broke. 'It happens, but Steve never mentioned it. Why the fuck are you asking me all these questions about Duncan and Paul? You hauled me in here to accuse me of killing Fairbairn, didn't you?'

'Because, Sian, in the immediate aftermath of the warehouse fire, you were heard to ask, and I quote, "Where's his fucking BA Set?" and then later, "We all saw this coming, and we did nothing." What did you all "see coming", Sian?'

Wilson chewed over her answer for long seconds. 'We all knew Fairbairn had been pressuring Steve to leave equipment in service long after he wanted to send it back to the manufacturer for maintenance.'

'How angry were you that both crews "did nothing", Sian?'

She shook her head. 'No. I'm not having that. Yes, I was angry, but not enough to kill a man. And you still haven't told me how he died. How can I discuss this with you without knowing exactly what you think I did?' She glanced at her brief, who nodded at her then looked to Malkie.

'Someone burned him to death in his home.'

Wilson's eyes flared. She looked to her brief again. 'Did you know this?' Her brief shook his head and didn't look happy.

'Oh, you bastards. You know I hate him and I'm a firefighter who knows how to set fires of course, so unless I can prove I've been at the caravan every day after I attacked him, you want to hang this on me, right?'

'The only person I want to "hang this on", Sian, is whoever did it.' Malkie realised too late his voice had taken on a harsh tone. He willed himself to calm down. 'If you can prove to us that you were – as you say – in East Lothian since your second attack on Fairbairn, which I note for the recording that you've confirmed without prompting from us, then it might help us to eliminate you from our inquiries, yes.

'But you've stated that you loathed Fairbairn and were furious at him for forcing Steve Grayson to push safety tolerances on critical safety equipment to their limit. You've also stated that you blame Fairbairn for Duncan's death, for allowing him to enter the warehouse on air without – in your opinion – the necessary experience. And your DNA will be all over his living room and on the shards of glass from the bottle you attacked him with.

'So yes. Without an alibi for your whereabouts between six thirty on Thursday evening and ten o'clock this morning, then I can see no reason not to charge you with Peter Fairbairn's homicide, Ms Wilson.'

Wilson clammed up. Malkie tried to rebuild some measure of a bridge between them, to elicit her cooperation in proving her whereabouts for the previous four days, but he got nothing more from her.

He suspended the interview, and they left her with her brief.

Back in the CID room, Thompson agreed that although they didn't yet have enough to charge her, she constituted a flight risk, so she agreed to hold her for twenty-four hours.

'Has she been cautioned?' Malkie looked to Steph, who nodded.

Steph offered to break the news to Wilson that she'd be spending the night in a cell, but Malkie refused to dump the task on her. He sent her home and they agreed to reconvene at 07:30, before the morning briefing.

THIRTY-EIGHT

'It's happening again, mate.'

Malkie brushed freshly mown grass from the small granite block that marked the grave of Walter Callahan, a tormented ex-squaddie who Malkie had vindicated but failed to save. Tormented by PTSD, he'd been an easy target to be framed for a hit-and-run on a young man who'd barely survived. Malkie had been right about him, about his total ignorance of the crime, but he failed to save Callahan from an armed officer's slugs to his chest. A fact he'd regret to his dying day.

Being a complete atheist – even a nihilist, as Thompson had described him – he had no reason to believe Callahan would hear him, but he was willing to suspend his disbeliefs just enough to convince himself that sharing his troubles with the memory of one of the finest men he ever knew at least honoured that man's memory, as well as helping Malkie deal with the ugliness that the job threw in his face too often.

'A firefighter. She admits she assaulted her boss for what would be understandable reasons if she's telling us the truth about him, but denies killing him. Although you never heard me say that, OK?' He smiled as he imagined Callahan scowling at him and telling him never to say anything to him that he wouldn't repeat to others.

He checked his watch. Dame Helen Reid had told him he could visit Deborah any time before eight but not a minute later. He'd called her to check she hadn't taken her meds yet. She'd told him Deborah had started taking them an hour later than she used to, just in case, which warmed his heart and did something to push the usual bitterness and cynicism out of his mind.

'She might be in the same situation that fucker Jake Fielding put you in, Walter. She's being held for questioning about the death of another firefighter, burned alive in his home. And – same as happened to you – even though all our evidence is circumstantial at the moment, it all points to her.'

He took a breath, needed a second to work up to saying out loud the kind of opinion that had so often got him a kicking from Police Scotland Senior Management.

'I can't believe she did it. And I think Steph – you remember Steph? – doesn't believe it either, but she won't admit it openly, because she's still infuriatingly addicted to objectivity. I know, I know; she's a good check and balance to my stupid emotional responses, and I do love her for that. But fuck's sake she can be annoying, sometimes.'

He stood. As much as he needed to imagine Walter Callahan giving him a well-deserved talking-to, he felt a far more pressing need to spend a half hour letting Deborah soothe him and remind him he had good things to value in his life.

'Thanks, Walter. You're a good listener, you know that?' He chuckled to himself as he left the small, gated cemetery and walked over to the entrance of the outreach centre.

He found Dame Helen's office door closed, and he saw no lights through the window from outside. After a moment's discomfort, he decided to grow up and assume Reid's previous conversations with him carried tacit permission for him to come and go as he pleased. Within reason, he reminded himself.

Deborah's face shone when he knocked and opened her door. She silenced the TV – another dreary soap opera – and raised the backrest on her bed.

'Hello, Mr Dirty Old Man. Oh dear. Sit. What's wrong, Malkie?'

He nearly swore. He'd been here before, fundamentally certain of someone's innocence despite mounting evidence to the contrary. Deborah had never met Walter Callahan, but shared Malkie's high opinion of the man based only on his stories about him. She also shared Malkie's regret that he'd failed to save Callahan and knew he might never forgive himself for that.

'Just like Walter, Deborah. Innocent person under arrest, and I can't believe she's guilty. This can't be happening again.'

Her eyes filled with affection for him. 'Then it's lucky for this woman that she has the best copper in Police Scotland fighting her corner then, isn't it?'

He managed a small smile to let her know he appreciated her effort but knew it wouldn't fool her. 'Anyway, enough about my rotten job. How are you?'

She held his gaze for a few seconds, before letting him off the hook. 'I'm great. I walked twenty metres without my crutches today.' She beamed with pride.

'Good for you. I think you're probably the only person who ever believed you'd walk out of here on your own pins one day.'

She grinned. 'Damn right. Then I'll learn to drive again, and you'll never get rid of me.'

'OK, OK. I know. I'll talk to Dame Helen about driving you out to the cabin again for dinner.'

'See you do, Mr Policeman. What can I do, Malkie?'

'How do you mean?'

'To help you through this. I don't want you clapped out and no good to any bugger when I'm fit to make your life hell, so what can I do to help you get through this? Without a repeat of what poor Walter's case did to you, I mean.'

He thought long and hard. Not for some tired old platitude that wouldn't stand a snowball's chance in hell of fobbing her off. He trawled his mind for what he could ask of her that would genuinely help them both through their respective troubles.

'You know what you can do? You can let me be there for you.'

She looked confused.

'I don't want to share my job with you. It's bad enough I have to see the things I have to without bringing it into one of the only two places I feel at peace. And caring for you matters a hell of a lot more to me than worrying about the stupid bloody job. So, let me in. Let me hear the worst of it, not just "I'm great" every time I ask you. Let me be there for you.'

Her undamaged eye glistened in the light from the TV, and she swallowed. She held her hand out and Malkie took it.

'Just shut up and hang on to me, old man. That's enough.'

Malkie relaxed back into his chair. His fingers stroked the leathery skin on the back of her hand, and they both closed their eyes.

Yes, it's enough, Deborah.

She unmuted the TV, and he found himself content even to sit and watch a soap opera with her. He marvelled at the simplicity of the storylines, the almost naive plotting that professed to depict awful things happening to both good and awful people, but pulled its punches. He suspected that the writers knew exactly what their target audience wanted: an illusion of the ugly side of life but with an assurance, or at least a glossing-over, of just how brutal, venal and loathsome the worst of the human species could be. He resented the fact that programmes like this allowed people to believe they were opening their eyes, acknowledging how rotten modern society could be, while simultaneously anaesthetising them to the full pain and desperation that even the lowest grade of crimes could inflict on those who deserved it the least.

He'd long ago decided that the worst mouth-breathers had to have had their brains rewired by callous, desensitising childhoods that allowed them to dissociate their violence towards others from the trauma they caused. They must develop a hunter and prey attitude where the old and the weak were fair game; survival of the cruellest. He'd seen too many complete animals let loose on the streets after leaving pensioners battered and bruised and terrified to open their front doors for the rest of their lives. Lives more often than not shortened by the sheer misery and fear they suffered for the sake of a few quid from their purses.

He looked to Deborah, needed to replace the hideous thoughts polluting his mind with something else, something better. She'd fallen asleep.

He watched her breathing, slow and steady, and hoped it would continue for decades to come. A woman he'd come to admire more than almost every other person he'd ever known; brave, determined, unbreakable.

Could he ever deserve her? Then it hit him. That wasn't for him to decide. He could allow her to know the real Malkie, warts and all, and show her the respect of allowing herself to make her own mind up.

He shook her gently. She took a second to wake, then a smile lit up the uninjured side of her face that he hoped he'd never forget. He helped her to take her meds, settled back in to watch TV's sterilised and declawed portrayal of modern life, and decided he couldn't blame Deborah and others for finding distraction in the anodyne half-truths presented as faux reality by scriptwriters who had probably never suffered anything ugly throughout their whole lives. When she started snoring, he kissed her on the forehead, wished her sweet dreams and closed her door as quietly as he could.

THIRTY-NINE

Steph found Dean waiting in his knackered old car outside her home. She walked past, tried to unlock her door and slip inside so she could slam it in his face.

He got a foot in the door and grinned at her. She struggled with an urge to slam her door on it again and again, send the bastard to A&E with multiple fractures, but she let him in.

He took a seat in her IKEA bendy easy-chair, pushed her Kahlua bottle and her glass onto the floor with his feet, and crossed both legs at the ankles. He clasped his hands over his belly and reclined. He bounced a couple of times. 'Love this chair.' It creaked; Steph knew Dean weighed more than its 100kg limit. 'Whoops.' He laughed, turned to study the wooden frame with fake concern, then bounced a few more times, his grin wider than ever.

Steph sat, refused to give him the satisfaction of a reaction. It was only a chair.

'What do you want?' She suspected she was about to find out what price Dean hoped to extract from her for his silence. If he'd taken a video of her pounding at Barry's face, he'd know her career lay in his hands.

As if he'd read her mind, he pulled his phone from his pocket and played a video. He didn't show it to her, just enjoyed it for himself, his eyes delighted and amused. She didn't need to see it to know what the grunts and muffled screams meant.

Still, she said nothing, gave no reaction.

Dean seemed to realise he wasn't going to get the first of his wish list from this visit. He put the phone back in his pocket and patted it, pleased with himself.

'What happens to police officers caught committing grievous bodily harm on an innocent man? Or even just someone who's been accused? Is that enough to fuck you up royally?'

She crossed her legs, clasped her hands in her lap, forced a bored and indulgent smile.

Dean failed to mask a double take, confirmed her already embedded opinion that he was out of her league, nowhere near up to taking her on, intellectually or emotionally.

She waited.

'You not going to say anything, you stuck-up wee bitch?'

An insult; always the first sign of a mind already out of options. She waited. Dean surged forward, sat on the front edge of the chair. 'Fucking answer me. Fucking had enough of your holier than thee attitude, like your shite smells sweeter than everyone else's. Fucking answer me, or I swear...' He put his hand on the outside of the pocket, holding his phone.

'Holier than *thou*, Dean. Holier than thou.' She smirked, knew it would unhinge and unbalance the idiot even more. 'And it depends.'

Dean scowled at her, never the sharpest knife in the cutlery drawer. 'What does?'

'Whether you could damage my career depends on how much evidence I can present in mitigation for my actions. I might be put on leave for a month, or suspended, or... aye, I could be sacked, I suppose.'

'So? What are you looking so fucking smug for, then? Fucking smug cow.'

'You don't need to say it twice, I got the message. I look "fucking smug" because if I learned anything from you and "Uncle" Barry and every other pathetic, loathsome, despicable piece of shit I had to endure growing up in your pathetic excuse for care, it's that...' She thought for a second, fished for the perfect punchline. 'I'll survive.' She nodded to herself, pleased with her words.

'My job is just that. It's just a job. Same as that's just a chair your fat arse is threatening to splinter under you. Actually, I'll probably need to burn it after I boot your sorry carcass out of here. Who knows how many lice you've dragged into my home with you. You really are a filthy wee animal, aren't you?'

Dean gaped at her; this wasn't going the way he'd have hoped it would go at all.

'Listen to me, you piece of—'

Steph surged forward now but didn't stop at the front edge of the sofa. She stood, placed her hands on the arms of her soon-to-be-incinerated chair, and stuck her face into Dean's. She nearly gagged at a stench of cigarettes and rarely brushed teeth, but refused to turn away.

'No. You listen to *me*. You ruined my mum's life. You bled her dry, got her addicted to your cheap coke and your third-rate weed and whatever brand of vodka was cheapest at the supermarket, and you killed her. You took years to do it and you made that poor woman suffer more than any person ever deserved to suffer, and that's how you killed her. I should execute you, and that fucker Barry, and I would feel not the slightest scrap of guilt about it. I'd consider it the wholly justified administering of natural justice. And being a "Pig", I know just how to do it so no one will trace it to me, and I know just how to dispose of your stinking corpses, so you'll never be found. So, you're going to hand your phone to me now and walk out of here while you still can.'

She leaned even closer, and Dean had to cower back into the chair. It creaked again and Steph didn't care a jot.

'Now. Are. We. Clear?'

Dean nodded, but his eyes held on to his fury.

Steph reached into his pocket and removed his phone. She dropped it into her own pocket and stood. She didn't worry about a copy of the video, him being too stupid to know how to do anything more technical than browsing the right porn sites. Dean jumped out of the chair, recoiled from her, all trace of his previous machismo evaporated except for a vindictive gleam in his eyes. He stepped sideways past her because she refused to move, and bolted for the door.

'By the way...'

He froze with his hand on the door handle, turned his head back to look at her with renewed dread.

'Chicken wire.'

Despite his fear, despite his fury, he frowned in confusion.

'Wrap you in chicken wire with a half dozen heavy rocks and drop you in a loch. Maybe wait until you're conscious before I do it.'

She smiled, as sweet as the little girl Dean had never bothered to appreciate.

'Fuck you, bitch.'

'And you, Dean. And you.'

He left, slammed the door behind him in one last defiant but ineffectual show of anger.

Steph sat for five minutes and shook. Only when she looked out her window and confirmed Dean had gone did she close the curtains, return to the sofa and break down. Not from residual fear or frustration or even adrenaline; she could be sure her heart rate and blood pressure hadn't deviated much from her normal resting condition while she traumatised him. She sobbed and punched the sofa and screamed rage into the cush-ions because of what the despicable bastard had reduced her to: ugly threats and undignified insults.

She undressed and crawled into bed and spent a sleepless night assessing the chances that she'd scared enough shit out of Dean to shut him up for good.

FORTY

Heads turned when Malkie entered the CID room at 07:00.

He checked the case notes for Fairbairn's murder, found Gucci and even Rab Lundy had worked late into the previous evening but found only one clip of Sian Wilson's cousin's car driving eastward on the A198 at two in the afternoon on Tuesday, fifteen hours after the fire had started and eight hours after Steph had interviewed her at home. They had found no CCTV of the same car driving back west towards the city. Gucci had confirmed that the footage came from a twenty-four-hour filling station a mile before the turn-off for the caravan park. The same cameras had captured Wilson going into the adjoining shop on her way east and returning to her car carrying two shopping bags before continuing her drive.

The evidence tended to confirm Wilson's claim that she had driven out to the caravan park after slashing Peter Fairbairn's tyres and posting the 'Tell them or I will' note through his door, then remaining there until the day Steph caught her. He added an instruction for Gucci to trace her whereabouts on the day Steph saw her drive back into the caravan park. She had to have driven further east and back again not to have appeared again on the same filling station's cameras, but Malkie needed to know where she'd gone.

He dialled Callum Gourlay's number but got no answer. He left a voicemail message for Gourlay to return his call.

When Steph arrived, Malkie dragged her straight into an interview room.

'What's going on, Steph? You look rotten. I can't stand seeing you like this, so tell me what's going on. Is it your pig of a stepdad and your uncle – sorry, that fucker Barry – again?'

She nodded, her eyes dull with exhaustion. She sat. Malkie joined her and waited.

She yawned and her head drooped. He waited. They had five minutes until the morning briefing. He didn't give a damn about being late for it, but them both doing so on top of Steph's obviously distressed state would attract unwelcome attention.

'Dean came to my house last night.'

Malkie sat back, rubbed his hand down over his face as if to wake himself, to prepare himself for the worst. 'What did you to do to him, Steph?'

Anger flared in her expression. 'Nothing. I never laid a hand on him. You think because I lost my temper once and attacked a man who had it coming that suddenly I can't be trusted to keep my hands to myself? Is that what you think of me now, Malkie?'

He waited a second for her breathing to slow again.

'Twice, Steph. Twice in the past week you've attacked Barry. And my whole point is that... It's just not you, Steph. You know you can mess up most people without breaking a sweat, and knowing that has always kept you cool. So, what's making you lose control now?' She seemed to hear the worry and affection in his voice and slumped in her chair.

'He's in me, Malkie. That bloody animal is in me, and always will be. Half of me is made of him, and I don't think I can stand that. He's a fucking disgrace, and his DNA is intertwined with my mum's, and I can never get rid of it. I'll always be his daughter, and that makes me want to throw up every time I think about it.'

She kicked the chair next to her. It clattered across the room. She seemed to flinch from her own loss of control. She crossed the room, picked it up and slammed it back down. She looked ashamed, disgraced, and Malkie knew only half of that came from her disgust at what ran in her veins.

'You're not him, Steph. You're nothing like him. If you've proved nothing else to yourself, isn't it that you've instinctively denied every shitty, filthy trait he forced on you but nurtured the very best of your mum? If she could see the woman you've grown up to be, she'd realise her pride in your achievements at school was nothing compared to what she'd feel about you today. If I ever had a daughter...'

The words came out before he realised what he'd said. He swallowed a lump of his own neurosis and forced himself back to Steph's welfare.

'If I'd ever had a daughter, I would have been fucking delighted if she'd grown into as fine a woman as you are. And there was zero per cent well-intentioned bullshit in that statement.'

She smiled at him, but it was weak and fragile.

'Granted, no daughter of mine would be allowed to grow up as gobby as you can be, but I didn't say you were perfect.'

She laughed. Genuine laughter born of an easing of her uncharacteristic mantle of self-loathing. Malkie had to hope he'd really got through, because he remembered how it felt to have his heart broken and seeing Steph hurting pierced him harder and deeper than anything his car crash of an adolescence had ever done to him.

She stood, and waited for Malkie to do the same. After checking the window in the interview-room door, she stood on tiptoes, placed her hands on his shoulders and kissed him on the cheek.

'We're late for the briefing. Let's go.' She straightened his tie, left her hands on his chest for a second then headed for the door.

'If you ever, and I mean ever, tell anyone I kissed you, you're a dead man, OK?'

'Goes without saying, Steph. Goes without saying.'

When they took their seats at the back of the chairs arrayed around one end of the CID room, Thompson glanced at them with annoyance, but seemed to take in Steph's fragile mood. She said nothing.

Malkie gave the briefing on their three parallel cases. Duncan Duffy's death would likely be subject to a fatal accident inquiry given that Callum Gourlay had so far voiced no suspicion of equipment failure or tampering, and the arson investigation would be separated out from that. He intended to interview Anna Galbraith again that day, to try to learn why her husband had been sleeping on a camp bed in the warehouse office when he'd claimed to be headed for Inverness. Gucci and Lundy would continue trying to trace Wilson's movements, if any, between her second attack on Peter Fairbairn and Steph arresting her.

Thompson thanked him for a comprehensive briefing. She ignored a raised hand from Pamela Ballantyne. In her capacity as cover for DI Gavin McLeish she covered his team's caseloads as well, but Malkie zoned out, as he usually did when he'd said his piece.

His attention snapped back to the room when just about every officer – Uniforms and detectives – in the room groaned and sighed, tutted and swore under their breaths.

Thompson snapped at them all. 'Oh, grow up. Try to pretend we're all professionals here. As I said, DI McLeish will take up his new role in MIT at the end of this month. Pamela, I need you to help me cover his role between us until we get a replacement. You OK with that?'

Ballantyne's smile told everyone present just how OK she felt about that. Malkie suppressed a 'Fuck's sake' of his own at the thought of *Acting* DI Pamela Ballantyne. The prospect almost made him want to reapply for a DI role, but he knew he'd never make that mistake again.

Thompson wrapped up the briefing and people wandered back to their desks, muttering to each other, some swearing and moaning loud enough for Thompson to hear but not seeming to care.

Malkie headed for the custody suite. He signed himself in and headed for Wilson's cell.

She looked like she'd had as bad a night as Steph.

'Have they given you a coffee or five?'

She managed a smile, but it couldn't mask the obvious misery of a woman suffering the mother of all hangovers from – if she'd been telling the truth – a three-day tequila binge. 'I feel shit, but thanks for pretending to care.' She sat up and Malkie sat beside her.

'How many bottles did you buy from that filling station?'

She glanced at him, her expression leaving him in no doubt she'd picked up on the fact that they'd traced at least some of her movements.

'Where did you go the night before DC Lang arrested you? You didn't drive past the same filling station, so you must have gone further east.'

Dismay darkened her face. 'The beach at Seacliff.' She lowered her head into her hands. 'Duncan proposed to me there.'

Despite him having had no way of knowing, Malkie felt a familiar rush of anger at himself for having asked yet another painful question. 'I'm sorry.'

He gave her a few seconds. 'Did you stop anywhere? Pub? Filling station? Anywhere that might have cameras?'

'I can't remember. I was wasted.'

'You drove while you were pissed on tequila?'

'Yes, Officer. Oh dear, am I in trouble now?' She sounded fatigued and resigned, rather than bitter or sarcastic, so he let it go.

'I'm trying to help you.'

She softened. 'Do you think you'll be able to confirm what I said? Apart from when I drove to Seacliff, I swear I went from Fairbairn's house straight to the caravan, and I only stopped at the filling station to stock up for my wee pity party, then I stayed at the caravan the whole time. I saw a gang of scruffs that spent the same four days pretty much camped outside their caravan drinking and smoking weed. Maybe they can confirm they didn't see me drive away except last night.'

'We'll check it all out, Sian.'

She stared at him. 'You do believe me, don't you?'

He wanted to, but he suppressed it. He'd been fooled before, been taken in by people naturally gifted at seeming to be the opposite of their true selves. As convincing as he might want Wilson to be, nothing changed the mounting pile of information that pointed straight at her.

FORTY-ONE

Malkie returned to the CID room. As much as he watched himself for the smallest sign of confirmation bias skewing his investigations, he couldn't shake a deep desire to discover that Wilson had told him the truth. Whether because he couldn't wish a life sentence on her after losing her fiancé, or because he just needed to hope his instincts about her proved to be correct. He'd been right about Walter Callahan; could his gut feelings be leading him astray this time?

Even if the beach at Seacliff held precious memories for her, could she have spent the whole night there? The weather across the Lothians had been dry but bloody freezing for days. She might have sat in her cousin's car, maybe listened to a favourite CD of hers and Duffy's, cried her eyes out, drank some more. He could see a credible and reasonable explanation for her having spent a whole night parked next to a bloody Baltic beach if she'd had a decent coat on, but he also couldn't ignore the window it created, a window he, Steph and Thompson had agreed begged the obvious question. Wilson had the means and the motive. Did that missing time imply opportunity?

Of course it bloody does.

He called the custody suite, asked the duty sergeant to bring Wilson to an interview room and call her brief. He checked his watch. He had three hours before they needed solid-enough information to seek authorisation for another twelve hours.

The hope on Wilson's face as he and Steph entered the room almost derailed him; he could not imagine anyone faking the desperation in her eyes, her whole posture.

After the legal and procedural preliminaries were dispensed with and Steph nodded at Malkie to confirm that the recording had started, the hope drained from Wilson's face as she heard Malkie's carefully intoned opening question.

'Where were you between eleven o'clock on Thursday night and when DC Lang saw you return to your caravan yesterday morning?'

Panic flared in her eyes. She looked away, up and to the right. Malkie reminded himself of the training he'd received on non-verbal communication; the theory that people who looked up and to the right were making up a story had been debunked years ago. He worried he felt too much relief that he could ignore her doing exactly that.

'Sian?'

She returned her gaze to Malkie but couldn't hold it.

'I told you. I went to the beach where Duncan proposed to me.' She looked again at Malkie, and he couldn't fight a feeling that she was looking to see how much he believed her, that she might be lying to him.

'For ten hours, Sian?'

'I fell asleep in the car, listening to a CD Duncan made for me. I was pretty wasted, too.' She glared at him.

'The temperature fell to two degrees on Thursday night through to Friday morning. If you sat in a car for that long, either you'd suffer hypothermia or you'd have run down the battery heating the inside. I have to ask you again – where were you for the whole ten hours?'

'I ran the engine all night. I fell asleep, in my car, at the beach. I swear.' Malkie couldn't believe he heard absolute conviction in her voice, and he sighed.

'If you don't tell me where you were, or if I can't confirm it, we may need to hold you for another twelve hours.'

Wilson lost control of herself in stages. Her eyes filled, then she seemed to shrink into herself, then she slid sideways, caught the edge of the table and sobbed.

Steph grabbed a handful of tissues and crouched beside her chair. Wilson took the tissues, smiled at Steph and blew her nose. Steph returned to her chair.

Malkie gave her a few minutes. As cruel as it felt, he needed to continue.

'Sian, can you do that? Can you tell us where you spent those ten hours?'

She sat up, straightened her back, and Malkie thought – hoped – she might be about to unburden herself.

A defiant gleam entered her eyes and Malkie cursed to himself.

'The beach. All day. And I'm getting sick of telling you.' She turned to her brief. 'How long can they hold me?'

He checked his watch. 'Twenty-four hours, initially, so until two this afternoon. Twelve more hours if they find some actual evidence.' He smiled at Malkie, a smile full of warning.

Wilson folded her arms, the interview over.

The Uniform took Wilson back to her cell. Malkie put Gucci onto a wider search of East Lothian, specifically traffic cameras on the A1. Gucci had compared journey times from the caravan park to Livingston via both the A198 and the longer but faster route on the A1, and discovered the longer journey to be a full six minutes quicker. He impressed on Gucci that they had only five hours to find something to allow them to hold Wilson for longer, but he knew she'd do the search faster than anyone else in Livi CID.

Malkie and Steph sat at their desks. Before they could talk, Thompson appeared at the door to the stairwell and called for Steph. Her tone of voice suggested something shitty had happened. Steph shared a look with Malkie. Malkie queried her with his eyes, but she gave him nothing, even though her face communicated only too well that she knew exactly what Thompson wanted to talk to her about.

Malkie settled in for a tense wait.

FORTY-TWO

'We've had a complaint, Steph.'

Steph's stomach sank. She stared at Thompson and could find no words to offer in response. She'd fully expected Dean to capitulate and disappear from her life. Hoped for it. The fact that he wasn't letting it go could mean career-ending trouble, and that would hurt her far more than she'd admitted to the bastard.

Thompson sat forward. 'From Dean Lang. Your stepfather.'

'My mum's husband.'

'Sorry.'

Thompson paused. Steph suspected she'd be bracing herself for one of the worst parts of her job.

'Let me make this easy, boss. I assaulted a man called Barry Boswell. We used to call him my uncle Barry, but I learned only recently that...'

Even in Steph's bloody-minded mood, determined to expose and confront her dirty little secret, she had to force her next words out.

'I learned recently that he raped my mother, and I'm the

result. My biological dad is a mouth-breathing, knuckle-dragging rapist. Ma'am.'

Thompson gaped at her. 'I knew none of this, Steph. It explains why—'

'Aye, it does. I've been a wee bit off my game for a while. Finding out that half the DNA in every cell of your body came from a complete scumbag. Takes a bit of adjusting to.'

She suspected Thompson wanted nothing more than to give her a hug, then take her out and get her royally pissed. But they both knew that a necessary wedge would be driven between them. She could rely on Thompson to conduct any required investigation and disciplinary measures with the utmost fairness and sensitivity, but their relationship – whether Steph got suspended or not – would have to change. Steph tried to take comfort from the knowledge that she couldn't be in better hands for the troubles to come.

'I'm sorry, Steph. I can't imagine...'

'It's no fun, boss.'

'Do you need some leave?'

'That's exactly what I really don't need, but I may not have any say in that, of course.'

'Aye. I'm not sure what the protocol is. I mean, I know what the books say, but I've never had to apply the regulations. This is new ground for me too.'

She went quiet. Neither seemed to think of any avenue of discussion that wouldn't be pointless at this early stage.

Thompson broke the silence. 'It could be worse.'

Steph laughed, a harsh sound full of scorn and cynicism. 'How?'

'If McLeish was staying on here, management might ask him to conduct the inquiry instead of me. People know we're friends as well as colleagues. I mean, I hope so.'

Thompson blushed.

'Do you need my warrant card?'

'Not for now. Keep working, please. We need you. I'll keep you advised, of course.'

Steph nodded. She stood and Thompson did too. As Steph reached for the door handle, she said over her shoulder, 'And yes, I hope we are too.'

'We are what?'

'Friends.'

Steph headed back to the CID room to drop the bombshell on Malkie.

Malkie dragged her to the favourite private meeting area of all in West Lothian CID: the top floor of the stairwell, at the roof access door.

'Dean has lodged a complaint about me attacking Barry.'

'Fuck's sake. Arseholes.' Malkie kicked a wall and winced. 'Shit, that hurt.'

'Idiot.'

They stood in silence for a while in their usual position, leaning their elbows on the railing so they'd know if anyone appeared on the stairs. Steph had caught McLeish sneaking out to eavesdrop on Malkie once, so she stood far to the left where she could see the door to the CID room.

'Does he have any proof? Video? Or just his word against yours?'

She pulled a mobile phone he didn't recognise from her jacket pocket and held it up in front of her, appraised it as if deciding what to do with it.

Malkie held his hand out. 'Bottom of Harperrig Reservoir?'

She considered him for what seemed like an age. Malkie watched her battle with her conscience: Steph the ever-consummate professional considering subverting the law. She handed it to him.

They stood in silence for a while.

'Am I on a slippery slope, Malkie?'

He pretended to give this some consideration before giving her the answer he was always going to.

'Aye, I think you are.'

She hung her head. Malkie didn't let her suffer for long.

'But the good thing is that for you, it'll be a very short slippery slope. One you were forced onto. But it won't take you anywhere near the kind of legendary fuckedupness that I achieve on a regular basis. You're just too good a copper and too strong a person to let yourself slide very far, or to stay slid for too long.'

He was happy to see her smile.

'Seriously? "Fuckedupness"? "Stay slid"? Do those come out of the same Malkie dictionary as when you say you have to interview a "witless"?'

'Aye, but I can't take credit for "mouth-breathers" and "knuckle-draggers". Much as I'd like to.'

She laughed and punched him on the arm. He feigned serious injury. 'Watch it. I'm delicate.'

They stood in silence again, but a different kind of silence. She would know as well as he that Dean's complaint would need to be investigated and would end up on her record in some way, but she'd also know that a full suspension – or worse – might yet be avoided.

'Thanks, Malkie.'

'You're welcome, doll.'

'Thin ice, mate.'

FORTY-THREE

Malkie knocked on Anna Galbraith's door then stepped back, his warrant card at the ready.

When she answered, she looked even more haggard and exhausted than before.

'Can we have another word, please, Mrs Galbraith?' His tone – he hoped – communicated the fact that he meant it as anything but a request.

She stepped aside and they entered. Her living room looked to reflect her apparent state: cluttered and messy. She sat in the same armchair as before but didn't invite Malkie and Steph to sit. Malkie did so anyway. Steph stayed on her feet.

'Mrs Galbraith, we wanted to ask if you've had any ideas about why your husband seems to have been sleeping in his office at the warehouse. We found the remains of a camp bed and a sleeping bag.

'When my colleague Detective Constable Lang first interviewed you, she got a clear impression that you already suspected the fatality might be your husband, before she gave you any substantial information. Why did you think that, Mrs Galbraith?'

The old geezer, Sidney, across the road from Fairbairn's home had been adamant that he'd seen a female running from the scene minutes before he saw smoke. Which pointed a huge finger at Sian Wilson or Anna Galbraith. He wrote Flora Beattie off because as well as seeming to be genuinely restricted in her movements, she'd struck Malkie as having suffered from months of inactivity and carried a few pounds more than he'd expected of a firefighter. She certainly wouldn't be capable of running anywhere.

Galbraith thought for a moment. 'I was afraid almost immediately that it might be my husband, because...' She dabbed at her eyes with a tissue from a box on the coffee table. 'William never, and I mean never, let himself be without at least two phones and spare batteries. Not since he got us stranded halfway up the back side of Ben Nevis; and the weather came in quickly and he'd let his battery go flat. He hated himself for putting us in danger, and he never did it again.'

Her attention drifted and a small smile touched her lips. 'I make him sound like a really boring man, don't I? He wasn't. Just obsessive about details.'

Malkie glanced at Steph. 'Nothing wrong with that in moderation, Mrs Galbraith.'

Steph stared back at him, blank.

'I believe I've told DC Lang already that the business has been struggling for some time. The night of the fire, William had told me he'd be in Inverness, discussing a buy-out by the Black Isle Distillery. I've not been involved because I have my hands full with my hospital lists these days. Too few surgeons to get through too many people who should have had operations months ago...' She tailed off, then flapped a hand at them. 'You both know how it is in the NHS these days. I'm sure your profession has been similarly affected.'

Malkie nodded. 'It has, Mrs Galbraith. So, when did you become certain?'

'The camp bed. You said you found the remains of what looked like a camp bed and a sleeping bag.'

Malkie nodded.

'William would be the only person who could possibly be in the building at that time of night. We even keep the emergency keys to the building here. If William can't open up for some reason, I do it, but I leave the running of the place to the staff; they've all been with us for many years and know how to run the place by themselves.'

'Aye, a colleague of ours, DC Gooch, interviewed them all. They all spoke very highly of your husband and confirmed that you'd done just as you say on several occasions over the years. But why would he...' – he didn't want to use the word 'lie' – 'Why would he mislead you about his whereabouts that night?'

She dipped her head, swallowed, looked to be fighting back a wave of grief.

'I called the Black Isle Distillery in Inverness. Their business manager has no knowledge of any proposed buy-out. I think William has been trying to find a buyer and failing, and couldn't bear to tell me. I think he got himself so backed into a psychological and emotional corner that all he could do was hide from me, hide from the problem, and drink.'

Tears fell now. 'I can't bear to think of him, alone in the office, in such pain, so frustrated and helpless. We have enough of a retirement pot not to have to worry about the business, but William knew every one of his staff personally, had trained them up from apprentices himself, and I can imagine the most critical factor for him would have been to make sure they didn't need to face redundancy. Fearing for their futures would have hurt him far more than allowing the business to fail.'

Malkie sat forward, tried to close the distance between them. He clasped his hands in front of him, relaxed his whole posture so as to seem as unthreatening as possible.

'Mrs Galbraith, I'm honestly sorry to have to ask you this, but is there any chance...'

She lifted her head, stared at him, intense and challenging. 'No.'

Malkie waited.

'William would never try to carry out an "insurance job".' She laced the two words with distaste, as if the very thought would be disgraceful to both her and her husband. 'He would never contemplate that.'

Malkie watched her try to hold herself together, but she managed only a few seconds. He'd expected either a simple rejection of the idea or maybe indignation, but Galbraith's reaction shook him. She leaned forward, folded in on herself, her arms clutched around her as if she feared she'd fall apart. She sobbed and screamed. She punched the sofa cushions. She howled. Malkie glanced at Steph, who shrugged and looked as confused as he felt.

What the hell?

Malkie's mind went into overdrive. This didn't look like grief; more like a massive over-reaction, fury even. At her husband because she suspected he may have set the fire after all, or...

Were you involved, Mrs Galbraith? Is that what I'm seeing here? Guilt? Did you kill your own husband? No, you loved him, that's clear. Did someone else burn the place for you?

It hit him. She thought he'd gone to Inverness. She believed that.

He felt a sudden and discomforting pang of hope that he might yet find an alternative suspect to Wilson, and kicked himself hard in his mind for being a fucking idiot. Both women had suffered bereavements, one a long-loved husband of decades, the other excited about their first steps on the journey of a life together. He had no reason to hope for one or the other to have been responsible.

Putting either one of them away would feel cruel, regardless of whatever justifications they might claim.

When Galbraith got a hold of herself again, Malkie continued, tentative and delicate.

'Might he have done something... ill-advised, out of love, Mrs Galbraith? Love for you and affection for his staff?'

'No. Never.'

'Mrs Galbraith, are you acquainted with a Mr Peter Fairbairn?'

She stared at him. Her mouth worked but no sound came out. She glanced from Malkie to Steph and back. Then she fell apart again. She fell sideways onto the sofa and wailed, tears pouring from her.

Oh nicely done, arsehole.

Steph cleared her throat, barely audible. Malkie looked at her and she shook her head, again almost imperceptibly.

Malkie stood. Steph stepped forward. She crouched beside Galbraith and eased her back into a sitting position. She took the sodden tissues from Galbraith's hand and passed her some more. Galbraith calmed down, again. Steph tended to have that effect on people; Malkie, the opposite.

'William would never risk that. He just wouldn't. Whoever did...' She stared straight at Malkie and the ice and fury in her eyes shook him.

'They deserve to burn in hell, Detectives.'

Something in her tone sent a chill deep into Malkie's guts.

Galbraith gathered herself with an obvious effort. 'I think I'd like you to leave now, please. I'm very tired.' She stood and as good as herded them to her front door.

After she closed the door on them, they heard her scream and sob and slide down the inside of the door.

Malkie and Steph shared a look.

'We need her back in an interview room.'

Steph nodded. 'And I want to see her phone, her smart watch and her laptop.'

'Why her smart watch?'

'I think I'm having a Columbo moment.'

Malkie's phone buzzed. Sandra Morton's name appeared on the screen. 'Aw, for fuck's sake. I need to take this. I'll see you in the car. Two minutes.'

He waited for Steph to close the driver's-side door, then accepted the call.

'Sandra.'

'Sorry, Malkie. I need to talk to you, and I need to talk to you today.'

Malkie thought through the next couple of hours of his day. It would take Thompson some time to get a warrant for Galbraith's gear. He remembered Rab Lundy's advice about 'ripping that bastard right off'.

'How about right now?'

'Are... Are you sure?'

'Aye, let's get this over with.'

Silence.

'Sandra?'

'I'm here. I can take a long lunch. Where would you like to meet?'

'Costa coffee in the McArthur Glen shopping centre. Twelve thirty.'

'I'll be there. Thanks—'

He hung up on her and got into the passenger side of the pool car.

'Everything OK?'

'Back to the station, please. Can you get Thompson's OK to bring Galbraith in for an interview? And ask her permission to look at her phone. I'd help but I need to meet someone for lunch.'

'Nice.'

'It won't be.'

FORTY-FOUR

Malkie spotted Sandra Morton sitting in one of the McArthur Glen shopping centre coffee shops. He watched her for long minutes but couldn't decide if he wanted some clue as to her state of mind and the reason she'd insisted on seeing him, or feared stepping around the corner and surrendering any chance to walk away without adding to his ignominy.

He had a harsh word with himself; if he didn't face her now, he harboured no doubt she would continue to pester him with texts or show up in person at the station reception desk as she had before. One thing that did not seem to have changed since their doomed relationship more than twenty years ago was her willpower.

He took a breath and walked towards her.

When she saw him, she sat bolt upright in her chair and looked flustered. Malkie had to wonder what she might have to say to him that could have her in such a state, and decided it couldn't be anything he wanted to hear.

He stood at her table but made no attempt to pull a chair out.

She glanced around her, uncomfortable. 'Can you sit down, please?'

'Ten minutes.' He pulled the chair out and sat, his arms folded over his chest.

'Would you like—'

'What I would like is for you to get to the point, Sandra. Why are you so insistent we talk? What do we need to talk about if the daughter you allowed me to believe I had never survived? What could we possibly need to discuss on that topic?'

He became aware that his tone had turned bitter, almost spiteful. He'd promised himself he'd stay on the moral high ground if he did this, would hold back from inflicting the full weight of his loathing on her. Despite what she had her brothers do to him all those years ago, despite them nearly ending his life before he'd had a chance to make a mess of it all by himself, he'd promised himself he'd remain civil. That resolve had lasted all of thirty seconds, and he heard how ugly his tone had turned.

Sandra took a drink of her coffee, a long slow sip he suspected she needed to give her time to summon up courage. She placed the cup back on the saucer, flexed her fingers as if preparing herself for a fight.

'She didn't die.'

Malkie reeled. He stood, stepped backwards, nearly collided with another customer carrying two coffee beakers out of the shop. He didn't apologise, his usual tendency eclipsed by the barely credible realisation dawning in his mind. He walked away a few paces, turned, stared at her, hoped for a sign she was pulling some sick joke, cruel beyond even what he still considered her capable of.

She stared back at him. She looked calm, if anything, as if glad she'd got the words out and now wanted him to sit back down so she could answer him.

He returned to his chair, watched her. Waited. Dared her to

retract, to admit she'd just wanted to lash out and hurt him, or that she was just softening him up for some even more brutal kicking down the line.

He saw nothing but shame.

His mind reeled and he realised she wasn't going to say anything until he told her what he needed to know or hear. Bereft of any better ideas, he opted for the obvious.

'You're lying.'

'I'm not.'

Fuck's sake.

She waited, patient but still visibly nervous.

Malkie's own patience ran out. 'What the fuck are you playing at, Sandra? Why are you doing this? You told me you lost your baby.'

Her eyes took on a pleading expression. '*Our* baby, Malkie.'

This hit him like a juggernaut. '*Our* baby.' *His* baby. Unless he could get her to admit to lying, playing some perverse game to punish him, he had a daughter, and had done for twenty-six years.

He leaned his elbows on the table and covered his face with his hands, like a child hoping that if he couldn't see the bogey-man, it wasn't really there. He felt her hands close on his arms and recoiled from them. 'Don't fucking touch me. Just... Don't.'

She shrunk back into her chair, looked bleaker and more guilt-ridden than he thought anyone without training could ever pretend to be.

'What's her name?' He couldn't believe he asked a question that would make the girl real, cement her in his consciousness as more than just a baby he knew nothing about.

'Jennifer. Her name's Jennifer.'

'Jennifer.' He tried it on his lips, almost felt it embed itself in his consciousness, as if it were already a fundamental part of his life. He couldn't walk away from her now.

Then it occurred to him. 'Why are you telling me this now?

You already put me through the wringer telling me I'd been a dad, then telling me I wasn't. Why tell me this now?'

Even as he asked the question, he knew what the answer would be.

'She wants to meet you.'

He felt a kind of paralysis seize him, a complete inability to even begin to process this. He hadn't stopped reeling from the news that he had a daughter after all, before she hit him with whammy number two.

'Why?' He could find no other words to express an immediate assumption on his part that he could only be a disappointment to the girl. Woman. She'd be twenty-six years old now.

'Because I've told her all about you, from when I knew you at school to what my family did to you – what *I* did to you – right up to the fact that you're a well-known copper who most people seem to respect. She asked me a thousand questions about you, then asked me to ask you if you'll meet her.'

'How long has she known about me?'

Sandra's face fell. 'Not long. I told her I didn't know who you were; one-night stand, you know?'

'And now?'

'When I met you at the Civic Centre, it was because she'd starting asking questions again, said she'd thought long and hard about it and she didn't believe me. She said I came over too emotional whenever she asked me about you for it to have been anonymous one-time sex.'

She took another drink, seemed to need this one for more than a delaying tactic.

'So, I told you I'd been pregnant. To see how you'd react.'

Malkie felt shame of his own sluice through him. 'And I didn't react very gracefully, did I?'

'No, but I can't blame you. Bad enough to find out you'd been a dad for twenty-six years without finding out it was by me of all people. After, you know... You must despise me.'

Malkie deflated. Both times she'd ambushed him at the station he'd been struck by how different she seemed from the Sandra he remembered. He'd allowed himself to admit that people can change that much. He'd changed himself since the trauma of his mum's death, could feel changes in him still in progress every day. Couldn't she have changed just as fundamentally? After all, she'd been the youngest of her siblings, and her brothers and dad had been some of the worst examples of Livi gang culture he could remember. Should he cut her some slack, allow her a chance to show him that she, and her daughter, had managed to crawl out from them and reject them?

She must have sensed these thoughts go through him, because a hopeful gleam shone in her eyes.

He sat forward again, unfolded his arms, clasped his hands on the table in front of him.

'What's she like?'

Sandra smiled now, looked relieved at Malkie's apparent softening and undoubted pride in her daughter. *Her* daughter? He felt far from ready to think of her as *theirs* yet.

'She's a hell of a young lady. I'm very proud of her and I think you will be, too.'

He flashed a warning glare at her.

'If you decide you want to get to know her, I mean.'

Suddenly, even considering the option of refusing his own daughter struck him as about as low as a snake's belly. This threatened to turn into one of those life events that gave him a chance to discover who he aspired to be, to face his own weaknesses and determine if he had it in him to beat them, to rise above them.

Step up. Grow up.

'Tell me about her. I'm not promising anything, but tell me about her.'

'That's fine. She didn't expect a quick decision. It's a huge thing to take in.'

She sat forward now, her whole manner less tense, almost eager to brag about the girl. Woman.

'She works in an advocacy centre. That's where people go to have someone assist them with legal cases and appeals and all sorts of stuff I don't understand.'

'I know what advocacy is, Sandra.'

She blushed. 'Sorry. Of course you do. Well, she's a front-line advisor. They offered her a promotion into management last year, but she refused it, said she could do more good in her own role. I was proud of her for that.'

Fuck's sake. I already have something in common with the girl.

'She's quite a woman, Malkie. Has her own flat on the south side of Livi, saved her own deposit and everything. She goes running most days, even all the way up the Pentlands at the weekends. She's very fit. Vegetarian. No, not vegetarian. She's a pesca... Something.'

'A pescatarian. Means she's mostly vegetarian but eats fish and seafood, I think.'

'Aye that's it. Anyway, she's smart and funny and makes me look like an under-achiever, and I couldn't love her more for that.'

She paused, waited for him to look up from his hands clasped on the table. 'I think you'd love her too, Malkie.'

He could believe that, but feared the girl's opinion of him if, as Sandra clearly wanted, they ever met. Sandra had made it sound like she'd sung his praises, but accepting compliments never sat well with him; he always looked for the 'although...' on the end of anything flattering said to him.

An ugly question bubbled up from his mind. He had no idea if it might be unfair to ask, but he needed to know just how far from the Morton tree Sandra's – and Jennifer's– apple had fallen.

'What does she think about her grandad and her uncle?'

Sandra's smile disappeared. She swallowed, held her fist up to her mouth as if holding in words she might regret. 'She has as little to do with them as she can, Malkie.' She paused, built up to her next comment. 'And so do I.'

He searched her eyes for a lie but found none.

'You might never believe this, but I didn't send my brothers to hurt you that night. I admit I wound them up, exaggerated what a big shite I thought you were and how much you'd hurt me. I was a teenage drama queen whose heart had just been broken and whose pride had been punctured. I was raging and hurting so... I didn't do as much as I could have done to stop them.'

She lowered her eyes again. She seemed to spend a lot of her time feeling humiliated, if he could believe it to be genuine.

'I'm sorry. I really am. But I can't go back and make it so it never happened. I wish I could, Malkie. Honestly.' Tears formed on her eyelashes. She wiped them away and Malkie could swear she did it not to cover her own embarrassment, but so he wouldn't think she'd use them to influence him, to soften him.

'And she wants to meet me? She said that?'

'She made me tell her who you were when she decided I'd been lying to her all those years, then yes, she made me promise to ask you.'

A penny dropped in Malkie's brain, and he felt shitty. 'So, you forced yourself to face a man you could only assume would despise you, to sound out his feelings. For her.'

'Aye. Sorry. I could have handled it better.'

'Me too.'

'When you stomped away like you did, I went to pieces because I thought you wanted nothing to do with her, and I knew that would devastate her. So...'

'You tried again. But when you thought I would never

accept her or want anything to do with her, you told me you'd miscarried to give me an easy way out.'

He thought it through and realised just how much Sandra had to have put herself through to do what her daughter asked.

'Did you tell her I wanted nothing to do with her?'

She grimaced, pulled a face that said *You're going to be angry with me.*

'I lied to her. I told her you were shocked and needed time to think about it. I told her your past with me and my family might make you want to walk away regardless of any feelings you might have towards her.'

Malkie had to reappraise her, found himself glad, after all, he'd given her a fair hearing. 'So, she knows exactly what you did to me, back then?'

'All of it. And she knows better than anyone else how much I regret it all. How much I hate what I did to you. It was unforgivable.' Shame dipped her head again.

Malkie found his decision easy when he forced himself to come to one.

'I'll meet her.'

Sandra's face lit up with relief and joy.

'But you need to be there. And I want to get my current case out of the way before I can concentrate on it. On her.'

'She'll be so happy, Malkie. She's waited three years since I told her, so she can wait another few days.'

'Weeks, maybe. I don't know.'

Without warning, she reached over and took both of his hands in hers. He pulled them away but found a part of him disappointed in himself for doing it.

She looked suitably abashed. 'Sorry. Wasn't thinking.' She tried to look penitent but couldn't keep a smile from her face.

Malkie stood. 'I've got your number. Give me some time to clear my mind a bit, then I'll call you.'

As he walked away, he heard her call after him.

'Thanks, Malkie. You're going to adore her.'

He returned to his previous vantage point and watched her through the glazing of a corner unit. She quick-dialled a number on her phone, said a few words, nodded with a delighted smile, then hung up.

He watched her sit for a few minutes more. She sagged in her chair, looked exhausted. She took a tissue from her pocket and wiped her nose. She didn't get as far as lowering her tissue again before she cried, hunched forward and struggling to hold herself together. People at an adjacent table leaned over and spoke to her. She nodded at them, spoke to them, and they let her be.

Malkie found it harder and harder to see any trace of the despicable and vengeful woman she'd turned into when he dumped her in their teens.

Aye, people can change, right enough.
Fuck.

FORTY-FIVE

After a sit in the cold February sun in the grounds of the Civic Centre to clear his head and settle his nerves, Malkie returned to the CID room and to the comfort of a world he knew, for the most part. The feeling of floundering in a mess of moral and emotional choices when Sandra had turned his life upside down a half hour ago had rattled him. He'd thought he had his past rationalised and compartmentalised and, if not dealt with, at least banished to a place where he could ignore it.

Now, he faced the prospect of meeting his daughter for the first time. His twenty-six-year-old daughter.

He dropped himself into his chair, leaned his elbows on his desk and covered his face with his hands. He knew that far from being concerned or worried about him, anyone but Steph and Thompson wouldn't take much notice, but put it down to yet another Malkie shitshow of his own making. And Gucci; she'd care. Why had he never noticed before that of all the people he came into regular contact with, the only ones he ever felt truly comfortable with, the only ones who seemed not to put him on the defensive, were women? Had he felt that way before losing his mum? Was he looking for a substitute? Could he really be that needy, even him?

He watched Rab Lundy at his desk. Rab had never progressed beyond two-fingered 'hunt and peck' typing, despite every officer in every division of the new, modern and efficient Police Scotland spending more time entering nonsense into on-screen reports than they did actually catching bad people these days. Rab's concentration amused him: intent, focused and determined. Could that be it? Did he find men too simplistic, too prone to convenience thinking, in a world where shades of grey mattered more than most would like to admit? Did men suffer from a form of mental colour-blindness that women didn't? A condition he feared rendered too many men – no, not just men, some women, too – blinkered and dependent on confirmation bias to avoid challenging them too much.

He knew his own life might be far simpler and more pain-less if his stupid head didn't insist on seeing the other side of everything, of playing devil's advocate at the most inappropriate of times.

Malkie saw Rab looking over at him and raised his eyebrows across the CID room.

'Oh, nothing, Rab. Just mulling.'

Rab turned back to his slow and deliberate hunting and pecking. 'I try to avoid excessive mulling unless absolutely necessary, Malkie. Never fails to complicate things.'

Malkie chuckled at Rab's concise summation of all that made the man both frustrating and unreliable at times, but inex-plicably popular.

'By the way, Lin Fraser called for you, said you need to call her about Peter Fairbairn's post-mortem results. And digital forensics emailed us. I think they've had a backlog again, because we've got loads through all at once: Fairbairn's crime-scene photos, his phone records and number, and something about CCTV from the warehouse?'

'Fuck.' Malkie had forgotten about that. Steph had noticed the melted remains of what could only have been a camera high in one corner of William Galbraith's office. He turned to his own desk and opened the case file with more eagerness than he'd felt about this case all week.

He called Lin Fraser first.

'Hi, Malkie. Thanks for calling. I've emailed you the report. Fairbairn did – as I thought – suffer blunt-force trauma to the head. From the burns on the lining of his lungs, it's also clear he regained consciousness and suffered before he died.'

Could you have done that, Sian? Did you need to see him suffer for what you think he did to Duncan?

'Thanks, Lin. Take care, aye?'

'You too, Malkie.'

He laid his phone down on his desk as if afraid it might ring again and further fuck his day up.

He opened the folder of notes from digital forensics. As he'd feared, they'd been able to salvage nothing from the melted lump of plastic and aluminium found beside Fairbairn's body. The call history of the other phone, the cheap Nokia found in his kitchen drawer, yielded two numbers: the first called multiple times over a two-week period, then the last call to a different number that lasted ninety seconds at 23:02 on Monday, the night of the warehouse fire.

The number tickled something at the back of Malkie's too often unreliable memory. He cross-checked it with the numbers of every Person Of Interest logged in the case notes. When he found it, he swore to himself, then reached for his phone and quick-dialled Steph.

'Malkie.'

'Galbraith told us she'd never met Peter Fairbairn, right?'

'Aye.'

'Her personal mobile was the last number Fairbairn dialled on that Nokia we found in his kitchen drawer.'

'Well, bugger me.'

'At 23:02 on Monday.'

'That's right before the 999 call came in for the warehouse fire.'

'Yep. We need her in here, pronto.'

'Are we going to release Wilson?'

'I think so, aye. This introduces enough of a doubt, and everything we have on Wilson is circumstantial. I'll take care of that. And I'll bring Galbraith in, OK?'

'Yes, boss.'

If this panned out the way he hoped it would, or rather the way that would cause him the least personal pain and regret, he'd be left with only the burning down of the warehouse and the death of Duncan Duffy to clear up. He called Callum Gourlay.

'Hi, Malkie. Your timing is perfect. I'm typing up my final FIU report now. I was planning to email you a copy in a couple of hours, but I can give you the good news now. Well, not good news, but better than it could have been.'

'I'd appreciate that, Callum. We've had a break in our other case, Peter Fairbairn's death, so I'm keen as mustard to hear you've made some progress on Duffy's death.'

'I have. I'd love to know what you've found on Fairbairn's case, but I won't insult your professionalism by asking.'

'Thanks, mate.'

Malkie heard Gourlay shuffling papers and humming to himself.

'The source of the fire was electrical. Overloaded socket at the back of the barrel storage area, old gear and a bodged fuse with the wrong rating of wire in it.'

'So, accidental after all?'

'Nope.'

Malkie could swear Gourlay sounded pleased with himself and wanted to be coaxed to impress Malkie with his technical proficiency. It seemed FIU investigators took as much satisfaction from cracking a case as the *polis* did.

'Well? Don't make me ask, Callum.'

'A large skylight directly above the temperature control unit had been opened. It was freezing that night, so cold air would have poured in the opening, right onto the electrics. That would have triggered the thermostat and put the unit into high-output mode. It would have been pumping heat out to balance the cold, to maintain the optimum temperature to mature the whisky.'

'So it drew far more power than usual.'

'Aye, and there were three such units. Even though the other sockets were only five feet away, all three were plugged into a single socket via an extension. Along with a high-wattage arc light someone had just happened to leave switched on. Massive power draw on that single socket, and that rubbish fuse wire.'

'And boom.'

'Well, sparks and flames, but that would have been enough, which leads me on to the clincher. Someone had also hammered a sliver of wood between the staves of a barrel at floor level. The weight of the liquid would have pushed the ethanol out under pressure and probably sprayed it close to, if not all over, the electrics.'

'So. Arson.'

Malkie's mind reeled. To imagine someone would deliberately set the fire knowing what it might do to anyone still in the building, to risk killing someone the way his mum died – he had to choke back a knot of fury that surged within him.

'Malkie? You OK, mate?'

Malkie realised Callum had spoken more than once to him.

'Sorry, Callum. Aye. Please, go on.'

Callum remained silent for a few seconds more, before continuing. 'I was saying that in my opinion born of twenty years in FIU, aye. But we call it willful fire raising, not arson.'

'OK, thanks. What about Duncan Duffy's BA Set?'

'You said Lin Fraser's post-mortem confirmed Duffy died of natural causes, and I can confirm that I've found nothing to indicate any fault in his equipment, or any interference by Fairbairn. That BA Set's regulator, gauge, warning whistle, everything to do with his air supply was functioning correctly and hadn't been tampered with. The neoprene face seal looked slightly degraded but still held its integrity. Steve Grayson agreed with me, confirmed that had been one of the issues he'd reported to Fairbairn repeatedly but been told to leave in service. The whole BA Set has been signed off by me and sent to the manufacturer to confirm our findings, but I can't see them coming to any different conclusions.'

'So why didn't Duffy or Turner hear his whistle?'

Gourlay's hesitated. 'It looks like he snagged his air hose on something, possibly all that junk in the corridor outside the office, and damaged the breathing valve. He must have tripped or fallen though, to snag it hard enough to damage it.'

Malkie remembered stumbling over chunks of blackened wood in the burned-out office, and his momentary feeling of losing his balance.

'So, Duffy just... What? Panicked?'

'I don't think he "just" panicked. I think he was stressed and breathing hard, but not so hard that his colleagues heard it on comms, so he burned through his supply in about half the time the standard calculations would predict for a man of his age, build, fitness levels, etc. A healthy man, that is. Then, when he snagged his air hose and damaged the valve, the remaining pressure in his cylinder expelled the remaining air so quickly that by the time his whistle went off he'd already realised he was in deadly trouble. So yes, he panicked. I defy any person not to panic if they suddenly realise they're ten minutes away from safety through a raging fire and their oxygen supply has dropped by fifty per cent in a minute. When that happened, he was starved of oxygen and his heart rate shot through the roof, and...'

'His cardiac condition.'

'Aye. Cardiomyopathy. Mild and undiagnosed through his entire life, but that night being his first time under real stress and on air, then his air running out so quickly, the stress on his heart, with his underlying medical condition, triggered a heart attack. Nothing more sinister than that. There's been a lot of attention on cardiac screening for SFRS firefighters recently, but either Duffy missed the screening, or his condition was too mild to show up. Until he put himself under so much stress, that is. Then, when he yanked his BA Set off in a compartment full of hydrogen cyanide, the poor sod had no chance.'

'None of that is good news, but better than other explanations might have been, I suppose.'

'Aye.'

'So, Fairbairn didn't cause Duffy's death, then?'

'No, that's down to whoever started the fire. It would only have been a matter of time though, if Fairbairn kept pressuring newbies to cut corners.'

'Which explains Sian Wilson's rage at him at the scene that night.'

They shared a silence for a few seconds.

Malkie sighed. 'I'll need to tell Sian Wilson.'

'Ach, that poor woman. I hope she...'

'Me too, mate. Me, too.'

'And about the other thing? Have you decided what to do about that? Not sure I would.'

'Not yet, Callum. My dad and I need to think it through. Thanks for making me look again, though. At your report, I mean.'

'Sorry it's causing you so much more pain, Malkie.'

'Not your fault. Move on to your next case and leave it to me.'

'Nah, I'm out, mate. Had enough. This one has left such a bad taste, I don't think I have the stomach for the job any more.'

'Want me to let you know what my dad and I decide to do? OK if I ask for your advice?'

Gourlay took a few seconds to answer. 'Aye. I think I do, and I'll help any way I can.'

'You're good people, Callum. Take care.'

'You too, Malkie.'

He headed for the stairwell and the custody suite to process Sian Wilson's release before her brief kicked up a stink.

FORTY-SIX

Steph reached Anna Galbraith's home in minutes. She knocked on the door and rang the doorbell, but got no answer.

She tried the door handle and found it to be unlocked. She and the Uniform she'd dragged along with her – Julie Faulds, a young woman but already with an old head on her shoulders – entered.

The living room had been tidied since her last visit. On the coffee table lay a laptop, a smartphone and a cheap Nokia mobile phone like the one found in Peter Fairbairn's kitchen drawer, Anna Galbraith's smart watch, and an envelope addressed to DS Malcolm McCulloch and DC Stephanie Lang.

Steph sent Faulds back to the pool car for evidence bags.

She unsealed and pulled on a pair of nitrile gloves and picked up the envelope. Galbraith had sealed it shut, so Steph would need to wait, which bothered her more than it should have.

The rest of the property looked show-house immaculate. If not for the items laid out on the coffee table, Steph might have expected her to walk in the door at any moment. When Faulds returned, she bagged and signed all four items and called for a SOCO team.

She apologised to Faulds for having to leave her on scene duty. Faulds shrugged her shoulders, no stranger to long periods of boredom. 'At least it's not raining.'

Steph took the pool car back to the station.

She found Malkie, head down, his brow furrowed in concentration. She peered over his shoulder and saw two sheets of paper, a call log and what looked like a timeline of the night of the warehouse fire. Sometimes, ticking off items on paper with a ballpoint pen felt more thorough than comparing lists onscreen.

She cleared her throat. As she hoped, he jumped in his seat.

'I wish you'd stop bloody doing that.'

'Sorry, boss.' She made sure her tone left no doubt she wasn't. It had become their 'thing' and she'd never tire of it.

She waited until Malkie sat back, threw his pen on the papers and turned to her, a rare look of optimism on his face.

'We found Anna Galbraith's number on Fairbairn's second phone,' he told her. 'Just once, after a succession of calls to only one other number over a two-week period.'

'You told me that already. And I found a second phone of the same model in Galbraith's home along with her laptop and her smart watch. And an envelope addressed to both of us.'

He waited.

'Oh, I don't know what's inside it; it was sealed shut.'

'Bollocks.'

'Quite.'

'And why her smart watch?'

'Not sure. I might have an idea, but it's a bit far-fetched, so ask me later.'

'Fine. I'd bet my pension and yours the number of Galbraith's Nokia is the one Fairbairn dialled a dozen times in two weeks on his.'

'Would be a surprise if not, but let's wait and see, aye?'

'Yes, Steph.'

'Oh, grow up.'

Malkie stood.

'Where are you going now?'

'The canteen. I'm starving.'

'I thought you had a lunch date?'

She saw his face darken, something unpleasant forcing his previous optimism out. 'It wasn't that kind of lunch date. I didn't have much of an appetite as it turned out.'

He left that hanging, refused to elaborate despite her holding her hands out and arching her eyebrows.

He waved her hands down. 'By the way, digital forensics emailed us. I think they managed to salvage some video from that camera you spotted in William Galbraith's office. I'll be back in ten mins, need a pish, too.' He pushed through the doors to the stairwell and almost skipped down the stairs.

Steph allowed herself a small smile at Malkie's apparent distraction by even a possible break in the case.

She logged on and pulled up the case notes, opened the digital forensics folder. An accompanying report advised that the SOCOs had found the camera in Galbraith's office, and several others with cables that led back to a steel cabinet in the corridor outside the office which contained recording equipment. The cables were melted through but the steel of the cabinet had protected the recorder from the fire. The report ended with a recommendation to check out a file called 'V-05022024-2214' first.

She scanned the list, found it and clicked on it.

A video window opened. William Galbraith's office, from

exactly the position where she had spotted the remains of the camera. Galbraith's feet and the corner of a camp bed were visible at the bottom right of the frame, the rest of him off-camera. The bulk of the picture showed the office from Galbraith's desk to the door and the glass walls that looked out into the corridor.

She watched, skipped forward until she spotted movement outside the door.

A man. Tall, dressed all in black. He peered through the glass of the door and down at the outside handle, as if trying to open it. He peered again through the glass, before disappearing.

Even on the grainy, low resolution video, Steph recognised Peter Fairbairn.

Malkie checking the calls against the timeline of the night of the fire made sense now. She scanned his sheets of paper, saw he'd underlined the time of the last call, the time that the 999 call came into the emergency call centre and the time that the SFRS confirmed they were leaving the station to attend. Fairbairn's last call, to Anna Galbraith, fell right in the intervening time period, as Malkie had told her over the phone.

Why use her identifiable number when they'd both had burners? The answer came to her without effort. To make sure Anna Galbraith went down with Fairbairn if his involvement ever came to light.

She checked Lin Fraser's post-mortem report, saw she'd signed off on the final version. Fairbairn had been assaulted then burned alive.

Had Galbraith been the woman old Sidney Baxter claimed to have seen leaving Fairbairn's home? Had she found out Fairbairn had killed her husband of more than forty years?

All of which cast serious doubt on Sian Wilson's guilt, and Steph was surprised to find herself happy about that possibility.

She started scouring every database she could for information that might reveal where Galbraith might have gone. Leaving her phone and laptop laid out so neatly smacked of finality, as if she didn't expect to return home again. A Uniform search of her home had turned up her passport, so they at least knew she'd be unable to leave the country.

FORTY-SEVEN

Three hours later, a package arrived from digital forensics.

Malkie opened it. Thompson and Steph sighed impatiently as he struggled to cut through the tape holding the box shut.

'Fuck's sake, do they not want us seeing what's inside, or what?'

'Language, Malkie.'

'Sorry, boss.'

He finally managed to rip the top flap open. Thompson must have escalated way above her own position to get them to act so quickly. Malkie pulled the contents out and spread them on his desk.

A printed call log from the second phone found on Galbraith's coffee table showed a complete match between it and Fairbairn's burner. Malkie compared them to the case timeline, confirmed that most of the calls had been made during the two weeks before the fire, the call to Galbraith's personal mobile only minutes before the warehouse fire was first reported. They now had CCTV footage of Fairbairn dressed in black and skulking around inside the warehouse less than an hour before the fire was reported, and calls between Galbraith and Fairbairn in the lead-up to the fire.

Thompson confirmed her opinion that the Fiscal would allow them to charge Galbraith based on this.

Malkie opened the evidence bag containing the envelope. Inside, they found a handwritten note signed by Galbraith.

I didn't know Bill had been sleeping in the warehouse, but his death is my fault. Peter Fairbairn set the fire. I've known Peter since we were at school together. He's a greedy, misogynistic pig and I knew he wouldn't say no to £50k. But he was careless and my Bill died. I went to Fairbairn's home to kill him. I once swore an oath to 'do no harm, above all' but Peter Fairbairn deserved to die. He stole everything from me, but I accept that ultimate blame lies with me. I just wanted Bill to stop spending so much of himself for the benefit of others. I wanted him to rest, for once in his life. But I killed him. As surely as if I had started that fire myself, I killed the man who made my life worth living.

After a blank line, it continued.

DC Lang, Remember what I said about smart watches?

'Smart watches? What the hell's that about?' Thompson lifted another evidence bag containing Galbraith's watch.

Steph smiled. 'First time I met her, the day after the fire, her watch buzzed, and she said...' She shook her head as if not believing her own memory.

'She said those things never let you get away with anything.'

'What did she mean by that?'

'I think I can guess. Give me five minutes.'

Steph removed Galbraith's smart watch from the bag and switched it on. She slid her finger around on the glass, sent menus, numbers and graphs sliding all over the screen so fast

Malkie couldn't follow. She showed it to Malkie and Thompson. Malkie saw a spiky graph the width of the watch face with one section of it elevated. He shrugged at Steph. 'Well? What is it?'

'Galbraith's heart rate. Between the time she got the call from Fairbairn on her personal mobile to about three hours later, it went through the roof. Exactly when the firefighters were tackling the warehouse fire; certainly not the kind of time anyone would be exercising.'

She swiped again. 'Same again a half hour before Sidney reported the fire in Fairbairn's home, and it lasted for two hours after that.'

'Fuck me. Any brief will tear that apart, though. Claim she's just been under massive stress because of her husband's death.'

'Except that she didn't even suspect her husband was dead until the day after the fire, when I talked to her. I think it's an apology.'

Thompson frowned. 'For what?'

Malkie got Steph's meaning. 'Could be. Her phone record and the note are as good as a confession, and she'd know that. I'm sure we'll find a fifty grand payment from her to Fairbairn. You think she needed to apologise to *someone* for killing her husband? The arson was deliberate, but her husband's death? Accidental. I think she really believed he'd gone to Inverness. Poor cow.'

Thompson scowled. 'Poor cow? Duncan Duffy died trying to fight a fire she paid Fairbairn to set, and you feel sorry for her?'

'She made a mistake, boss. A stupid one, aye. But remember the CCTV footage? Fairbairn checked inside the office and down the corridor outside, even though he set the fire. If he was – as most people seem to believe – a low-life pig, would he have bothered to check no one was in a building he'd expect to be empty at that time of the night?

Galbraith must have told him to. She wasn't taking any chances.'

'Ach, this is all conjecture, Malkie. It makes a kind of sense, but it's only one possible explanation.'

'I agree, but we have her note, her burner-phone log, and I'll bet my pension we'll find a fifty grand payment from her account to Fairbairn.'

Thompson stretched her arms above her head and arched her back. She grunted as she straightened again. 'Where the hell is she now, though?'

An idea tickled the back of Malkie's mind. 'Steph, that smart watch of hers – does it have any routes saved in it she might have walked or run?'

Steph fiddled with the watch again and nodded. She handed it back to him. 'Knock yourself out, mate.'

She stood, yawned, stretched her back and grabbed her jacket. 'I need some air. I might just head home if you don't mind, bosses. I'm knackered. If I'm honest, I feel like I might need a wee breakdown after all the shite with Dean and Barry, but you tell a soul I admitted that and I'll kill you, right?'

Thompson stood too. 'Is it really affecting you that badly, Steph?'

'Aye, and that infuriates me, boss. I think – in time – I can deal with what that bastard did to my mum, and maybe even process the fact that half of me comes from such a piece of shite and there's nothing I can do about it, but...'

Thompson waited.

'I lost control. I've been all over the place this week, and I think I hate those bastards more for making me such a waste of space this week than for any of the rest of it.'

She looked mortified. 'I let you down, bosses.'

Thompson made a move towards Steph, but Malkie beat her to it. He gripped her shoulders in his hands. 'You stop that shite, right now. You've never let us down. Never.'

Thompson nodded. 'He's not often right but he's bang on about that, Steph.'

Malkie ignored her. 'You're the best Police Scotland detective constable called Steph I've ever met, and I don't care who hears me say that.'

Both laughed and Steph pushed him away from her. He suspected tears were not far from her eyes.

Thompson pulled her own coat on and grabbed her bag. 'You're an idiot, Malkie. Both of you, get yourselves home. It's been a rotten week and there's not much we can do now until we locate Galbraith.'

Steph gave her a Girl Guide salute. 'Yes, boss.' Thompson left.

Malkie grabbed his wallet and car keys from his desk. 'An early night sounds perfect, but I have a stop to make on the way.'

'OK, I hope it's nothing too stressful. G'night, mate.'

Stressful? Fucking shitting myself, Steph.

FORTY-EIGHT

As soon as Dean Lang opened his front door, Malkie piled into the fucker before his nerves could talk him out of it.

He manhandled him backwards until he fell on his sofa and stood over him.

Lang stared up at him, his eyes wide and bewildered, but furious too. 'Who the fuck are you?'

'My name is Malkie, and if I ever find out you've lodged a complaint about Steph again, I'll fucking kill you.'

He leaned close, forced Lang to back up, even draw his legs up in a defensive posture.

'Now, have I made myself clear?' Malkie could barely believe he was doing this, struggled to believe the man wouldn't see through his genuine rage to the terrified coward beneath.

'Ye... Yes. Fine. I'll withdraw my complaint.'

'No, you won't. You'll say that fucker attacked her first and she lost control only because he goaded her. You'll say she defended herself, and you'll say fuck all more about it. Steph will weather this and come out of it stronger than ever, and you will never – and I mean fucking never – talk to her again or come within a hundred yards of her. If I see or hear about that happening...' He cast his eyes around the room and inspiration hit him. He opened the balcony door then pulled Lang up and out of the sofa by the front of his jumper. The man was bigger, but Malkie was running on fury. He dragged Lang, too stunned to resist, out into the freezing night air, pushed him against the parapet, and leaned him over.

Lang squealed and whined, all fight draining from him.

'If any of what I just said happens, or if that fucker Barry tries to lodge a complaint, I *will* come back here, and you *will* suffer an unfortunate accident. And I'll sleep well for having improved the West Lothian gene pool immeasurably. Now, have I made myself crystal fucking clear?' He punctuated each word with a push that could have tipped Lang over if Malkie had let go.

'Yes. Fuck's sake, aye.'

Malkie let him go. He slid down onto his backside and trembled. Malkie turned to leave.

'Fuckin' wee skank isn't worth it, anyway.'

Malkie's foot had buried itself in Lang's gut before he knew he was going to do it. He pulled himself away and felt he'd had a small taste of what had made Steph do so much worse to Barry.

Inspiration hit him again. 'Did she mention chicken wire to you?'

Lang's eyes widened in renewed fear.

'I thought she might. Chicken wire and big fuck-off boulders. Don't forget, because *I* won't.'

Back in his car, seven floors below, he sat at the wheel and shook and choked back stomach acid until the adrenaline drained from his system.

He hoped he'd never have to follow through on his threat, but realised, in a dark part of himself where he rarely looked, that he could.

. . .

Malkie almost couldn't bring himself to get out of the car when he reached the LESOC. He knew which window was Deborah's now, and her lights still burned. He remembered Dame Helen Reid telling him she'd started taking her meds an hour later than before, just in case. He didn't find that nearly as 'sweet wee crush' as him knowing which window was hers, but it did mean she'd placed him high on her list of people who mattered to her.

But as of this evening, he wasn't the man she believed belonged on that list. Far from proud of his treatment of Dean Lang, but at the same time devoid of doubt that it had been the right thing to do. He felt more conflicted than he could remember, even in the days after his mum's death.

Had he stepped over a line he might never be able to justify to himself, never mind in the opinion of others? Steph's future just could not have been left in the gift of that animal. A good copper and a fine human being, not to mention the best mate he could wish for, being at the mercy of the whim of a low-life mouth-breather like Dean Lang offended natural justice.

But still... If Steph ever found out, he couldn't decide if she'd thank him or crucify him.

He reached for the door handle but let it go again. He'd been in this situation before: desperately wanting the company of another but fearful of the things he might feel obligated to say. Things that might ruin something good in his life, another reason to believe himself redeemable.

Would Deborah understand? Or would she lose all faith in him, replaced with disappointment he could never recover from?

He reached for the door handle again, but again let it go. He felt like weeping, wanted Deborah's comfort but knew – at least until he'd had a chance to process his actions – he'd confess all to her, wouldn't be able to hide his worry from her and wouldn't be able to refuse her plea to understand. He drove off again and hoped to hell neither she nor Dame Helen had seen him pull up in the first place.

Malkie's dad expressed his delight in seeing his son home for dinner before the bats had started their nocturnal dances for a change. His delight lasted until Malkie sat at the table, pushed his meal aside and placed a sheaf of papers in its place.

His dad reached for it, never one to shy away from something he needed to face up to. Malkie slapped his hand down on it, stopped him from sliding it towards himself.

It took him long moments to choose the most appropriate – or at a minimum the least hurtful – way to warn him. He saw that his dad had picked up on his concern anyway, and lifted his hand.

Malkie waited, counted the pages, his anxiety building with every new sheet his dad started on. When he got to page seven, Malkie leaned forward, clasped his hands on the table, braced himself.

He couldn't be sure if his dad made it to the bottom of the page, but he certainly didn't turn to page eight. He dropped the papers on the table.

Malkie waited, couldn't think of a single fucking thing to say.

His dad stood, seemed to try to find words but gave up. He turned away, then back, again failed to find words, then walked away towards the reservoir shore like a man in shock.

No, not like a man in shock. A man in a state of total emotional crisis.

Malkie gave him three minutes, then joined him. His dad stood on the shore, staring off into the darkness towards the lights of the scattering of houses that gave the reservoir its name and the glow of Edinburgh beyond the intervening hills.

'Does that mean what I think it means, Malkie?'

'I don't know, Dad. Could she have got herself out of bed to light one of the candles on her windowsill, the ones she'd never lit before in twenty years?'

'No, son. She couldn't. Towards the end, she...' He couldn't finish.

'I don't know what to do with this, Dad. I really don't. And I don't know what you want me to do with it.'

His dad crouched down, stirred the surface of the water, smooth as glass in the absence of the slightest breeze until his fingers made both their reflections fragment and dance. Malkie looked for tears falling into the water but saw none.

When he spoke again, his dad's voice chilled him more than he could ever remember in his forty-five years.

'If you decide someone did this, son, then I want the fucker found. You find him and...'

He stood, wiped his hands together and walked back towards the cabin. He didn't look back.

Malkie wanted to throw up. He couldn't bring himself to believe someone had murdered his mum, despite his career having left him with no remaining capacity for doubt that any one of the worst examples of humanity he'd helped to put away could do this and worse.

He headed for his bed, his meal still on the table, uneaten and ignored, his dad's bedroom door closed and the light off.

Maybe he would be able to think more clearly in the morning.

He knew he wouldn't.

FORTY-NINE

'I'm getting a distinct feeling of déjà vu, Dirty Old Man.'

Dame Helen Reid tutted and shook her head but didn't lift her eyes from her book.

Malkie's dad spluttered a mouthful of cocoa. 'Are you talking to me, young lady?'

'No, Dad, she's talking to me. It's a long story.'

Deborah beamed an evil grin at Malkie, and he couldn't help but smile.

'Well, that's progress, at least.'

'What is?'

'A smile. You've been a misery guts since we arrived.'

'I'm sorry. Just work stuff.' He cast his eyes out across the black waters of the Harperrig Reservoir, hoped she wouldn't dig any further.

I'm so tired of feeling guilty for doing the right thing.

Dad stood. 'Time for bed. It's been lovely seeing you again, Deborah.' He leaned over and kissed her on the top of her head. 'And you, Helen.' He did the same to her. She looked up, scandalised, but they all saw a delighted gleam in her eyes. Deborah and Malkie looked at each other, then burst into laughter like Malkie had been thinking he might never enjoy again.

Dame Helen adjusted her cardigan and her coat and patted the bun in her hair as if checking her decency remained intact after Dad's scurrilous attack on her person.

Dad winked at Malkie and Deborah, then headed inside.

Dame Helen closed her book. 'I'm going to get the van ready, Deborah. It's late.' She stood.

Deborah pouted, petulant and pleading. Only the undamaged side of her face changed but as always with her, it made Malkie's heart sing.

Dame Helen's shoulders sagged. 'I might need some time to disentangle the anchor straps, or something.' She winked at them and walked off towards the LESOC minibus.

Deborah turned a serious face on Malkie. 'Fess up, Dirty Old Man. What's wrong?' The worry on her face melted his resolve and he decided to share some of it with her, figured he owed her that much.

'It's this case we're hoping to wrap up tomorrow. It's been a bit ugly.'

'How?' He knew she needed to ask out of concern for him, maybe an attempt to make him share some of his load with her. For a woman with trouble enough on her own plate she seemed to possess vast reserves of compassion and affection for others. He'd never deserve her.

Stop that shite. We deserve each other.

He gathered his thoughts, wanted to give her the whole story, but without the ugliest parts.

'Someone did something technically naughty but not actually bad. But it went wrong, and her husband died because of what she did. A firefighter died tackling the fire that she'd had someone start, that she'd caused, albeit indirectly. Then the guy she paid to start the fire was murdered. We had one person in custody for it, but I couldn't believe her capable. Same as

Walter Callahan all over again. She's been released now, but the firefighter who died was her fiancé. They were supposed to get married next month.'

Deborah's mouth hung open, revealing perfect white teeth that her accident had somehow failed to damage. She licked her lips and swallowed.

'That's horrible. Is every case you have to work as ugly as that?'

Yes. Sometimes uglier.

'No. This one just got a bit messy. Unpleasant. That's all.'

She stared at him. Her expression told him she saw straight through his well-intentioned fib.

Dame Helen returned from the minibus. 'Are you ready, Deborah? I know it's a beautiful evening...' She breathed deep and scanned the glow on the dark horizon from Edinburgh, across the peaceful water. 'But you need your meds, or you'll feel rotten in the morning.'

'Yes, Mum.' Deborah's eyes glittered and she half-smiled.

Dame Helen reached for the handle of Deborah's wheelchair, but she waved her away.

'No. I'm doing this.'

Dame Helen tried again. 'I don't think that's wise, Deborah. The ground here is quite uneven.'

'I'll be fine. Won't I, Malkie?'

Malkie smiled, felt his heart swell in his chest. 'Aye. You will.'

He stood and walked around the table to the side of her chair. He didn't take her arm, didn't touch her, knew she had something to prove.

She placed her arms in the plastic loops of her crutches and stood, with difficulty and a pained grunt. Dame Helen stood in front her, within catching distance, her face a picture of concern.

Deborah walked, unaided, the fifteen feet to the minibus.

Malkie walked beside her, ready to catch her if needed. Dame Helen followed with the wheelchair.

Sweat beaded on Deborah's brow. She bit her lip in concentration. Twice she had to stop, but Malkie refused to touch her.

Dame Helen went past her with the chair and waited at the ramp into the minibus.

Deborah took five more steps before wobbling. 'Oh shit. Chair, please.'

Dame Helen pushed the chair under her bottom and Deborah flopped into it. She breathed hard for a few seconds, then beamed at them both.

'I'm going to be on Indie again in no time.' Her eyes crinkled with glee.

Malkie looked to Dame Helen. 'Indie?'

'Her horse.'

'Ah.'

Dame Helen wheeled a knackered and sweat-soaked Deborah up the ramp and into the minibus. While she fastened the retaining straps, Malkie opened the side door and leaned in.

'You're unstoppable, you are.'

She grinned. 'Better believe it, Dirty Old Man.' She reached for his hand, and he laced his fingers in hers, felt the soft touch of her scarred skin, and had to choke back tears of pride.

'Oh, stop that. You'll set me off.' Her eyes glistened.

'Sorry. I'm just so damned proud of you, you know?'

'And I'm proud of you, Malkie.'

He frowned at her, felt about as undeserving of her admiration as he thought possible.

'I know you doubt yourself. Every day. And I know you underestimate yourself, too. And it annoys me.' Deborah leaned forward and beckoned him closer with one finger. He leaned in. She grabbed his jacket collar and pulled him to her. She kissed him, then rested her forehead on his.

She whispered to him. 'I see you, Malkie. And I couldn't be

happier that I met you. And I'm known for being an excellent judge of character. Isn't that right, Dame Helen?'

Malkie looked behind him and saw Dame Helen waiting to get in to fasten the last of the anchor straps. He stepped back and she fastened the last buckle. When she turned back, she winked at Malkie.

'In most cases, Deborah, yes.'

He reached in again and they held hands for another few seconds, then he stepped back and slid the side door closed. Deborah yawned. Dame Helen climbed into the driver's side.

As the minibus pulled away, Malkie saw Deborah wave to him, and wondered what the hell he'd been doing to deserve such a blessing to enter his life.

He returned to his seat on the deck. Dad would be asleep by now. He watched bats flutter and listened to the soft gurgle of a stream feeding into the reservoir off to his left somewhere. He remembered nights like this as a boy. He and his mum used to sit in the dark and she'd hum old songs to herself.

Tomorrow, he'd find Anna Galbraith and bring her home to face the tragic fallout from her misguided actions. He couldn't bring himself to despise her. He almost pitied her, until he reminded himself of the damage she'd done.

His thoughts returned to Callum Gourlay's FIU report sitting in a file box under his bunk.

What do I do about that, Mum?

FIFTY

In the cool night air of Inverkip Marina, Anna Galbraith decided to give herself ten more minutes before ending her life.

She slipped her shoes off and stretched her legs out across the cockpit of the boat on which she and Bill had planned to cruise into a long retirement. She sipped her Chardonnay, the best bottle from their ridiculously expensive temperature-controlled wine cabinet back at home. It had taken a monumental amount of pressure to get her solicitor to amend her will and find someone to witness it in just a single afternoon, but she'd known she had limited time to leave her affairs in order. Three cousins and the six employees of the William Galbraith Independent Bonded Warehouse would soon become wealthier to the tune of three hundred thousand pounds each after the sale of the house, the liquidation of the company's few remaining assets and the sale of the ground on which a burnt-out shell of a once bustling building sat.

She believed William would have approved.

Even so, she wept. The lights from the cluster of houses in Ardhallow, across the sea loch, turned into blurred sparkles of red and white and green, until she pulled a tissue from her sleeve and dabbed at her eyes. She'd taken the utmost care in choosing an outfit and applying her make-up in order to leave this world looking as good as the night William had dropped to one knee and proposed to her within three minutes of their first meeting, in front of a laughing and cheering mob of friends and family on the night of Hogmanay 1979. She remembered feeling – even as she'd helped him to his unsteady feet and dragged him under a sprig of mistletoe – a deep attraction to him and maybe, deep down, had known this drunk but charming man would form a significant part of her life in some way.

And now, forty-five years later, she missed him. More than missed him.

She'd never been a religious woman and even now felt no desire to undergo some convenient deathbed conversion in a vain effort to ease her passing. And besides, she didn't deserve any such comfort.

She downed the last of her Chardonnay and checked the weather forecast again. Not long now. The sky had clouded over, and she prepared herself. She fingered the syringe of morphine she'd stolen from her ward at St John's. She'd already fitted a cannula into the crook of her elbow, and she now inserted the needle into it and laid the syringe on her arm.

While she would never be so self-delusional as to blame Fairbairn completely for William's death – ultimate culpability for that lay firmly with her and she meant to settle that account now – but the man couldn't have looked carefully enough if he genuinely hadn't seen William asleep on the floor of his office.

Fine drops of rain landed on her hands. Tiny, soft, gentle prickles of cold. She leaned back in her chair and turned her face to the heavens. To the sky, she corrected herself.

It had rained on the day they were married, and she remembered William refusing to allow it to dampen their day. He had ordered an open-topped carriage for their departure from the church, without checking the forecast for the day. They had laughed like teenagers as rice and rain fell on them together. By the time they climbed into the carriage, they were both soaked and loving every second of it.

She enjoyed the feel of the soft drops on her face for a few minutes. Something inside her ticked over and she knew the time had come.

As she reached for the syringe, she didn't ask her husband for forgiveness because she simply didn't believe anything of him – of any of us – survived beyond death. She did, though, feel a brief pang of envy for those who did.

Before she could complete her final crime, she heard footsteps on the pontoon. Curiosity stilled her hand, and she pulled her sleeve down to her wrist to hide her intentions.

* * *

Malkie stopped beside the boat and looked at Galbraith as if awaiting permission to board.

She sighed. 'How?'

'GPS on your smart watch. Every second weekend, out and around the sea loch then back. Those things really don't let you get away with anything, do they?'

She smiled, and Malkie figured she was happy to realise her message had been interpreted correctly.

He placed one foot on the gunwale of the deck. 'May I?'

She nodded.

He boarded, stepped into the cockpit and sat opposite her.

'You're used to boarding a boat, Mr McCulloch.' She smiled at him, looked gracious and appreciative, but haunted, too.

He tried to smile. 'Aye. My dad owns a boat. We've yet to make much use of it, but we plan to. He and my mum wanted to cruise the Scottish coastline, but we lost her.'

Galbraith's smile evaporated. Something like shame crossed her face. And empathy.

Malkie leaned back against the inside of the cockpit and stuffed his cold hands into his coat pockets. 'I'm guessing you and your husband had similar plans?' He poured all the sympathy he could muster into it, his voice gentle.

She nodded. Her eyes glittered and reflected the lights from the marina behind him.

'I need you to return to Livingston with me, Mrs Galbraith. You need to come back.'

She rubbed her arm, used the motion to lift her sleeve and reveal the syringe sticking out of the cannula.

No, no, no.

'Don't, Mrs Galbraith. Please don't.'

She placed her fingers on the end of the plunger. Malkie realised he had no chance of stopping her if she decided to do it.

'This isn't the path to take, Mrs Galbraith. This isn't right. Can't you see that?'

She stared at him. Tears brimmed and spilled from her eyes, and Malkie knew she intended to never see another new day. Grief filled him. Despite what this woman had done, he found himself unable to think of her as evil. Misguided, yes. Foolish and naive, her actions as understandable as they were unforgivable.

'Bill wouldn't want this, would he? For you to do this? I can't imagine that.'

Her eyes hardened, and Malkie knew he'd – yet again – said exactly the wrong thing.

'Bill is gone, Mr McCulloch. There's nothing left of him except how I remember him. I'm not following him, because he's nowhere and nothing now. As I deserve to be.'

Before he could reach for her, she depressed the plunger. He threw himself across the space between them and yanked the needle from her arm, even as he feared the action to be futile.

'Morphine, Mr McCulloch.' She studied the syringe in his hand. 'Probably still enough, but I accept that you had to try. This is my area of expertise, so please take my word for it that there's nothing you can do now. So, please, just keep me company for a few minutes. Can you do that for me, Mr McCulloch, after what I've done?'

Malkie's heart wept and a cold wave of regret sluiced through him. He watched her fade. It took only minutes. She settled herself into a position she wouldn't easily slide from, closed her eyes, heaved in three sudden and desperate breaths, then went still.

Malkie checked her pulse and found only the faintest sign of her fading life. He figured that given her circumstances he might well have chosen the same for himself. Or rather, old Malkie might have. Now, he rejected the thought, found it offensive to even consider throwing away what he'd worked so hard to learn to appreciate in his life.

He watched Galbraith, still and quiet, and realised a part of him envied her.

'No. Fuck that.' He stood, put two fingers to his lips and whistled. The two Uniforms he'd instructed to wait at the head of the pontoon appeared. One stopped short, his shoulders sagged as he reached for his Airwave and requested an ambulance. Malkie heard the words, but they washed over him. Nobody would blame him for failing to stop Galbraith from taking her own life. Or rather, no one other than himself. But he knew if he'd done nothing he'd carry her death with him for an age before letting it go, if he ever could.

He called Steph. She answered after only one ring, then he found he could get no words out.

FIFTY-ONE

Malkie stared at the back of Steph's head, and he could swear –
somehow – she knew.

'I can feel you watching me. It's annoying.'

He smiled but erased it when she turned her chair to look
at him.

'Well? Have you decided?' She crossed her legs and folded
her arms, and her eyes dared him not to answer.

'Yes. I'm going.'

She shook her head, her eyes disbelieving. 'Why? What the
hell do you think it can achieve? Shouldn't you make any
conversations on the record, now we've charged her?'

He shrugged, found some imaginary fluff to pick from his
trousers. 'I feel like I owe her that much. Sian Wilson, too.'

'No. Steer clear of Wilson. I spoke to her. She doesn't blame
you for suspecting her but she's still hurting far too much to
make time for you.'

She unfolded her arms but only to run her hands through
her hair and stretch her head back, as if she needed to ease a
kink from her spine before starting on him.

Malkie wondered for only a few seconds if he'd get a chance

to clear the air with Wilson, apologise to her, before deciding that was one itch he'd never get to scratch.

Steph, as ever, seemed to read his thoughts.

'We did our job, and she knows that. If anything, she appreciates you listening to her, but best to leave well alone there. And as for Galbraith, I can believe she never wanted anyone to get hurt, but that doesn't forgive her for setting off Fairbairn's actions. I almost feel for her. I really do. But she brought this on herself, and on her husband. But Sian Wilson – totally different. You can't help who you fall in love with, and by all accounts she was doing what she could do to secure herself a transfer, to fix things so she and Duffy could stay together. If you ask me, Sian Wilson deserves a hell of a lot more sympathy than Galbraith ever will.'

She took a breath, and her look softened. 'You can't keep doing this, mate. You did what you could. You always do. Sometimes it's enough, but sometimes...'

'I know. You're right. You're always right. It's one of your most endearing features.'

She gave him a look. *Really?*

'But I can't help it, Steph. Galbraith did what she did out of love, too. She'd been watching her husband eat himself up from the inside trying to save a business they had no need to save, except for the people whose jobs depended on it. Who knows how long he'd been lying to her, trying to find a buyer and failing. Can you imagine the sense of failure that poor sod must have felt? More than a dozen people relying on him for their livelihoods. Their families. Their retirements. The man was a bloody saint. No wonder he'd turned to the bottle. I just hope he was so pissed he didn't suffer too much. Fuck's sake, he was ten times the man—'

She cut him off with one of her infamous hard stares, dared him to turn his admiration for one man into habitual criticism of himself.

'OK. You know what I mean.'

'Yes, mate. I know exactly what you mean and what you mean is complete shite.'

He held his hands up in surrender. No point arguing with someone who knew you better than you knew yourself and who was never afraid to re-educate you accordingly.

'So, you're insisting on visiting her in hospital?'

'Aye, and I'm going to the Glasgow Necropolis for that memorial service that Gourlay told me about. He said the numbers dwindle every year, so I thought I'd pay my respects.'

He stood, grabbed his jacket from the back of his chair.

Steph stood too. 'You want me to come with you?'

He studied her, knew only too well how uncomfortable she'd be facing Galbraith. 'Thanks, partner, but no. This is personal, and I'm not sure I even understand it myself.'

Galbraith lay in a private room in St John's, a Uniform seated outside the door looking bored. Malkie nodded at him as he reached for the door handle. The man nodded back.

Another new face. Looks barely old enough to shave. I'm getting too old for this shite.

As he eased the door closed behind him, Galbraith opened her eyes. The look she cast on him would haunt him for years. Had he expected gratitude for saving her life? Shame at what she'd done? Resentment at him stopping her from releasing herself from her self-imposed purgatory?

He saw only grief, and he knew in a second that she'd not live beyond her first month in prison. He doubted she'd spend long on suicide watch; she was too smart and savvy a woman to languish long in self-pity and self-recrimination that would give any therapist cause to extend her heightened scrutiny. Then she would find a way. A way out.

He pulled a chair to her bedside. Her eyes followed him. He saw no ill-feeling, saw nothing. She was dead inside already.

'I'm sorry.' The words shamed him even as he said them, sounded pitiful and inadequate for what he'd done to her. He'd imposed a second life sentence on her, above and beyond whatever the court would hand down. One sentence she'd cut short by ensuring the other lasted only as long as she could endure.

He'd hoped for a 'You were only doing your job' or maybe a 'Not your fault' but got nothing. A tear dropped from her eye onto her cheek and ran down to her lips. She seemed not to notice.

He leaned forward, rested his elbows on his knees, brought himself closer to her, felt all wrong to look down at her, as if she might think him sitting in judgement on her.

'You understand I—'

'Was only doing your job? Yes, I get that, Detective McCulloch. Don't worry, your conscience should be clear. You had no choice.'

He wondered if she meant what she said. Did some scrap of compassion remain in her for the situation she'd put him in? Did her own sense of right and wrong demand she do what she could to minimise the damage her actions inflicted on others? Or had she just reprimanded him for his self-indulgence, his need to hear her forgive him?

'I was going to say I couldn't let you throw your life away.'

Pain flashed across her features, and more tears spilled.

You idiot. What life, now?

He couldn't hold her gaze. He found no blame in it, no condemnation, no resentment, but the bleak misery in it burned him to his core. As much as he'd tell himself a thousand times he had no moral choice but to yank that needle from her arm before she pushed the whole dose of morphine into herself, he suspected he wouldn't stop regretting his actions until – if – he got word she'd finished the job from inside a cell in Cornton

Vale. Until he knew she'd got what she wanted without him having been party to it.

She turned onto her side, away from him. He stood, scoured his mind for something, anything, to say that wouldn't sound hollow, and failed. As he reached for the door handle to leave, he heard her voice one last time, small and weak and lost.

'Why couldn't you tell me, Bill?'

He swallowed tears of his own and left.

He found himself ashamed to hope she wouldn't make it as far as the court hearing, because he didn't think he could bear to testify against her.

Back at the station, he spotted Steph's car still parked long after dark, and figured he owed it to her to report back in. The climb up the stairwell to the CID room took him an age, as he chewed over the past hour and what he could possibly take away from it.

Steph stood as he entered. From anyone else he might think she was offering a hug, but she folded her arms and made no move towards him.

'How did it go?'

He sighed, folded his arms in front of him as if to hold himself together. 'Oh, you know. Hugs, tears, mutual support. She asked if we can be pen-pals, maybe do lunch when she's done her time.'

'That bad, eh?'

'Worse. I don't think she blames me for saving her, but fuck knows she wishes she'd never met me. I think she'd have preferred some other copper who might have had the guts to just watch her die. I think my wanting to reach out to her just made her more ashamed of what she'd done. Like she felt the last thing she deserved from anyone was understanding or compassion.'

She arched one eyebrow but didn't pursue the obvious next comment.

Malkie sat. She pulled her chair over and did the same. 'So, don't expect her to survive whatever time she gets in Cornton Vale?'

'Not if she can help it. I think she'll display the perfect mix of remorse and acceptance of her sins, just long enough to get herself off suicide watch, then she'll finish the job.'

Steph sighed, and Malkie had to wonder if she finally felt something for Galbraith or just feared Malkie would be counting the days until the news of her death let him off a hook he'd hang himself on.

'What about you?'

She scowled at him. 'What do you mean? I'm fine.'

'Bollocks.'

She shrugged. 'I will be.'

He waited. She buckled.

'I will. Thompson told me my pig of a stepfather seems reluctant to follow up his complaint about me. I'll still have some difficult questions to answer, and even the abandoned complaint will stay on my record, but Thompson's confident no further action will be taken.'

Malkie forced his face to remain neutral; if she'd heard about his visit to warn the fucker off, she'd have said something by now. Looked like Dean Lang and Barry Boswell had taken Malkie's warnings seriously, which amazed him, given he'd been shitting himself throughout the incident.

'Good. I have no trouble believing that lowlife deserved whatever you did to him.'

'He did, but that didn't give me the right to do it. I need to be better than that, Malkie.'

'You are. We all have our limits, our triggers. I'm just amazed you took as much as you did before you snapped. I'd have kicked the shit out of the fucker long before now.'

She laughed. 'You? Bless. I can't imagine you giving anyone a kicking, mate. You just don't have it in you, poppet.'

Yes, I bloody do, Steph.

'But how are you coping with it? You know? What you found out?'

She thought for several seconds, then turned a look on him he found himself beyond happy to see. She'd survive this, come out of it stronger.

'Ach, when I think it through, what can I possibly find to blame myself for, or hate myself for? It all happened, by definition, before I was born. And...' She considered again. 'We're not our parents, are we? Or rather, we don't have to be. I can choose to hang on to the best of my mum and wipe out every trace of my rapist uncle. It's my choice, right?'

Malkie's heart swelled. He had ten years on her but knew he'd never meet a wiser person. Not for the first time, he realised he fully expected to have to call her 'boss' one day – Gucci, too – and he found himself perfectly comfortable with that prospect.

'You're twice the man I'll ever be, Steph.'

She stared at him, but he saw the twinkle in her eye that nobody else would. 'Is that supposed to be a compliment? Rab Lundy told me to "man up" last week. He won't do that again. Point taken, old man?'

Malkie winced, then chuckled. He opened his mouth to reply, but she stood.

'Just say "Yes, Steph."'

He grinned at her, cared not a jot if the depth of his fondness for her came across loud and clear.

'Yes, Steph.'

She nodded her approval, punched him on the arm, then left.

Malkie stared at his PC and his desk phone for long minutes. He had two jobs to do before he'd allow himself to go home to his dad, to the cabin and – he hoped – a rare weekend off which he intended to spend doing as little as possible beyond drinking coffee and napping on the porch.

He typed up an email to Thompson, informing her that new evidence may have come to light which might cast doubt on his mum's accidental-death verdict. He felt bile rise in his throat as he considered the effect a new investigation might have on him and on his dad. Callum Gourlay's revelations about the candle that started the fire threatened to stir up a huge amount of grief and pain that they'd only just begun to process, but he knew that neither he nor his dad would be able to settle for anything less than a full re-investigation, regardless of what else might come to light.

He saved the email in his drafts folder, to reread before hitting the send button on Monday morning and spinning his life and that of his dad's off into unknown and doubtless harrowing directions.

Then he called Sandra Morton to ask her to arrange dinner for three.

Time to meet Jennifer, the daughter he realised he now couldn't wait to meet.

A LETTER FROM THE AUTHOR

I hope you enjoyed this, my third book, and I hope you found yourself enjoying Malkie's slow and painful journey to repairing and redeeming himself. If you'd like to join other readers in hearing all about my latest releases, you can sign up here:

www.stormpublishing.co/doug-sinclair

And can I ask you to be kind enough to leave a review of this book on Amazon? Let me know what you liked and what you didn't like, what resonated with you and what really didn't. I need to know so I can grow as a writer and help Malkie be a better man.

Book four will see Malkie meet a man whose small but precious life falls apart because of his own actions, but for reasons Malkie struggles to blame him for. Meeting another person who messes up trying to do the 'right thing' and the fallout from his appalling discovery during book three drags Malkie back to the edge of a deep, dark, hole of self-doubt and self-recrimination, and he finds himself relying on the love and support of his small circle of friends more than ever.

As I said about books one and two, I never set out to write police procedurals in the traditional sense. I want to write books about the impacts of terrible acts inflicted by ordinary but desperate human beings on others. I admire all good, decent, police officers who face the ugliest aspects of society every day, and who more and more suffer scorn and abuse arising from the awful acts of only a tiny minority of their ranks, from the very people they clock on every day to serve and protect.

Similarly, if I've messed up any of my research into the practises and processes and rules and regulations that firefighters have to navigate every time they risk their lives to save those of us, the great unwashed public, please accept my apologies. Knowing what technical facts to leave in and what to take out of a book like this cause me much worry that I'll offend or insult the brave and inspiring professionals of the SFRS and other firefighting forces.

Please check out my website at www.dougsinclair.co.uk for information on coming books and some free short stories, some of which were written decades ago and languished in a drawer until I dusted them off and decided to believe in them. I write an occasional blog, too, where you can get to know me a wee bit better.

You can connect with me on Facebook, or Twitter, and I'd love to hear your comments. The more 'honest', the better.

facebook.com/doug.sinclair.12382

x.com/DougASinclair

ACKNOWLEDGEMENTS

My amazing wife, Maaike, is still by far the primary reason that my first book, *Blood Runs Deep*, ever saw the light of day. Without her, books one and two, and now book three, simply would have felt 'beyond me'.

So, yet again, my biggest thanks go to my wife, Maaike, and my mum, who kept faith in me, always. Also to Donna, my fantastic sister-in-law and always my first beta reader.

Thanks to John 'Tonka' Coughlan for his invaluable advice on the lives and experiences, the bravery and resilience, of firefighters everywhere. I'm bound to have taken the superb research John helped me with and screwed some of it up in the interests of story, for which I can only apologise and beg the indulgence of him and firefighters everywhere, for whom I have nothing but admiration.

Thanks, again, to Gordon Brown who recommended my debut to Kevin Pocklington at The North Literary Agency. I'm also as grateful as ever to Storm Publishing's Oliver Rhodes and Claire Bord for 'getting' Malkie, and to Kate Smith for helping me to polish and refine and find the book this deserved to become. Also, to Alex Holmes and Shirley Khan and Laurence Cole for guiding me through the editing process, and Anna McKerrow for selling me so well on social media. Finally, thanks to the annoyingly talented Angus King for signing on to narrate the third of my audiobooks.

Thanks, also, to all who supported and advised me, and kicked my arse when I needed it. Craig Robertson, Caro

Ramsay, Douglas Skelton, Lin Anderson, Mark Leggatt, Neil Broadfoot, Gordon Brown, Michael Malone, Carla Kovach, Zoe Sharp, Alex Gray, Graham Smith, Alison Belsham, Noelle Holten, Sharon Bairden, Jacky Collins, Kelly Lacey, Suze Bickerton, Pam Fox, Gail Williams – thank you for helping me finally accept that I'm at least not a terrible writer.

The Twisted Sisters of Dumfries – Irene, Fiona, Linda, Ann, Jackie, Hayley – and the rest of the Crime & Publishment gang – Les, David, June, Angi, Steve & Karin – thank you just for being the nutters you all are.

Andy & Al, Rich, Dave T, Meesh, Wendy – thank you for pretending to care.

Eleanor, Fergus, Rosie, Lorne, Kathy, Helen, Colin – thank you for reminding me that I *do* deserve you all.

As ever, if I've missed anyone I really shouldn't have missed, please feel free to get me at playtime. With a big, pointy stick, even.

Printed in Great Britain
by Amazon

55028204R00180